The Stolen Sisters

BOOKS BY ANN BENNETT

The Stolen Sisters

ANN BENNETT

bookouture

Published by Bookouture in 2024

An imprint of Storyfire Ltd.
Carmelite House
50 Victoria Embankment
London EC4Y 0DZ

www.bookouture.com

The authorised representative in the EEA is Hachette Ireland
8 Castlecourt Centre
Dublin 15 D15 XTP3
Ireland
(email: info@hbgi.ie)

ISBN: 978-1-83525-890-3
eBook ISBN: 978-1-83525-889-7

For Will

PROLOGUE

Joanna's legs were trembling, and she clutched her sister's hand as tightly as she could. The soldiers ordered them to walk through the station entrance and stand on the platform to wait for their train. People stopped and stared at the group of terrified children, escorted by SS officers, as they walked through morning crowds on the station concourse.

When they reached the platform, Joanna found she was standing in the middle of the huddle of children, so she couldn't see out. She was short for her ten years. But soon she heard the loud blast of a train whistle, and a huge, black engine came puffing into the platform in front of them, hissing out great clouds of steam and smoke. It came to a stop with a great squealing of brakes.

'Get onto the train. All children onto the train. This door!' the SS officer commanded, and they all crowded around the open door of a carriage. It was a struggle for some of the little ones to get up into the train; one boy stumbled, grazing his knee. Soon they were all on board a carriage with wooden bench seats. The window blinds were pulled down so it was impossible to see out. One little boy tried to pull his up.

'Don't do that!' the SS officer yelled at him, and the boy dropped the blind immediately and looked terrified. 'Those blinds must stay down for the whole journey. You must not look out.'

Joanna sat down beside her older sister, Marta, on one of the bench seats.

'Why can't we look out?' she asked.

Marta shrugged. 'They probably don't want us to be seen by people. They don't want everyone to know that they are stealing children from their mothers.'

The twenty children, ranging in age from little ones of three or four years old to twelve-year-olds like Marta, occupied a whole carriage. Just as the train was about to leave, the three nurses, led by Nurse Weiss, came on board and took seats in different parts of the carriage. Joanna was relieved to see Nurse Weiss sit down across the aisle from her and Marta. She looked over and gave them a reassuring smile. Nothing could make Joanna feel good about the journey, but having Nurse Weiss there at least made her feel a little better.

With another blast of the whistle, and a great hiss of steam, the train pulled forward with a jerk and soon they were moving out of the station. Joanna was fearful about what the journey would bring. One of the older children had told her they were going to Litzmannstadt. She'd never heard of that place. Where was that? Was it in Poland or Germany? She had no idea. All she knew was that this train was probably taking them even further away from Jasło and from Mama and Tata and that her heart ached painfully to see them again. She couldn't help a sob escaping from her, although she'd promised herself she would try not to cry. Crying didn't help. It gave her a headache and made her feel wretched. Marta put her arm around her and held her tight, but it didn't stop Joanna's fear.

She felt a soft hand take her own, and looked up to see Nurse Weiss leaning over towards her, holding her hand, a concerned expression on her face.

'Don't worry, Joanna. I will be with you all the way. You will be looked after. I know it's hard,' she said, in her funny German accent.

The journey to Litzmannstadt in the north of Poland from Kraków took around five hours. No one spoke much. Some of the children dozed, others sat there under the harsh electric lights in the carriage looking dejected. When they'd been travelling a little while, Agata, who was sitting behind them, leaned forward and said, 'You know where Litzmannstadt is, don't you?'

Joanna and Marta shook their heads. As long as they had each other, surely everything would be all right.

'That's the German name for Łódź.'

Joanna had heard of the city of Łódź. She'd heard Mama and Tata talking about it during one of their whispered late-night conversations that she and Marta had overheard.

'It's awful what they're doing in Łódź,' Mama had said. 'I heard from the neighbour. Her husband had to go there on business. Did you know that the Nazis have created a ghetto there, like in Warsaw? The Jews are forced to live in one area, sealed in by wire fences. There are thousands of them crammed in there and they're made to work for the Nazis as slaves in the factories.'

Joanna shivered just thinking about it. Why were they being taken there? Would they be put in the ghetto too and used as slave labour? She swallowed hard, trying not to think about it. She didn't want to tell Marta her fears, nor Nurse Weiss, so she stayed quiet, but she was terrified of what would happen when their train finally pulled into Łódź station.

When they'd got down from the train they were herded out through another huge station. An open-backed lorry was waiting for them, a guard sitting by the tailgate, an icy expression on his face.

'Get up in there,' one of the soldiers said, directing the children with his rifle. Everyone scrambled on board, terrified of the soldiers. One boy tripped as he was climbing and a soldier picked him up by the arm and threw him bodily onto the back of the truck.

The nurses who'd been travelling with them until that point were directed to get into a waiting car.

'Goodbye, children, I will see you very soon,' Nurse Weiss said, but her face wore an anxious expression.

Here, the Germans didn't seem to care who saw a lorry-load of children being driven by SS officers. But here, just as in Kraków, most people in the street cast their eyes down when they saw the SS emblem on the doors of the truck.

Joanna looked around her at the forbidding station entrance, hung with swastikas, as were many of the buildings in the streets they drove through. Everyone they passed on the pavements seemed downtrodden and afraid. Why had they been brought here? What was going to happen to them?

Joanna glanced at Marta, who squeezed her hand and gave her a timid smile. Her big sister was trying to reassure her that everything was going to be all right, but Joanna could tell she was just putting a brave face on things. Everything felt far from all right.

When they'd been travelling for a couple of kilometres, they turned in through some wooden gates topped with coils of barbed wire. The buildings here were shabby and dilapidated, paint peeling from doors, broken windows patched up with boards. It was very crowded, and the people wandering about looked even more dishevelled than those in the town. Everyone wore the yellow star on their arm that marked them out, even to Joanna, as Jews.

Fear sliced through her. This was what Mama and Tata had

been talking about; the Łódź ghetto, where all the Jews in the city had been forced by the Nazis to live in cramped conditions. She stared out, aghast. Everywhere she looked, people looked thin and cowed and were dressed in rags, even the children. There were many beggars sitting on the pavement on bundles of rags, amongst them several children. They had the saddest eyes Joanna had ever seen.

The truck turned in through another set of gates, which swung shut behind them. Looking back at the gates, Joanna noticed that a high fence, once again topped with barbed wire, ran either side of the gate, enclosing the whole area. German sentries were patrolling it with dogs and guns. Beside the gate was a wooden watchtower and another guard stood with a gun on the top.

This seemed to be a camp within the ghetto. They rumbled past a group of children marching in line. They were all desperately thin, just like the Jews in the ghetto, but unlike them, these children didn't wear the yellow star. They must be Polish, just like her, Joanna realised. Their heads had been shaved, and they wore shapeless grey tunics and baggy trousers, and were hobbling along in clumsy clogs. It was impossible to tell who was a boy and who was a girl. SS guards walked either side of the column holding guns, sometimes poking a child who walked too slowly with their rifle butt.

'Who are those children?' she asked Marta, but, just as she was, her sister was staring at them incredulously, her face white with shock. Marta shook her head, her eyes still fixed on the children.

'I don't know,' she whispered.

'Will that happen to us?' Joanna asked, shivers of fear going through her, and again Marta shook her head.

'I don't know, darling,' she whispered again and she squeezed Joanna's hand.

ONE

MARTA

Munich, 2005

It was pure chance that Marta happened to put the television on that Wednesday evening in late November 2005. She was exhausted, and felt every one of her seventy-three years. It had been a long day at the clinic, and she'd been later than usual getting home. Once she'd cooked her meal, eaten it and cleared up – even mopping the floor, because she couldn't bear to wake up to an untidy kitchen – she sat down in the living room and, for once, allowed herself to relax.

She thought back over her day and all the patients she'd treated. Her heart went out to each and every one of them for the difficulties they'd already faced to travel to Germany, and continued to face on a daily basis. Most had come from North Africa or the Middle East and almost all were young men, who had entered the country illegally and were searching for work in an alien land to provide for their families back home. They were all bewildered, so far from home with very little language to help them. Marta recognised that look in their eyes – homesickness mingled with desperation – because, despite her outward appearance as a middle-class German citizen, she too had once been an immigrant into this country, and it had felt equally alien to her back then.

Since retiring from her job at a private clinic, she volunteered two days a week for a Catholic charity that ran clinics for immigrants who didn't have the correct papers to be treated in a state hospital. Most of them had waited until their condition was serious before seeking medical help, not wanting to alert the authorities to their existence, so the job was a constant challenge. Without much in the way of equipment, today Marta had had to treat chest infections, septic wounds, gastroenteritis and broken limbs. It was so different from her old, ordered job at the clinic, treating private patients with high blood pressure and diabetes with the most modern equipment and drugs available. But helping these people who existed on the edge of society was so much more rewarding; she felt a real connection with them, and it made her feel that she was making a difference.

The remote control was on the arm of the chair and, without really thinking, she picked it up absently and flicked the TV on. She surfed through the satellite channels, skimming past the pop videos, the reality TV shows, the quiz shows and soap operas, until she reached a channel that she knew and felt comfortable watching. It was a satellite news network, *Nachricht* 24, that she'd watched a few times before.

She was familiar with the presenter, Kristel Meyer; the long blonde hair, the appealing blue eyes, the serious, intelligent but accessible manner. That face was made for the television screen, Marta thought, and, not really listening to the broadcast, she closed her eyes momentarily and began to drift off. But the words Kristel was saying soon made them snap open again.

'This is my fourth report on the Lebensborn programme, and I have to tell you that, with the help of Margarete Weiss, a former nursery nurse for the programme, and her bravery in keeping her secret notebooks, we have been able to reunite many mothers with their sons and daughters. Almost all of them had given up hope of ever seeing each other again.

'So far, we have been focusing on the Nazi breeding programme that took place in secret locations throughout Germany and occupied countries, but there was another side to the Lebensborn programme that is, in some ways, even more heinous and reprehensible than what we've heard about so far.'

Marta sat up straight and the hairs on the back of her neck stood up. *Lebensborn.* That word struck terror right through her. It was something she'd never spoken about with any of her colleagues or friends. The word conjured something so hideous that she could hardly acknowledge it even to herself, and yet those terrible memories had always been with her – a constant, shameful companion that would never let her rest.

'When the Nazis occupied neighbouring countries such as Poland and Ukraine,' Kristel went on, 'they were struck by how many blond-haired, blue-eyed children there were in those territories. Since the birth rate in the Third Reich wasn't what they'd hoped, they decided that these children were true Germans and that it was their duty to "repatriate them" and give them the chance of German citizenship.'

Marta sat there open-mouthed, staring at the screen, as Kristel gave details of the plights of several such children, and explained how Margarete's notebooks had helped unite them with long-lost families whom they'd given up hope of ever seeing again. Marta had never heard anyone speak openly of any of this in Germany before. It was something few people were aware of; and, if they did know about it, they usually had reason to sweep it under the carpet.

She was mesmerised by Kristel's report, horrified yet fascinated. Part of her wanted to switch the TV off, to bury her head in the sand and try to banish it all from her thoughts, but there was something compelling about these stories. Many people had come forward to tell how they had searched for years for their family with no success, but Margarete's records had helped them fulfil their dream.

A thought struck Marta. Perhaps she could be one of those people who found their family after a lifetime of separation? She shook her head. She'd been old enough during the war to know where she'd come from, but when she'd returned to her home town years later, after the fall of the Iron Curtain, her dreams had been shattered. None of her family was left, and the town was unrecognisable. It had been bombed heavily during the war and most of the population expelled. The trip to the place that she'd held in her memory as a beacon of hope had been so disappointing, so desolate and stark, stripped of all the old buildings she'd known and loved and all the friendly faces, that she'd returned to Germany devastated, and resumed her old life, an empty shell.

After that, she'd tried to put it all behind her. To focus on the present and not dwell on the past. But there was one loose end that wouldn't let her rest. She swallowed a lump in her throat thinking about it now.

She stood up, wandered into her bedroom and sat down on the bed. She picked up the fading black and white photograph from the nightstand that she'd kept by her side for sixty-odd years. Two young faces stared out at her, unsmiling, eyes wide with apprehension about what the coming days would bring. There was her own twelve-year-old face, framed with blonde hair, long plaits falling forward over her shoulders, and her ten-year-old sister beside her, with an identical expression on her face, her plaits a little darker.

'Joanna,' she murmured, tracing her sister's face with her finger. 'Whatever happened to you?'

She returned to the living room to watch the end of the report, clutching the photograph. Kristel was addressing the camera, winding up her presentation.

'So, if you have a story to tell, if you were part of the Lebensborn programme and think Margarete's notebooks might be able to help you, please don't hesitate to give us a call. We'd love to hear from you and to help you in your quest.'

Marta's hand hovered over the telephone beside her as the TV network's phone number came up on the screen. Her heartbeat sped up. Should she call? Would it make a difference? But her hand shook at the thought of going back to that time and place, and she let it fall to her lap. She'd already tried everything she could to find out what had happened to Joanna, but had always drawn a blank. How would this woman's secret notebooks help her?

But then the shard of a memory went through her mind. *Margarete.* Wasn't that name familiar? She paused, trying to remember the features of the nurse who had shown them such kindness, who had done her best for them despite her position as a senior nurse in the Lebensborn programme. It was she who had taken that photograph, wasn't it? Marta had to know. As the programme credits rolled, with shaking hands she turned the photograph of her and Joanna over, unclipped the pins and prised the cardboard back off the frame. She recalled the nurse scribbling them a message on the back of the photo before she gave it to Marta.

She gasped and stared down at it. The writing was still there, faded and indistinct but legible still. Proof that she hadn't dreamed it all.

To my darling Marta and Joanna. Never give up hope. With love,
Margarete Weiss.

She stared at the name. Wasn't that the name Kristel had mentioned? She was almost sure it was. If so, how amazing it was that all these years on, Margarete was still trying to do her best for the babies and children she'd cared for during the war. She must be a very old lady now. Marta closed her eyes and tried to remember Margarete's face. She had blonde hair, always pinned up neatly in a bun, and kind, blue eyes. Marta would never forget those kind eyes. But despite her good intentions, Margarete hadn't been able to prevent what happened to them.

TWO

MARTA

Jasło, Poland, March 1944

That day, early in 1944 when the world stopped for twelve-year-old Marta, would be etched on her memory for ever. Decades later, she could still remember every detail of that morning, of her home and of the little town of Jasło, near Kraków, where she lived with her mother and father and younger sister; the weather, the first hint of spring in the chilly air, the sounds in the street, everything.

Mother was unwell that day and unable to get out of bed. Marta had crept into her room and held her hand.

'Are you all right, Mama?' she asked, but she could tell from the droplets of sweat standing out on her mother's brow and the sunken look in her eyes that she wasn't all right. She was often ill. It was the result of a poor and insufficient diet and the fact that she always put the rest of the family before herself when it came to food.

'Could you get your own breakfast, my darling? And give some to your sister?' Mama asked. 'There's some bread in the kitchen. You're such a good girl. What would I do without you?'

Marta returned to the tiny bedroom she shared with Joanna and the two of them got themselves dressed. Then, downstairs in the cold kitchen, Marta found some crusts of bread for breakfast. Her stepfather, whom she thought of as her own father and called Tata, had already left for work on the railway. Before the war, he'd worked at the chemical factory on the edge of town as a foreman and had earned good money, but the factory had been closed and destroyed by the Germans after the invasion in 1939. Marta knew that Tata was active in the resistance in the town, that he took great risks in the name of the cause, and that Mama worried desperately about him.

'What shall we do this morning?' Joanna asked when they'd finished their meagre breakfast. 'Will Mama read to us?'

Marta shook her head. 'She's not well again, sweetie,' she said, and Joanna hung her head but said nothing. They both worried about their mother. They'd not spoken about it but Marta knew that, young as she was, Joanna worried about her mother dying, just as she did. When Mama was sick, they both found it hard to concentrate on anything.

There was no school; the Nazis had forbidden children over the age of eight to receive any sort of education.

Marta had overheard her parents talking about it shortly after the Nazi invasion: 'They say all Poles are slaves, not fit to be educated,' Tata had said, tight-lipped with anger. 'They've closed all the schools down.'

'God help us,' Mama had said and there had been a long silence, after which Tata had lowered his voice and said, 'But Stanislaw Broz has a solution. If we take them to his house early each morning, he will hold classes in his cellar.'

A few days later, they had attended their first classes in the cellar of their former teacher Mr Broz's home alongside about eight other children from the neighbourhood. It was exciting at first, going there in secret. Learning took on a whole new meaning now there was something illicit about it. In order to avoid being reported to the Nazis by neighbours, the children had to arrive before dawn and leave by a back entrance in twos and threes after their classes. This had gone on for over a year, but one day an army lorry had arrived out of the blue after class and, according to neighbours, Stanislaw Broz had been bundled on board by SS officers. People said afterwards that the lorry was full of professors and teachers, whom the Nazis classed as their enemies. Stanislaw had never been seen again and there was no longer any school at all.

Mama had done her best to make sure the girls practised their reading and arithmetic each day. She also read them stories, but it was no substitute for going to school and being with other children.

After breakfast, Marta climbed the stairs again and went into her mother's darkened room.

'What's wrong, Mama?' she said, reaching out and holding her mother's floppy hand.

Mama smiled wanly at her. 'I'm just feeling a bit weak, that's all. Will you go to the market for me this morning? Take Joanna and get some fresh air.'

'Of course,' Marta said, desperately wanting to ease her mother's suffering. At least if she went to the market, that would be one less anxiety for her. Mama always worried about food and with good reason: there was simply not enough to go round. They normally all went together to buy provisions. It was their daily ritual that they all looked forward to, despite the fact that they might have to queue for hours at the butcher's, or that the vegetable stall might have run out of produce, and they could well come home empty-handed.

Marta went downstairs and she and Joanna put on their threadbare coats and boots. Although it was March, it was still chilly and there was slush on the pavements from the snow earlier that week.

'See you later, Mama,' she called up the stairs and her mother called back, 'Take care, my darlings.'

Take care, my darlings. Years later, when Marta closed her eyes, she could still hear her mother's tremulous voice calling down the stairs.

Marta took the shopping bag from the kitchen and they left the house together and walked, hand in hand, up the road towards the local market.

'Do you think Mama will be all right?' Joanna asked anxiously.

Marta bit her lip. 'Of course. It's just a little cough, you know that. She always gets better.'

The wind whipping up the street was fierce that morning. It made the branches of the trees that lined the pavement bend and bow. Marta shuddered as she and Joanna made their way towards the market square in the centre of town. They reached the end of the road and turned into Kościuszko Street, one of the wider roads in the little town. It was lined with pretty two- and three-storey gabled houses painted in pastel colours. This road led towards the marketplace.

There was slush underfoot, as Marta had predicted, and in order not to slip over they walked slowly, shivering as they went. Their coats weren't thick, and they weren't very warm, especially in the biting March air. Nearing the top of the street, Marta suddenly became aware of the rumble of heavy tyres on the cobbles behind them, and a German army truck overtook them, moving slowly. Out of the corner of her eye she noticed the swastika painted on the door. The sight of Germans struck fear into Marta. She looked away quickly, casting her gaze down to the wet pavement, but not before the officer in the passenger seat, with his black and grey cap bearing the SS skull insignia, had caught her eye. His cold, blue eyes lingered on her a moment longer than necessary and she shivered as she watched the truck draw away from them and disappear up the street.

'Keep away from those Nazis,' Mama and Tata always warned the girls. 'And always keep your heads down.'

At first Marta had wondered why, but, after she'd witnessed uniformed SS men beating and kicking old Jewish men in the marketplace and rounding up innocent citizens to load them onto a lorry and take them away, she was terrified of them. She'd overheard Tata and Mama speaking about it late at night and from those conversations she knew that through his work with the resistance, Tata had been instrumental in helping many Jewish people to hide and to escape deportation. Mama constantly urged him to be careful, but he'd told her not to worry. 'I'm as careful as I can be, Maria. You have to trust me. This has to be done.'

At last, they arrived at the market square. It was filled with covered stalls, some of them bearing little produce, and as usual it was thronging with people. Most of them were thin and shabby, dressed in rags, in their eyes the desperation of not knowing where their next meal might come from. All pretence at manners had long been abandoned, and women were elbowing each other out of the way to get to the stalls.

As they walked across the square, with a shiver Marta noticed the German army truck pulled up on the opposite side of it.

The girls approached the vegetable stall that Mama normally bought from. Women thronged around it, pushing and shoving. Mama often left Marta and Joanna on a nearby bench while she fought her way towards the stall.

'You stay there and wait for me,' she told Joanna now, pointing towards the bench.

'Can't I help you?'

'No, look how busy it is. It will be easier if there's only one of us.'

Reluctantly, Joanna went over and sat down on the bench. Marta turned back towards the stall and entered the crowd. She looked back at her sister. She looked so thin and pale, her legs dangling. Then Marta turned back towards the stalls. Being short, she could easily worm her way to the front between the women and she was soon at the head of the queue. The stall-holder recognised her instantly and smiled.

'Potatoes and cabbage for you, my little one?' he asked with a wink, and she nodded.

'And beetroot too if you have it, please.'

'Of course. I've kept some just for you.'

The other women huffed and grumbled, scowling at Marta as she produced Mama's coupons and paid the stallholder with coins from her purse, but soon she was turning away from the stall, clutching three bulging paper bags to her chest. She elbowed her way back through the throng to the edge of the crowd. There she stopped and stared.

Shock washed through her. Joanna was still where she'd left her, sitting on the bench, but a Nazi officer in his peaked cap, greatcoat and long boots was standing over her, speaking to her. Nothing good would come of this, of that Marta was sure. She approached, unsure how to deal with the situation.

'And where do you live?' the officer was asking Joanna in broken Polish.

'In Floriańska Street,' Joanna replied.

The officer glanced at Marta. 'And is this your sister?'

Joanna nodded.

'Good. Now, you two girls are coming with me,' he said. 'It's nothing to worry about, just a routine check-up.'

Shock and fear sliced through Marta at those words. 'No!' she said, 'Come with me, Joanna.'

She held her hand out to Joanna, but the officer had already grabbed Marta's arm. He pulled Joanna to her feet with the other hand.

'Don't make a fuss,' he growled. 'This is the law. You are coming with me for a medical inspection.'

Marta felt tears of terror prickle her eyes, but there was no escaping the officer's iron grip. She tried desperately to wriggle out of his grasp, but he dug his fingers into her arm, making her cry out. Then he began to drag the girls across the square towards the waiting army truck.

'Help!' Marta shouted and several of the townsfolk in the market square turned to stare at the unfolding scene, but something told her that they wouldn't intervene. Everyone in the town was terrified of the Nazis and there was nothing they could do anyway. Struggling to get free, she dropped her bags of precious vegetables, which scattered all over the cobbles. Instantly people swarmed to grab them, pushing each other out of the way in their desperation to snatch a beetroot or potato before someone else got it.

Joanna was crying too when they reached the truck. There was a ladder at the back. The man pulled the back of the truck down and shoved Marta onto the ladder.

'Get up in there and stop making a fuss,' he barked. 'You're coming with us. You have no choice about it so get used to it!'

THREE

MARTA

Jasło, Poland, March 1944

Marta had no choice. She climbed into the truck. She could feel Joanna right behind her, her hot hand inside her own. They were both shaking. To her surprise, the benches that ran down either side of the truck were already full of children. Boys and girls ranging from around three to her own age. All of them were crying, and looking at their terrified faces she knew that they too had been snatched, just like her and Joanna. How could this be happening? It was like a bad dream, but one from which she knew she wasn't going to wake up.

The soldier jumped up inside the truck and sat at the end by the tailgate with his rifle poised. Another slammed the gate shut and shoved the bolts across, then disappeared. Marta heard the truck door in the cab slam. The engine started up and the truck roared into life, the boards beneath her feet vibrating. With a bump, the truck moved off the market square and started moving slowly through the town. Staring, through her tears, out of the back of the truck at the familiar streets of the little town where she'd been born and had spent her whole life, Marta wondered when she would ever see it again.

They drove out through the suburbs and left the town behind, and were soon speeding through the countryside. Marta counted ten other children in the truck and they were all still crying. She knew that tears were streaming down her own cheeks, and she held tightly to Joanna, but she could feel her shaking with sobs too. Marta had no words of comfort for her sister. She had no idea where they were going or why they'd been taken.

The road was straight, and the farmland surrounding Jasło looked especially barren at that time of year – flat brown fields devoid of crops, a few bony animals shivering beside hedges, the occasional spinney of bare trees on the horizon. Marta knew this road. They had been along it a few times as a family on bus trips; it was the road to Kraków.

The lorry didn't stop once during the journey. At one point, a tiny boy, who could have been no more than three years old, got up from his seat.

'Sit down!' the guard shouted instantly, waving his gun, and the little boy returned to his seat, tears streaming down his face.

Later on, another little boy stood up. He was holding his fists to his face, crying his eyes out. There was a wet patch on his trousers and he was shivering in the cold March air.

'I told you. Sit down!' the soldier shouted.

After that, the children stopped trying to get up, and sat on the bench, tears streaming down their sad faces.

Within a couple of hours, the truck was rolling through the outskirts of Kraków. Straggling houses lined the road and people trudged about, wrapped in rags, their heads bent against the cold. No one noticed the lorry full of stolen children rumbling past.

The streets gradually became narrower and more built up, the traffic heavier, but eventually they rattled into a courtyard through some high gates, and drew up in front of a stark, white-painted building. The lorry came to a stop and Marta looked around at the terrified faces of the other children. She could see that they were all thinking what she was thinking – where were they and what was going to happen to them?

The officer stood up and someone else let down the tailgate.

'Get down from the truck and form a line by the front door,' he ordered, jumping down from the lorry.

The children all clambered down and did as he said. Marta and Joanna brought up the rear.

'What's going to happen to us?' Joanna muttered, looking up into Marta's eyes. Marta wished she had answers.

'No talking!' barked the officer.

Gradually a ragged line formed, then the officer waved them inside the building. One by one they walked up a shallow flight of steps and in through the front door. There they waited in an echoing corridor with a tiled floor and high ceiling. Marta recognised the smell of disinfectant. Perhaps this was a hospital? The officer had said they were going for a medical inspection. Maybe that was all this was, and they would be going home soon, but she didn't dare to hope.

Marta longed to be back home, sitting by the fire with her mother, listening to a story or helping prepare the evening meal.

They stood there shivering, waiting. No one was speaking and no one was crying. Whatever was happening was just too bewildering for tears.

A door in the corridor opened and a fierce-looking nurse dressed in a striped uniform with a starched white cap put her head round.

'First child. Come inside.'

The first in the queue, a little girl, detached herself from the column and went to the door. The nurse grabbed her by the shoulder and pulled her inside, then slammed the door behind her. The children all looked at each other wide-eyed, wondering what it meant, but no one spoke.

After a few minutes the nurse opened the door again.

'Next!' she barked and the next one stepped forward, a little boy this time.

The children in the corridor were restless. What had happened to the little girl? Was she still in the room with the nurse? Would the little boy come out? These were questions to which there was no answer.

This repeated itself again and again. No children came out of the office, but one by one, they all went inside. Finally, only Marta and Joanna remained.

'Will you go first?' Joanna said, her voice shaky.

'If you like. Or shall I ask if we could go together?' Marta said and Joanna nodded.

The door opened and the nurse appeared.

'Next.' Her eyes were cold, her face unsmiling.

'We are sisters. Can we come together?'

'Of course not. One at a time. Who is coming first?'

'I will.' Marta let go of Joanna's hand and stepped forward.

The nurse pushed her into the room. It was narrow, with the same high ceiling as the corridor, and reminded Marta of the doctor's surgery that they'd sometimes been to in Jasło when they were ill. There was a sink with a mirror above and a cabinet under it, a trolley with medical equipment beside one wall and a desk. On the other side of the room was another door. That explained why the children hadn't come back, Marta thought. Beside the desk sat an SS officer in uniform.

'Sit down there.' The nurse indicated a hard, wooden chair between her and the officer. The woman was large and square. She had a large, square face too and no warmth in her eyes.

'We are going to ask you some questions and give you some preliminary tests today. More tests will follow.'

'What tests?' Marta asked, sitting down.

'Don't ask questions,' the nurse said. 'Now, what is your name, date of birth and address?'

Marta reeled off the answers and felt a little reassured. If they wanted their address, that surely meant that they were intended to go home at some point?

The nurse wrote the answers down laboriously on a form. Then she looked up.

'Who are your parents and what are their occupations?'

Marta told them that Mama was a housewife and that Tata worked on the railway. When she said Tata's name, the nurse wrote it down, then underlined it heavily. Prickles of fear went through Marta. What did that mean? Should she have lied about his name?

The nurse then asked her about her grandparents and other relatives and wrote down the answers. Then she asked about family illnesses.

'Mama is often sick. She has a bad chest,' she said, and the nurse exchanged an exasperated look with the officer.

'Not that sort of illness. Heart disease, epilepsy, schizophrenia, cancer. Anything serious.'

'My father died,' she said, and the nurse stared at her. 'Of tuberculosis.'

'But you said your father is alive and works on the railway.'

'He's my stepfather,' she said. 'I didn't think.'

The nurse glared at her. 'I need accurate answers. It makes a big difference,' she said, scribbling notes frantically on the form. Marta hung her head, wondering how they would have got on with some of the tiny children who'd passed through the office already. Surely none of them would have had any idea about all this?

Finally, the nurse stopped writing and put her pen down.

'Now, I need to take some quick measurements. You will have more tests later on, but these are for our preliminary assessment.'

Marta wondered what a preliminary assessment was and what the tests were for, but she didn't dare ask.

'Stand up,' the nurse said, then she produced a tape measure and measured Marta's head, her forehead, the distance between her eyes, and wrote several things down on her form. Glancing at what she was writing, Marta saw, 'Blue eyes. Perfectly spaced. Blonde hair. Good stature.'

When the nurse had finished writing all this down she handed the forms to the officer, who read them, bowing his head down over the papers. Marta watched him anxiously, still wondering what it all meant. She noticed that his grey hair was clumped together with hair oil, and she could smell it from where she sat. Finally, he looked up and, to her astonishment, actually smiled.

'Well done,' he said. 'You have passed the preliminary tests. You will be staying with us here for a day or two, then we will explain what will happen. You're not to worry, your future is assured.'

She stared at him. What did he mean? All she wanted was to go home.

'What about my mother and father?' she asked. She thought of Mama. She would be frantic by now because they hadn't returned from the market. They had left the house well over three hours ago. She pictured Mama struggling to get out of bed, her face streaked with anxious tears. She would pull her clothes on and go out into the freezing cold street to look for them. Would someone tell her they had been taken? Would she and Tata try to find them?

'Don't worry about them,' the officer said. 'All will become clear.'

'Now, come along, we're wasting time with all these questions,' said the nurse, beckoning Marta towards the inner door. When she opened it, another nurse stood outside in another tiled corridor. This nurse was a little younger but no less fierce-looking.

'Follow me,' she said and set off down the corridor at a fast walk. Marta hurried behind the young nurse, slipping on the polished tiles.

At the end of the corridor was a concrete staircase.

'Come on, keep up,' the nurse said and went up the stairs, up and up at least three flights. Marta was out of breath when they reached the top. She wondered what had happened to Joanna. Where was she? The nurse paused beside a door.

'This is the dormitory for the older girls,' she said, pushing the door open. Inside were four beds. Two of them were already occupied. Marta recognised one of the girls from the lorry. She was a little younger than Marta herself, the other about her own age. Both were dressed identically in blue pyjamas.

'Can my sister stay here with me?' Marta asked anxiously.

'I'm not sure at the moment. Perhaps, if all goes well.'

Marta wondered what that meant.

'You can change out of your clothes and put those pyjamas on,' the nurse told her. 'Place your clothes in that bin over there. Keep your coat and shoes, but you won't be needing the rest of them any longer,' she went on, pointing to a crate on wheels in the corner. Then she left the room.

'Do I have to get changed?' Marta asked the other girls.

The one she didn't recognise shrugged. 'Everyone does. They won't let you have food if you don't change.'

'What's this all about? Do you know?' Marta asked her. Nothing here felt right; the tests, the uniforms, the dormitory. She had no idea what it meant for her and Joanna. All she wanted to do was to go home to Mama and Tata.

'I came yesterday but I've already heard rumours. I overheard two of the nurses speaking in the passageway. They are going to take us to a camp tomorrow, to get us ready to go to Germany one day.'

'To Germany? Are you sure?' Marta swallowed, her heart hammering. Why were they taking her to Germany? Would Mama and Tata be joining her? Was Joanna going too?

'We are going to become Germans. That's what I heard. It's called Lebensborn.'

'Lebensborn?' Marta repeated. She'd never heard that word before. What did it mean? She hoped fervently that the girl was wrong, but still she took off her coat and undressed, shivering in the unheated room, and pulled on the scratchy cotton pyjamas.

She was just buttoning up her pyjama top when the door opened and the younger nurse reappeared and ushered Joanna into the room. Marta felt relief wash over her, seeing her sister at last. The nurse repeated the same instructions to Joanna that she'd just told Marta. Then she left.

Joanna rushed over to Marta and put her arms around her, dissolving into sobs.

'I don't like it here, I want to go home,' she said.

'I know, I know,' Marta said, hugging her tight.

'How long will we be here?' Joanna asked.

'I'm not sure, little one,' Marta replied.

'Didn't they tell you anything?'

Marta shook her head. 'I'm sorry, Joanna. I don't know what's going to happen.'

Marta stroked her sister's hair and tried to comfort her, all the time wondering how she was going to break the terrible news to Joanna that they wouldn't be going home, that tomorrow, they were being taken to a camp to prepare them for a life in Germany.

FOUR

JOANNA

Kraków, Poland, March 1944

The fear and confusion that had engulfed Joanna when they were dragged to the truck on the market square by the SS officer had stayed with her all day. It hadn't lessened now that they were sitting in the dormitory in the old hospital building in Kraków. The longer she was there in that cold, miserable place, the worse she felt. She snuggled closer to her sister. At least Marta was there too. Most of the poor children who'd arrived on the same truck didn't have a sister or brother to take care of them, and Joanna was comforted by her sister's presence.

She'd always looked up to Marta. Two years older than Joanna, Marta was strong and brave, capable too. She would often cook and tidy the house when poor Mama wasn't well enough. And in recent years, Mama had been unwell so often. Joanna was sure that Marta would do her best to take care of her, whatever happened to them, but Marta didn't seem to know what was happening any more than Joanna herself did. That was partly what was so worrying.

Joanna stared across the bare dormitory at the two girls

sitting on the opposite beds and it struck her that they looked a
lot like Marta. At least, they both had long blonde hair and blue
eyes like her. In fact, nearly all the children on the truck had
had similar colouring, now she thought about it. Joanna glanced
down at her own thick plaits. They were a little darker than her
sister's. Joanna had Tata's colouring and complexion, whereas
Marta took after Mama, whom Tata always said looked like an
angel.

Joanna sat there on the bed, still sobbing, while Marta
hugged her tight and rocked her back and forth. She couldn't
stop thinking about the horrible experience she'd just had down
in the office. The nurse had asked her a lot of questions about
her home and family, and her health, most of which she couldn't
answer. The SS officer with the hard face, who sat on the other
side of the desk, had stared at her through narrowed eyes the
whole time. He hadn't smiled once.

The nurse had measured Joanna's head with a tape
measure. She'd been rough, touching Joanna's skin with her
cold, hard fingers, making her flinch.

Joanna had noticed some of the things the nurse had written
down on the form and she was still wondering what they meant.
The nurse had scribbled, 'Brown hair' followed by a question
mark. 'Grey eyes', and, at the end, one word. She had no idea of
its meaning: 'Borderline'.

Now she turned to Marta and asked her: 'Why did the
nurse and that man ask us all those questions?'

Marta shrugged. 'I don't know, Joanna. I've no idea.'

But the girl on the other side of the room, the one who
hadn't been on their truck, piped up. 'They're testing us to see if
we are Aryans,' she said.

'What's an Aryan?' Joanna asked.

'It's something special,' the girl said. 'The Nazis think
Aryans are the master race.'

Joanna stared at her, still not understanding, but she didn't want to show her ignorance to this bossy-looking girl who seemed to know a lot.

'The food is good here at least,' the girl said. 'But you'll need to get those pyjamas on, or they won't let you have any.'

'I'll help you,' Marta said. 'Come on, take your coat off.'

It felt odd undressing in that cold, stark room in front of those two strange girls. She could feel their eyes on her all the time, but soon she was in the pyjamas, which were slightly too big for her.

'Roll the sleeves up,' Marta said, tying the belt around her waist. When Joanna was dressed, she sat down miserably on the bed, next to Marta.

'What are your names?' the girl opposite said. 'I'm Agata and this is Maja.'

Marta told her their names.

'They will probably give you new ones – when you go to Germany, that is,' Agata said.

'Germany?' Joanna asked, alarmed, feeling fresh tears prickle her eyes. She looked to Marta for reassurance, but Marta's lips were pursed and her cheeks were wet with tears too.

'We're not really going to Germany, are we?' Joanna asked.

'I don't know,' Marta said. 'Let's wait and see.'

Joanna stared across the room at the other girls. Agata sat there expressionless, hugging her knees, but Maja was crying. She'd arrived on the same truck as Joanna and Marta. She looked a little younger than Joanna herself. She was very pale and thin and was biting her nails. Joanna felt sorry for her: she looked so alone. At least Joanna and Marta had each other.

The afternoon dragged. There was nothing to do. No toys to play with, no books to read, no possibility of playing outside. Joanna wanted her mother with a physical ache and, every time she thought about her, she burst out crying again.

Agata told them that she'd arrived the previous day.

'I live in Kraków, so they didn't have to bring me far,' she said.

'Did they grab you off the street, like us?' Marta asked.

For the first time Agata dropped her gaze and shook her head.

'They broke into our house and took Mama and Tata away,' she said. 'They came in a lorry. Lots of them with dogs and guns. I don't know where they are now.'

'Why did they take them?' Marta asked and Joanna felt fresh chills run through her. Would they do that to their mama and tata too?

'I don't know. The SS kept shouting "traitors" at them. It might be because they sometimes help Jewish people to hide or escape.'

Joanna stared at Agata, thinking how brave her mama and tata must be. She must be as proud of them as Joanna and Marta were of their own parents.

'Tata said I wasn't to breathe a word about it,' Agata replied. Despite her bravado, Joanna could see that she too had tears in her eyes.

'What about you, Maja?' Marta asked.

'The same happened to me,' the little girl said. 'They took my parents away too. They said they were being taken to Germany to work.'

Both Joanna and Marta fell silent. Joanna screwed up her eyes to stop the tears, but instantly, an image appeared in her head. It was of a group of Nazi soldiers hammering on the front door of their house, then, without waiting for an answer, kicking it down with their jackboots. They plunged inside the house, grabbing Tata from the kitchen and Mama from her bed, pulling them outside, then making them march to a truck. They had to climb in, then the back of the truck slammed and the truck drove away. The fear coursing through Joanna was so strong when this vivid image came to her that she could barely move. When would she ever see her parents again? She felt for Marta's hand and held it tight, hoping the feel of it would lessen her fear, but it didn't seem to. The fear was still there, filling her senses, fogging her mind.

Later, a bell rang somewhere downstairs and Agata got off her bed and put her shoes on.

'It's supper time,' she said. 'Let's go down. I'm hungry.'

Joanna was hungry too, despite everything. She hadn't eaten since the scraps of stale bread at breakfast that morning and her stomach was rumbling fiercely. She hadn't had anything to drink either, not even water.

Agata led them down some stairs to the ground floor, then along a corridor and into a big, high-ceilinged hall that was empty except for a long trestle table with chairs along each side. Some children were sitting down already. Marta pulled out a chair for Joanna and she sat down. Other children were arriving and soon the table was full. There must have been around twenty of them there, of all ages from around three to twelve. Nearly all of them were flaxen-haired with blue eyes, just like Marta. Most were gulping water from the tin mugs set out at each place beside empty bowls. Joanna sipped hers gratefully.

A miserable-looking porter in grey overalls pushed a trolley up to the table. On it was a great black cauldron. The man took the lid off and, with a ladle, doled out some watery-looking stew into the first child's bowl. Joanna found that her mouth was watering. The stew didn't look very appetising, but she would eat anything right now.

For as long as she could remember, she'd been constantly hungry. German rule meant that food was scarce, and with her ration books Mama could rarely afford meat. Sometimes Tata would bring an illicit parcel of unknown meat, smuggled in from his friends on the black market, wrapped in newspaper and hidden inside his jacket. But that was a rare thing. Joanna knew that it was very risky for all concerned.

The meat in this stew was full of gristle, but it was definitely meat. Joanna picked up her spoon and took a mouthful. It was watery and greasy, and the meat was chewy, but Joanna chewed it quickly and swallowed it down, the juice dripping down her chin.

'Don't eat too fast, little one,' Marta said. 'You'll be sick.'

Joanna knew she was right and tried to slow down and chew every mouthful a dozen times just as Mama always told them, but it was hard to restrain herself. Looking around her, she saw that other children were gulping their food too and soon most of the bowls on the table were empty.

When they had all finished, the SS officer who'd been with the nurse in the office earlier strutted into the hall. He stood at the head of the table and held up his right hand. All the children instinctively fell silent.

'Heil Hitler!' he said.

Those words sent chills through Joanna. She'd seen SS officers in Jasło greeting one another like that, holding out their right hand stiffly in a rigid salute.

The officer went on in his broken Polish.

'I have come to speak to you children to let you know what the coming days will bring. But first, let me say how lucky you all are, to have been selected from amongst all the other children in your neighbourhoods to be part of the Lebensborn programme and to be tested for Aryan blood. Aryans are special, German people. They are members of the master race and you must not ever forget that.

'Tomorrow, we will take you all to a youth camp at Litzmannstadt on the train, and you will undergo more thorough testing there. Eventually, if you pass the tests, you will be sent to Germany as German citizens.'

He paused and looked around the table. The children stared back at him, their faces full of terror, their eyes wide. Some were crying again, rubbing their eyes with their hands.

Joanna felt like crying too, but she managed to hold back the tears – she didn't want to show these Germans that she was afraid of them.

The officer clapped his hands above his head.

'Silence! Please, children, there must be no crying. This is a great opportunity for each and every one of you. You must forget your old, Polish families now. You will become German citizens and you will realise that you will soon be superior to the Poles in every way.

'Now, you have already met one or two of our wonderful nurses. They are members of the Brown Sisters, specially selected by the Nazi Party. More of them will accompany you on your journey tomorrow. I'd like to introduce you to the nurse who will be in charge. She has arrived today from Lebensborn HQ. Come forward please, Nurse Weiss.'

Joanna hadn't noticed the woman sitting quietly at the side of the room, dressed in a nurse's uniform. She stood up and approached the table. Joanna saw with surprise that, unlike the other two nurses she'd seen, this lady had a kind look about her, and was smiling. It was a genuine smile that reached right up to her blue eyes. To Joanna she was beautiful, like Mama; her blonde hair was coiled up in a plait around her head and she had a graceful look about her.

'Good evening, children,' she said in a soft, melodious voice, with a German accent that somehow sounded softer than the SS officer's. 'My name is Margarete Weiss and I will be in charge of your transport to Germany tomorrow. I'm sorry, I do not know very much Polish, but I just want to ask you not to be afraid.'

Joanna looked at Marta with hope and surprise in her eyes. Nurse Weiss was the first German she'd encountered who wasn't harsh and terrifying.

'We will be with you all the way to look after you,' Nurse Weiss went on. 'I know it's hard leaving home, and that you all must be missing your parents and families, but I, and the other nurses, will do our best to help you through this difficult time, I promise.'

The SS officer stepped forward and said something sharply in German to Nurse Weiss, and she raised her chin defiantly and said something in return. The man addressed the children again, his cheeks flushed with anger.

'As I said, children, you need to forget all about your families. The nurses are here to look after you, but you all need to be brave. One day you will realise how lucky you are. Now, let us have no more talk of home. Tomorrow we will all be taking our first steps towards a life in Germany, the Fatherland, so let us rejoice about that!'

FIVE

MARGARETE

Kraków, Poland, 1944

When the SS officer, Untersturmführer Winkler, had finished speaking to the children, he strutted out of the dining hall, giving Margarete a withering look as he passed her. She knew that he hadn't approved of the gentle way in which she'd spoken to the children, in fact he'd said so in no uncertain terms: 'Whatever are you doing, Nurse Weiss? These children have to be toughened up in accordance with Nazi policy. Please don't pander to them!'

She'd lifted her chin and, looking him in the eye, and had retorted instantly: 'Some of these little ones are only three or four years old, Untersturmführer. They've just been torn from their homes and families and are bewildered and unhappy. I'm only doing what I can to help them through this.'

He'd scowled at her, but he must have been acutely aware that he needed her help.

Once he'd left the dining hall, Margarete breathed more easily, despite the fact that the Brown Nurses, both committed Nazis, who would join her on the journey to Litzmannstadt the next day were standing by the wall, grim-faced, staring at her with deep disapproval. She smiled at them sweetly. It didn't really bother her that much. They were her juniors and had to report to her, so they had to follow her orders. Their disapproval was irrelevant.

She turned her attention back to the children sitting around the long table and her heart turned over with pity just looking at their woebegone faces. She counted twenty little heads turned towards her, every single one with questioning, terrified eyes. It made her feel the true weight of the responsibility she'd taken on.

Each and every one of those children had been ripped from their home within the last couple of days and she knew that they must all be in deep shock. When she'd been working at the Lebensborn home, Schloss Schwanburg, in Bavaria, she'd first heard that this Nazi policy was being carried out all over occupied Europe. She'd been incredulous, shocked to the core. How could anyone even conceive of stealing innocent children from their parents? But nothing she ever heard about the Nazis surprised her. They were zealots who would stop at nothing. They'd convinced themselves that these blond-haired, blue-eyed children were natural Germans by birth and that it was their duty to return them to the Fatherland.

Now it wasn't just an evil rumour, it was happening, here before her very eyes. And she was caught up in it despite her true feelings.

She approached the table and asked the children to tell her their names. She started at the end of the table and repeated the names after each child had said them. Margarete had a talent for names; once she'd fixed a face and a name in her mind, she wouldn't forget it. But of course, she knew that the poor little things would all be given German names once they arrived in the Reich, and she would have to memorise them all over again.

All the children deserved her pity, but there were two

sweet-faced girls seated at one end of the table. The way the older one was taking care of the younger one reminded her of the way she'd been with her own sister, Alicia. She felt an instant connection with these two young Polish girls.

'What's your name?' she asked the older girl.

'Marta,' said the one with blonde hair.

'And yours?' she asked the darker one sitting beside her.

'Joanna,' the girl said, and Margarete realised how alike they were.

'Are you sisters?' she asked, and they both nodded. They looked up at her with their big, pleading eyes and it melted her heart. There were tear stains on their cheeks, and in their wounded, shocked expressions Margarete had a glimpse of the hell that they must have been through that day.

She laid her hand on Marta's shoulder. 'I can see that you're looking after your little sister,' she said. 'It must be hard for you. Be strong, Marta. I will help you as much as I can.' She could feel the disapproving eyes of the SS officers on her as she spoke, but that didn't worry her. She was here for the children, to help them through this terrible time in their lives as best she could.

'Thank you, Nurse Weiss,' Marta said with a ghost of a smile.

Margarete went to the head of the table and spoke to all the children then, telling them where the washrooms were and that they must all now get ready for bed.

'Tomorrow, we have a long journey ahead of us. We need to be up early so we have time for breakfast before we go. A bell will ring at seven o'clock and breakfast is at seven thirty. I will call in on each of you to say goodnight later and switch your lights off. Now, off you go. And please, do your best not to worry.'

She watched them get up from the table and stream out through the door, then she left the room by the opposite door and hurried to her own quarters at the end of the building. She sat down on the bed, shaking all over with shock and revulsion. It had been such a challenge to see the children for the first time. Until then, the whole exercise had only been theory.

Margarete put her face in her hands and breathed deeply for a long minute, trying to calm herself down, to come to terms with the fact that she was part of this heinous Lebensborn experiment, carrying out the orders of an evil regime. She would never get used to it, and the only thing she could do in order to live with herself was to be as humane as she possibly could, to do her best to treat the little ones as if they were her own children.

She slipped off her shoes and lay down on the bed, staring at the ceiling. She wasn't sure if she could do this, now she was here. All the way here on the train from Berlin, she'd told herself that she could. If she could preside over a Lebensborn home in Norway, doing her best to ensure the humane treatment of mothers and babies, she could surely carry those ethics to this reception centre in Kraków. But now, faced with twenty living, breathing children who she was convinced would be scarred for life by their experiences, she wasn't sure if she actually had the courage to go through with it.

She'd been numb when she'd been given her mission, two days before, unable to properly process what it actually meant. Numb with shock and grief.

SIX

MARGARETE

Berlin, Germany, 1944

A few days beforehand, Margarete had been standing on the deck of a ferry that had brought her back to Germany from Norway. She'd had mixed feelings as the ship docked in Hamburg. She was looking forward to seeing her family again, but going back into the heart of the Reich made her feel claustrophobic and afraid.

She'd just returned from Norway after three months overseeing a Lebensborn home there. When she disembarked, she went straight to the station and caught a train to Berlin to see her family.

She was worried about them. At the start of her posting, they'd exchanged letters frequently, but lately the letters from her mother and sister, Alicia, had dried up.

Margarete had carried on writing to them, asking for news of her baby, Tomasina, who her mother was taking care of, but they hadn't replied.

She'd been racked with anxiety. Alicia worked secretly for

the resistance, and Margarete was terrified that her work been discovered, and the whole family sent to a concentration camp.

She worried about her mother's health too. Had Mutti fallen ill? Papa had died the previous year – he'd been ill for a long time – but Mutti, although she wasn't in the best of health, had soldiered on. Seeing little Tomasina growing up and being responsible for her welfare seemed to have given her a new lease of life.

When the train finally puffed into the outskirts of Berlin, Margarete stared out of the window, shocked, at the extent of the recent allied air raids. Piles of dusty rubble lined the track on each side. They passed whole streets of bombed-out buildings, where just the façades or inner walls remained, teetering precariously on the point of collapse. There had been bombing raids earlier in the war, before Margarete had been posted to Norway, but nothing on this scale.

At last, when the train ground into Anhalter Bahnhof station, she gathered her luggage, got down from the carriage and pushed through the crowds on the concourse to find a tram to her district. Looking around, she saw that part of the station itself had been bombed, the roof on one side had been blown off and only half the platforms were operating. She was shocked to see how gaunt and dishevelled people had become as a result of wartime rationing, too. There were beggars in the station, dressed in rags, holding out cups, entreating passers-by with pleading eyes.

She went out through the grand station portico, which miraculously was still standing. Out on the street, where the swastikas still fluttered from the fronts of buildings, she discovered there were no trams running. The traffic on the street seemed to be gridlocked too.

'The lines were cut by last night's raid by the British,' an old man at the tram stop told her.

'I've been away for a long time,' Margarete said. 'I had no idea Berlin had suffered so much damage.'

'There have been air raids every night since last November,' the man replied. 'You've been well out of it.'

Looking around, it was apparent that there were no taxis anywhere. Margarete realised that she would have to walk the few kilometres to the district where her family apartment was. It would be a struggle – she had two heavy suitcases – but she was sure that the left-luggage office in the station would not be open amidst all this chaos.

She braced herself, picked up her suitcases and set off with them through the once-familiar streets to the apartment. Everywhere looked different and was shrouded in a film of dust. The bombing had clearly been extensive. Sometimes whole streets had been reduced to rubble, sometimes single buildings had gone, leaving a gaping hole in the façade. The place seemed transformed. Sometimes damaged cars, buses or trams blocked the street, forcing Margarete to change her route; sometimes the pavement had a crater in it or was barriered off in case a building collapsed.

As she made her way through the devastated city, a terrifying thought occurred to her: what if her apartment building had been bombed too? She'd never really considered it a serious possibility as it was a little way away from the centre, but the closer she got, and the more evidence she saw of how extensive the recent raids had been, the more possible she realised it was.

The horrible truth became clear when she arrived at the old, familiar square in front of the apartment building and looked across it towards her former home. Either side of her were the places she'd known since childhood. The café where Papa used to take them for lunch when he was feeling flush, the tobacconist, the newspaper stall, the tram stop, all now stood empty. But ahead of her, on the other side of the square, all that was visible under the grey sky in the place where her red-brick apartment block had been were piles of rubble. She stared, scarcely able to process what her eyes were telling her.

Shaking with shock, she sank to her knees, too stunned for tears. What had happened to them? Mutti, her sister Alicia, her precious little daughter Tomasina? Had they been in the apartment when the bombers came? Had they all died in the blast? Had none of them survived? She couldn't bear it. Poor little Tomasina, less than a year old. The little mite didn't deserve to suffer. Margarete stifled a sob. She didn't want to cry out here on the street with people milling to and fro, but there was no holding back. The sobs came, and soon she was convulsed by them, on her knees on the pavement, doubled up, crying her heart out.

She felt a hand on her back and looked up, fearing it was a soldier or policeman, but it was an elderly woman, with a kind face. She was stooping down to look at her.

'Are you all right, my dear? Can I help you?'

The old lady helped her to her feet and took her into the nearby café and bought her a strong coffee. 'I have lost people in the war too, my dear. I know what you're going through.' She didn't linger, but Margarete was deeply grateful for her kindness.

The café owner was new, not the friendly woman Margarete had known her whole life. When Margarete asked her about the bombing of the apartment block opposite, she shook her head.

'It happened a couple of months ago. When I came to work one morning the building had gone and people were sweeping up. I know nothing about any survivors.'

Margarete asked her if she would look after her suitcases and the woman reluctantly agreed she could leave them behind the counter for a few hours in exchange for a few pfennigs. Margarete left the square and hurried to the nearest hospital, which was a few blocks away. When she went up the front steps, the entrance hall was in chaos, full of people on stretchers waiting for treatment – victims of the previous night's raids. Nurses and doctors ran to and fro in bloodied uniforms, looking harassed.

Margarete approached the desk, where a receptionist was speaking on the telephone. When she'd finished, Margarete thrust a photograph in front of her. It was of her mother, her sister Alicia and baby Tomasina, sent to her by Mutti in her last letter. They were all smiling broadly.

'Have you seen any of these people in the last couple of months?'

The woman shrugged and held up both hands in a gesture of exasperation. 'I have seen so many people. How would I know?'

'Could you check your admission lists for the last three months? Their names are Weiss – Hilde, Alicia and Tomasina.'

The woman glared at her, but opened her register and ran her painted nail down the columns. She was quick, but Alicia could tell she was being thorough. Finally, she looked up and shook her head.

'I'm sorry, Fräulein. They are not here. Have you tried other hospitals?'

'Not yet. You are the closest.'

'Well, do try. Not all casualties are taken to their nearest hospital.'

The woman's telephone started ringing again. Margarete thanked her and picked her way between the stretchers and went out into the fresh air. She took a deep breath. The stench of blood and vomit had been overpowering in there.

Margarete knew all the hospitals in Berlin. She'd once tramped the city trying to get a job when she'd first been forced to work for the Brown Nurses at the Charité Hospital. The next one was a few kilometres away. She was exhausted from her journey, but that didn't matter. If her family had survived and had been taken to a hospital, she needed to find them.

For the rest of the morning she tramped the streets of the devastated city, going from institution to institution clutching her photograph, asking the same questions she'd asked at the first hospital. The answer was always the same: no one remembered her family and they weren't in the register of admissions. The last hospital she went to was the Charité. It seemed like an age since she'd walked through those imposing gates, up the front steps and into the echoing entrance hall. Like the other hospitals, the reception area was inundated with people injured in last night's raid, only here seemed a little more ordered.

The woman on the reception desk recognised her. 'Margarete! How are you? I haven't seen you for years.' She was all smiles, but when Margarete told her about her sad mission, the receptionist looked sympathetic and scoured the admissions book. But it was to no avail and Margarete turned away with a heavy heart.

There was a bench outside the hospital entrance and she sat there to try to process everything that had happened that morning. She sat for a long time, listening to the sounds of the hospital, the traffic on the road outside, the twittering of birds in the trees. How long it seemed since she'd first come here as an auxiliary nurse and had sat here in the garden to gossip with her friends. That was before the Nazis had come to power. How simple life had seemed then; how happy and carefree she'd been. It was a long time since she'd felt like that.

She thought about her mother, Alicia and baby Tomasina. What had it been like for them in that bombing raid? They must have been terrified. Had they been buried alive in the falling building? She shuddered to think of them suffering. The apartment was on the top floor, so if the roof had been hit... She drew in a sharp breath and tried to stop thinking about it.

After a while she realised that she was shivering in the cold air. She glanced up at the hospital clock. When she saw that it was almost two o'clock, she started. She had an appointment at the SS Race and Settlement Office, which was in the Reich Security Main Office, at half past two. She had to report in to the ministry there for a debrief about the situation at the Lebensborn home in Norway. She'd all but forgotten about it in the turmoil that followed the discovery that her home and family had disappeared. But reporting to the ministry was non-negotiable. No excuse would be accepted for non-attendance and an order would go out to the Gestapo in the city for her arrest and detention if she failed to attend.

She got up from the bench and hurried out onto the street. Then, turning left, she headed quickly down Luisenstrasse in the direction of the Reich Security Main Office.

She arrived a minute late and the SS officer on the desk gave her a disapproving look. Soon she was ushered up the grand staircase and into the office of one of the officials in charge of the Lebensborn programme. It was a woman, and, looking closer, she recognised with surprise that it was Fräulein Koch, the grim-faced nurse who had come to establish the Brown Nurses in the Charité hospital in the 1930s. She looked a lot older now, her face harder than before, her hair brittle with blonde dye. She wore the SS uniform with evident pride.

'Sit down, Fräulein Weiss,' she said. 'You are a little late. Is something wrong?'

Fräulein Koch was the last person Margarete wanted to confide in, but there was no hiding her distress.

'I went to my home to see my family, but the building had been bombed,' she said quietly, not able to meet the fräulein's judgemental gaze. 'There was nothing left of it. I've been searching the hospitals for news of my family.'

'I'm sorry to hear that,' Fräulein Koch said. 'Yes. We knew that your family were no longer with us.'

A bolt of shock went through Margarete. This was doubly

surprising – both that the SS knew that her apartment block had been bombed and that Fräulein Koch had said, 'no longer with us'.

'You knew?'

Fräulein Koch nodded. 'Missing presumed dead, I'm afraid. Your mother, your sister and... er... your sister's young baby. I'm very sorry for your loss, Fräulein Weiss.'

Margarete hung her head. She didn't want Fräulein Koch to see her tears, or her fury. She'd known that Alicia had been a person of interest to the SS, but she had no idea that they were still watching her family. She'd thought that her long service with the Lebensborn programme would have put them off the scent.

'Why didn't you tell me before?' she asked, bewildered. 'This happened months ago.'

Fräulein Koch drew a deep breath. 'Because we wanted you to complete your mission in Norway. No purpose would have been served by your coming home early.'

'But... but...'

She knew there was no use in protesting at the inhumanity of this decision. These were sadists; people who took babies from their mothers, who consigned whole families to live in ghettoes and suffer in work camps simply because of their race.

'Now, Nurse Weiss, let us move on and discuss your orders. You are urgently needed at a reception centre in Kraków, Poland. We will soon have a new batch of children ready to bring into the Reich. We want you to accompany them on their journey and to settle them in a new Germanisation centre in Bruczków in Poland. They will stay there until they are suffi-ciently assimilated into German ways to transfer into the Reich. In fact, once you arrive, we want you to take over the running of that centre. That is the Reichsführer Himmler's personal order.'

Margarete stared at her. She'd hoped that she would never have to get involved in this side of the programme. The whole idea of taking children away from their natural homes both sickened and appalled her.

'I'm sure you will do what you can for these children,' Fräulein Koch added. 'If you would like a couple of days off to get over your shock, then I will speak to the Reichsführer myself... But if you decide to go now, there is a night train to Kraków. It departs at ten o'clock this evening. We have booked you a sleeping compartment.'

Margarete wanted nothing to do with Himmler and, if she had to go, she had to go. There was nowhere for her to stay in Berlin. There were no hotels open and she'd lost touch with all the people she'd once known here. She could sleep on the train.

'It's all right. I'll go tonight,' she said and shuddered to see Fräulein Koch's smile of evil satisfaction.

SEVEN

JOANNA

Kraków, Poland, 1944

Joanna was missing her mother with a physical ache. She couldn't get rid of the lump in her throat. Once all the girls had visited the chilly washrooms, they got into their beds, which were hard and lumpy without nearly enough blankets. There was a knock on the door and Nurse Weiss came into the room.

'I've come to say goodnight, girls,' she said, hovering by the door. 'I know it must be hard for you, away from your parents for the first time, but please do try to get some sleep. You'll feel much better if you do.'

Joanna stared at her. She found Nurse Weiss confusing. She wanted to hate her because she was German. But Nurse Weiss wasn't like the other nurses; she was doing her best to be kind. Her eyes had a gentle look in them, and she was always smiling. Joanna wondered if Nurse Weiss would give her a goodnight kiss and cuddle if she asked, but she didn't dare. The other girls would surely laugh at her, especially Agata.

'Goodnight, girls. I'm going to put the light out now, so get comfortable in your beds, please,' Nurse Weiss said.

Joanna pulled up the scant covers. The sheets didn't look or smell very clean and she wondered if other children had slept between them before.

The lights went out and Nurse Weiss went out of the room and shut the door behind her. Joanna listened to her footsteps echoing away down the corridor. It felt even worse now it was dark in the room. Joanna couldn't help thinking about Mama and Tata. How would they be feeling now that night was approaching? They must be as sad as she was. How she longed to be back at home in her own bed, for her mother's arms to be around her. She let out an involuntary sob.

'Are you all right, Joanna?' Marta whispered.

'Not really,' Joanna admitted. She heard Marta pushing back her sheets, the sound of her metal bed creaking, then she felt her getting into bed beside her. The bed was tiny, but they snuggled up together as they often did at home. Marta put her arms around Joanna's middle and held her tight. Feeling Marta's body so close was warming her up as well as comforting her. Her sobs gradually subsided and she closed her eyes. It didn't take long for her to drift off to sleep.

When the bell sounded at seven o'clock the next morning, Joanna was still in a deep sleep. She woke with a start, then remembered where she was, and her spirits plummeted. Rubbing her eyes and looking around her, she saw that Marta was sitting up and yawning. When Marta got out of bed, she pushed the covers back and the chill air of the room enveloped Joanna and she shivered again.

'Come on, we need to get dressed for breakfast,' Marta urged.

Joanna turned her face away. 'I don't want any,' she said.

'Oh, yes, you do,' Marta said. 'I know you're hungry, little one. Come on, the food is better here than we've had for ages. Let's make the most of it.'

It was true; her stomach was already rumbling, and it would

be good to eat. The stew at supper last night, although greasy, had made her feel pleasantly full and had warmed her insides. She pushed back the covers and got out of bed.

'Put your blue clothes on,' Marta said. Maja and Agata were already out of bed and getting dressed.

'But they are pyjamas too,' Joanna complained, and Marta smiled.

'But these ones are thicker. For the daytime.'

Joanna sighed, took off her night clothes and got into the blue pyjamas, then pulled on her socks and shoes. There was a hole in one of her shoes that let in water. It was still wet from the walk to the marketplace in Jasło yesterday. Putting it on reminded her of the terror of being grabbed by the officer and bundled into the truck. That feeling was still raw and fresh in her mind. She wondered if it would ever leave her.

Agata opened the bedroom door and led the four girls along the passage. She stopped outside the washrooms.

'If you need the bathroom, go now,' she said. 'You don't want to miss breakfast.'

'I need to go,' Joanna said and went into the cold, tiled washrooms and to the smelly lavatory with the hard, wooden seat. When she'd finished, she washed her hands in cold water and rejoined the others.

In the dining room they sat in the same places as they had for supper the previous day. Breakfast, which was doled out from a trolley by the same grim-faced orderly, consisted of hard-boiled eggs, some dry-looking ham and some bread that, although hard, wasn't as stale as the bread at home. All the children ate greedily and a hush descended on the room while they shovelled food into their mouths. Joanna had finished hers within a matter of minutes.

The SS officer entered the room. He stood at the head of the table, clicked his heels together and gave a Heil Hitler salute.

'Go upstairs and get your coats on,' he said. 'Then come straight back to the dining room. Make sure you have been to the bathroom – we don't want accidents on the way. You will be taken to the train station on lorries. When you get to the camp at Litzmannstadt, you will be given new clothes. Now hurry, please, children.'

Upstairs in the dormitory, Joanna pulled her coat on. Mama had given it to her for her last-but-one birthday and it was getting a little thin and worn now. But it was a reminder of home. Even now she could remember the excitement of unwrapping it. 'It's not new,' Mama had said apologetically, watching her anxiously as she tried it on, 'but it's in good condition. And I think that shade of blue really suits you, my precious.'

She followed the others back down to the dining room, then they were herded out onto two waiting lorries. When they climbed up the ladder onto the back of the truck, Joanna saw that it was the same one that had transported them from Jasło the day before. Just sitting down on the bench reminded her of her terror once again. This time, the soldier unrolled a tarpaulin to cover the back of the lorry so they couldn't see out.

'They don't want people to know they're kidnapping Polish children,' Marta said under her breath.

'Hush,' said Agata. 'You don't want to be punished!'

It was dark inside the lorry, but Joanna, who was sitting near the end of the bench, could see out through the gap between the tarpaulin and the lorry's metal frame.

They pulled out of the courtyard of the old hospital and onto a main road. It wasn't far to the city centre. As the lorry rumbled over the cobbles, people on the pavements quickly looked away. Joanna could see how the sight of an SS vehicle struck fear into everyone. If only they knew what the cargo was, she thought, they would be even more disturbed.

The buildings became taller and the streets more crowded

as they neared the centre of the city. Joanna saw many queues of women on the pavement, waiting patiently outside shops for bread or meat. This was a daily feature in Jasło too; many a time she'd gone with Mama to wait in the queue for bread. They could wait for hours just to receive a single meagre loaf.

From the bigger buildings, red, white and black swastika banners flapped in the morning breeze, and Joanna spotted German soldiers patrolling the streets, some with guns, some with dogs. The truck rumbled through squares and past a great church with twin towers. Joanna didn't know Kraków well, but the sight of all the magnificent buildings made her afraid. This place felt so much bigger than her home town.

The train station was an imposing stone building with an arched entrance above which flew more swastika banners. Crowds of pedestrians, horse-drawn vehicles and cars jostled for position in the forecourt, but they all stopped and waited for the trucks to pass. They drew up outside the front entrance and came to a halt with a jerk.

The officer rolled up the tarpaulin at the back of the truck.

'Everybody out,' he ordered, pulling the tailgate down.

One by one the children climbed down from the truck and stood in a group on the cobbles in front of the station entrance.

Joanna nudged Marta. 'Why don't we run away?' she said. 'We could go right now.'

Marta shook her head. 'Don't be silly. They would set the dogs on us or shoot us. Look, they all have guns.'

Joanna fell silent. She'd known Marta would say that. Her sister was always the sensible one and Joanna knew she was right really.

Once the children were loaded onto the carriage and the blinds were pulled down, the train set off with a blast of its horn. The train journey passed quickly, but it was boring sitting there under the harsh lights of the carriage, unable to look out at the countryside. And Joanna was besieged with worries. Worries about where they were going, worries about Mama and Tata. Where were they now? Some of the stories the other children had told her about their own parents had made her wonder if she and Marta would ever see them again. Nurse Weiss reached out and held her hand, which was comforting, but nothing could erase the pain and fear she was feeling about being wrenched from her home and sent on a long journey to a place she'd never heard of.

When Agata told them that they were bound for Łódź, Joanna remembered Mama and Tata talking about the horrors of the Łódź ghetto. She became even more anxious and so, when the train puffed into Łódź station and they were ordered out and onto a waiting truck, she was almost paralysed with anxiety.

'Don't worry, Joanna,' Marta said, squeezing her hand again. 'At least we are together. And Nurse Weiss is with us. We will look after you.'

Joanna turned to her sister and tried to smile, but she knew that her eyes betrayed her true feelings.

When the truck turned in through some gates topped with barbed wire, guarded by SS soldiers, and drove on through the shabby streets full of stick-thin people dressed in rags, her worst fears were confirmed. She noticed that everyone here was wearing the yellow star. This must be the Łódź ghetto. They passed a girl of about her age sitting on the pavement in an over-sized overcoat, eating from a bowl. As the truck passed, the girl looked up and met Joanna's gaze. In those eyes Joanna saw a reflection of her own feelings: desperation, terror and defeat. She watched the girl until they had driven past and left her behind.

When they were deep inside the ghetto, the truck stopped in front of some more gates topped with barbed wire and guarded by a watchtower. The gates were dragged open and the truck passed through. They passed a sign that said *Camp for Polish Children and Youth, Łódź Ghetto*. So, this was where they were going: a prison within a prison. Looking around her, Joanna saw columns of children and teenagers marching, all dressed in a drab grey uniform and clogs, their heads bowed, eyes fixed on the ground. Chills went through her. Would she and Marta be amongst those children this time tomorrow?

The truck drew up in front of a two-storey building. The door of the cab slammed, and the officer came round to the back of the truck and let down the tailgate.

'Get down, all of you,' he said, 'and form a line in front of the door.'

Joanna climbed down from the truck and stared up at the austere building with its blank windows. It looked forbidding and struck more fear into her. She didn't want to go inside.

'We will take you to your dormitories,' the officer said. 'This is where you will stay while you complete your tests.'

Joanna stared up at the building. She really didn't want to go inside. And the thought of all these tests terrified her too. She hesitated for a few seconds, then felt the prod of a rifle in her back and walked forward quickly.

EIGHT

MARTA

Camp for Polish Children and Youth, Łódź Ghetto, Poland, 1944

Marta watched her sister's face anxiously while they were marched up the dirty concrete staircase and into a large dormitory on the first floor. She knew that Joanna was less resilient than she was, as well as being two years younger, and she was worried for her sister. Marta was aware of her own strength. She'd always had to help Mama, who'd suffered from ill health for several years, and she'd had to help care for Joanna throughout that time. Her mother's frailty had meant that Marta had to grow up before her time.

Joanna on the other hand had always been the baby of the family, the 'precious one' as Mama used to call her. She'd been sheltered and, as far as was possible in wartime, indulged. Perhaps it was to make up for the harsh conditions they were forced to exist in that Mama wanted to spoil and cosset Joanna. Perhaps it was also a way of compensating for her own frequent periods of inability to care for Joanna because of her ill health.

Now, Marta watched Joanna's face as she looked around the

dormitory. The place was dingy and dirty. The thin mattresses were heavily stained, and the place stank of urine. There were no sheets on any of the beds, which looked as though they had been thrown together from old wooden boards. On each bed was a greying, frayed blanket. Joanna's face registered shock when she looked around at their new accommodation and her shock quickly turned to dismay. Marta half expected her to start sobbing. Understandably, she'd done a lot of that since they'd been abducted in Jasło marketplace, but today she seemed to be making an effort to keep her tears at bay.

'This place is horrible,' Joanna said, her bottom lip trembling. 'I don't want to stay here.'

'Hush,' Marta said, 'I know it is, but we don't have a choice.'

She glanced nervously at the guard, who was allocating beds to the other children. Here, there weren't separate dormitories for girls and boys, or for different age groups; they were all lumped in together in one big, draughty room.

The guard approached them with a severe expression on his face. He tapped them both on the shoulder and pointed to two beds beside each other. Obediently, Marta and Joanna went and sat down on the beds. They didn't take their coats off – it was too chilly in the room. What would it be like at night with just one dirty blanket to keep you warm, Marta wondered.

The guard was just about to leave the room when Nurse Weiss came through the door. Everyone fell silent while she walked around the dormitory inspecting the beds, occasionally bending down and picking up a blanket and holding it up to the light or to her nose and shaking her head. Finally, she stopped in front of the guard and spoke to him sharply in German in a tone that showed that she was disgusted with the place. The guard replied and shook his head a few times, but Nurse Weiss persisted until he finally left the room. Then, she turned to speak to the children.

'I'm sorry that this place is so dirty, children. I have asked the guard to bring you more blankets. I asked for sheets and pillows too, but I'm told that there aren't any in the building. At least if you have more blankets, you shouldn't be cold at night. I also asked for the room to be cleaned, but was told that if we wanted it cleaned, we would have to do it ourselves. The other nurses and I will do that this afternoon if we can find anything to clean with.'

Marta felt a rush of gratitude towards Nurse Weiss. She seemed genuinely to have the care of the children at heart and to be shocked at the conditions they were expected to endure.

Later, Nurse Weiss and the two other nurses came back with dusters, brooms, mops and buckets. They set to work trying to make the dormitory more habitable, sweeping the floors, removing the cobwebs from the eaves, cleaning the blackened windows so a little light could come through. For a while, Marta sat on her bed watching them, but that made her feel guilty. She knew it was because she was so used to doing the cleaning at home, but it seemed wrong somehow to sit there and watch others work.

She got down from the bed and approached Nurse Weiss, who was kneeling up on a wooden chair, cleaning one of the windowsills.

'Can I help?' she asked.

Nurse Weiss turned and smiled.

'That's very kind of you, Marta. You don't have to, but if you'd like to, you could take that broom and sweep under the beds on that side of the room.'

Marta did as she suggested and soon several of the older children, including Joanna, had come forward and offered to help. It meant that within an hour the dormitory was far more habitable than it had been when they arrived, although no one could do anything about the smelly mattresses and blankets. A little later, a group of teenagers, dressed in the grey uniform of the camp, brought extra blankets and handed them out. These were a little less dirty than the existing ones, but still could hardly be described as clean.

Marta watched the older boys and girls as they went about their task. They looked terribly thin and unhealthy. None of them spoke or made eye contact with any of the other children. All had pale faces, many with sores round their mouths, and their hair looked filthy and matted. She felt desperately sorry for them and wondered why they were in the camp. It looked as though they were here to work. She'd heard of Nazi work camps before, but she didn't know that anyone other than Jews and gypsies were sent to them. These children were clearly Polish, like all the children in this dormitory.

When the cleaning was finished, they sat down on their beds once again.

'I'm so hungry,' Joanna said. 'Do you think they'll give us any food today?'

Marta realised that they hadn't had any lunch. They must have arrived in the camp after lunchtime. Glancing out of the window, she saw that the light was fading. It must be late afternoon.

'It will be supper time soon,' she told Joanna, more to stop her worrying than anything else. She had no idea when supper time actually was. She was hungry too.

To Marta's relief a shrill bell sounded soon after that and one of the guards appeared.

'Line up by the door. You are going down to the canteen to eat.'

They all trooped down the concrete stairs and entered another dingy room on the ground floor. The floor was covered in scraps and filth from previous meals, and the place smelled of rotting food. The room was laid out with long trestle tables and benches. Dozens of children were already seated, shovelling food into their mouths. No one was speaking. They were all dressed in the same grey uniform and, like the teenagers Marta

had seen earlier, every one of these children looked malnour-
ished and unhealthy.

Marta's group were told to sit at tables on one side of the
room. An orderly came and put bowls of watery soup and
spoons in front of them. Another brought water in tin cups.
Joanna started spooning her food into her mouth immediately
but Marta tried to take it slowly. The soup was lukewarm and
tasteless. Marta could tell that it was made from some sort of
vegetable but couldn't work out which one. At one point she
picked up some solid matter on her spoon and saw that it was
potato peel. She pulled a face, but was so hungry, she put it in
her mouth and chewed it anyway.

After supper they were sent back upstairs and told to get
into bed. Pyjamas were waiting for them on the beds, but they
appeared not to be the ones they'd worn the night before.

Nurse Weiss came and said goodnight. 'Tomorrow you will
each be examined by a doctor and take some more tests,' she
told them. 'I'm hoping that all this will be over very quickly and
that you will all be able to go somewhere better than this camp
very soon.'

At these words, Joanna began to sob. Nurse Weiss came
over and stroked her cheek.

'Don't worry, Joanna. Things will get better from now on.
And you are lucky to have your sister here with you.'

Marta was grateful to Nurse Weiss for her kind words. She
wanted to ask her what the tests would consist of or were for,
but she didn't want to alarm all the children around her. She
hadn't really understood Agata's explanation about the Nazis
testing whether they were Aryans or not. What did that even
mean? She wondered if the other girl had made it up in order to
look knowledgeable.

The lights of the dormitory went out and Nurse Weiss left
the room.

'I'm cold. Will you come into bed with me, Marta?' Joanna

asked after a few seconds, and Marta immediately got out of bed
and in beside her sister. As she had the night before, she slid her
arms around Joanna and held her tight. Soon she was warming
up and Joanna's steady breathing told her that she was fast
asleep. But Marta lay awake for a long time, listening to the sobs
and moans of some of the younger children. The poor little
things, they must be missing their mothers terribly. Marta
wished she could do something to alleviate their pain, but knew
she was powerless to help them. She thought of her own mother
and father. They must be desperate. Had someone from the
market told them what had happened? But even if they knew,
they would still be beside themselves with worry. Finally,
exhausted with the stress of it all, Marta closed her eyes and fell
into an uneasy sleep.

In the morning, they were given breakfast in the canteen.
This consisted of two slices of stale bread and a cup of coffee
that didn't taste like coffee at all.

'Do you know what it's made of?' Agata, who was sitting
beside Joanna, asked.

All the others shook their heads.

'Acorns,' Agata said triumphantly.

Marta wondered how she knew this and whether she was
making it up.

After breakfast they were told to go back to the dormitory
and wait. Then, one by one, they were called downstairs for
their medical examination. Lying on the bed, waiting, Marta
began to feel nervous about the forthcoming tests. What would
happen if they didn't pass? Surely whatever it was would be
worse than what might happen if they did pass the tests? She
told herself not to think about it. Whatever happened, she
would have to deal with it, but, glancing at Joanna, whose eyes
were wide with fear, she wasn't so sure about her.

'Shall we play I-Spy?' she asked, and Joanna brightened
instantly.

Marta was one of the first to be called by one of the unsmiling nurses who came to collect her. She followed the nurse downstairs to the ground floor, through some corridors, to a wing at the back of the building. There, she was told to sit down on a hard, wooden bench and wait. This place smelled the same as the hospital in Kraków.

At last, another nurse called Marta into a room and told her to sit down on a chair in the middle. A man in a white coat approached her with a clipboard.

'Marta Kaminsky?' he asked, surveying her with cold, blue eyes.

She nodded.

'I need to take some measurements,' he said, and produced a tape measure.

As before, he took various measurements from her face and head, then, muttering to himself, he wrote something down in a ledger. Then he asked her to stand up, and measured her waist and hips. Once again, he turned away from her to write something down. Then he produced a metal frame and asked her to rest her chin on the bottom of it while he made some adjustments and scribbled some notes down on his clipboard. He cut a lock of her hair off and put it in an envelope. This all felt very strange to Marta. She just wanted it to be over and done with.

He then brought a camera into the room, set it up on a tripod and photographed her from several different angles – both close up and from a distance. Marta began to tire of sitting up straight and staring into the camera. How much longer was this going to go on?

Finally, he took a needle from a cabinet and asked her to roll up her sleeve.

'I am going to take some blood from you for testing,' he said and plunged the needle into her arm.

She gasped. She'd had blood taken before but this hurt far more.

'You can leave now,' the doctor said blithely while she was still feeling faint from the shock of the needle. 'We will have the results of the tests in a day or two.'

She went out of the room and sat down on a chair for a few moments, and put her head in her hands to recover.

'You need to go back to the dormitory,' the nurse said. 'There is no room for you to sit here. Come along.'

Still feeling dizzy, Marta followed the nurse through the corridors and back into the main part of the building. As she was climbing the stairs she passed Joanna coming down, behind another nurse.

'Good luck, Joanna. It's not too bad after all. But they will take your blood, so be ready for the needle.'

'Hush!' The nurse turned round. 'You must not speak about the tests,' she snapped.

Joanna looked white-faced and terrified as she followed the other nurse down the stairs. Marta wished she could do something to alleviate her suffering. She would gladly have undergone the tests all over again in her place if it would take that terrified look off her sister's face.

The next few hours were taken up with children coming and going from the dormitory. Some returned crying, others rubbing their arms, looking bewildered. When Joanna came back, she sat down on the bed, tears streaming down her face.

'That doctor was so rough,' she said. 'He was horrible. He hurt my arm when he took blood.'

Marta stroked her hair. 'It's over now, my darling,' she said. 'You won't have to go through that again.'

Later that day, Nurse Weiss brought a hand-held camera upstairs. It had a lens that folded away on a metal frame. One by one, she photographed all the children sitting on their beds. She took a picture of Marta and Joanna together. Marta looked into the lens of the camera and tried to smile, but she was feeling so wretched, no smile would come.

'Why are you taking photographs?' Marta asked and Nurse Weiss smiled.

'Because I like to keep a record of what is happening. For the future,' she said. 'It might come in useful one day.'

The next morning, Marta woke very early. The sky was still grey and some weak sunlight was struggling over the rooftops opposite. She could hear the sound of many, many footsteps in the yard outside. Curious, she got out of bed and went over to the window. Dozens of children and teenagers were marching in columns across the yard, flanked by SS soldiers with guns and dogs. They were all dressed in the same grey uniform and clumsy wooden clogs. All looked cowed and reluctant, dragging their feet. She guessed they were being marched to work in factories or workshops, wherever they might be.

Gradually the rest of the children in the dormitory stirred, sat up and yawned and stretched. On each of their faces Marta saw bewilderment as they looked around, wondering where they were, then the change on their faces to misery as they gradually realised where they were and what was happening to them. Some of the little ones began to cry and moan, rubbing their eyes pitifully.

Joanna sat up and at first her face went through the same transformation. Then she caught sight of Marta and she smiled.

At that moment, the officer who had accompanied them from Kraków entered the room. He was carrying a clipboard.

'Sit up, children. I have the results of your tests.'

A murmur went through the room, then it fell silent.

'Listen very carefully because these results determine what happens to you today. Those who have passed the Aryan tests will be leaving today for a Lebensborn home in another part of Poland. You will then go on to the Reich, or Germany as you probably know it. The others will remain here for a while until decisions have been made about your future.'

He began to read out the list. It was in alphabetical order. When he came to the 'Ks' Marta was taut with anticipation.

'Maja Kaczmarek, Marta Kaminsky, Janick Kovac, Bartek Kowalski...'

A bolt of shock shot through Marta's body and she stared, open-mouthed, at the officer.

'What about me? Where's my name?' Joanna was saying, tears in her eyes.

'Hush, please,' the officer said. 'Let me finish.'

When he reached the end, all but three children's names had been read out. The other two, Marta quickly worked out, were a three-year-old boy and an eight-year-old girl. Both had darker hair than the others, a similar shade to Joanna's.

The officer turned and walked towards the door. Marta scrambled off the bed and ran after him.

'Please, please, sir. My sister isn't on the list,' she said. 'That must be a mistake. I am on the list and we are sisters. Please.'

He stared at her. 'Those not on the list were found to have gypsy or Jewish blood in their ancestry. She cannot be your sister. Now, get dressed and ready yourself. We will be leaving for Bruczków straight after breakfast.'

He pushed Marta away brusquely and marched out of the room. Marta turned towards Joanna with tears in her eyes. It was true – they were only half-sisters by blood – but it had never felt like that.

Joanna was collapsed on her tummy on the bed, sobbing into the filthy mattress. Marta rushed over and flung her arms around her sister and they lay together, clinging to each other, sobbing their hearts out.

NINE

MARGARETE

Camp for Polish Children and Youth, Łódź Ghetto, Poland, 1944

When Margarete saw the results of the tests on the children she couldn't believe her eyes. She had thought they would pass the Aryan tests without exception. After all, they had all got through the initial screening, so she'd expected them all to fulfil the rest of the strange and random criteria dreamed up by the Nazi racial theorists.

Shock went through her when, scanning the paper handed to her by the SS officer, she read the results and saw that three children had not got through. In particular, she could hardly believe that Marta Kaminsky had passed, but her sister Joanna had not.

She looked up at Untersturmführer Winkler, who was hovering over her, and asked to see the full results of Joanna and Marta's tests.

'Are you questioning the experts, Nurse Weiss?' the officer asked, frowning deeply.

'No, not at all. It's just that these two girls are sisters. It's extraordinary that one has passed while the other has failed.'

Muttering under his breath, Herr Winkler handed her two sets of papers and she studied them quickly. To her surprise, Joanna's tests showed a trace of Slavic ancestry, while Marta's ancestry was what was regarded as impeccable for an Aryan. She then scanned the answers the two children had given to the nurse at the reception centre at Kraków and it became clear to her that the girls had the same mother, but different fathers. She sat there, in the oppressive medical room at the back of the building in the Łódź ghetto, feeling horror running through her.

'If only I'd known...' she said.

'What's that, Nurse?' the officer asked.

'Oh, nothing,' she said quickly. But her mind was racing. If only she'd known that the two were half-sisters in advance, if she'd taken the trouble to look at the papers before, she would have foreseen this problem. But even if she had known, could she really have done anything to alter the results of the tests? She had no idea what the blood tests consisted of, or how the blood was analysed in the laboratory. How could they tell, she wondered, from a simple vial of blood, that buried deep in someone's family tree was a Slavic, Jewish or gypsy ancestor?

She thought again about the three poor children who had failed the tests: Joanna, Lili and Josef, a three-year-old boy. All they had in common was that their hair was a shade darker than all the others. That must be it, she decided. That was what had led to the conclusion that they had ancestry that the Nazis considered less than desirable. Their future had been decided simply on the colour of their hair.

'Can I come upstairs with you when you deliver the news?' she asked.

'Absolutely not, Nurse. This is an SS matter and I've already witnessed how you encourage weakness in the children. There is no sugar-coating what I have to tell them.'

'I must protest, Untersturmführer,' she said, raising her voice. 'We are talking about a three-year-old boy, barely more than a baby, and two girls aged eight and ten years old. These are young children; they are not soldiers, or even adults. The news will be devastating for them, especially for the sisters who will have to be parted, I'm assuming.'

'Half-sisters, Nurse,' he corrected her. 'And the answer is no. I repeat: I will deliver this news alone. I may have to report your concerns to the Reich Main Office if this dissenting behaviour continues.'

Margarete turned away, exasperated. The man had no feelings whatsoever. She watched him gather up the papers on the desk, straighten his cap with the SS death's-head skull on the front and adjust the buttons on his collar.

'As a matter of interest, what *does* happen to the children who fail the tests?' she asked.

'No decision has been made as yet,' he replied, avoiding her gaze. 'For the time being, they will stay here in the children's camp. In time, they may be transported elsewhere.'

'Elsewhere?'

'Use your imagination, Nurse.'

What could that mean? To an adult labour camp? Margarete had heard that more and more of these terrible, inhumane places had been built all over Germany, Poland and the other occupied countries. Why ever would anyone want to send an innocent child to one of those terrible places where people died all the time of overwork, starvation and disease?

'Now, I'm going to tell the children the news right away. When I come back, you may go up and see them yourself. You'll need to prepare them for the journey.'

She watched him go, powerless to stop him. She wanted to scream, but in order to stop herself, she clenched her fists and dug her nails into her palms.

She promised herself she would ensure that she had the

details of all the children noted down in code in her secret note-books. She had already written down their names, addresses and the dates they were taken from their families. Later, when they reached the assimilation camp at Bruczków, they would be given new, Germanised names, so she would note those down beside their original Polish ones. She'd reached the conclusion, when she first started working for the Lebensborn programme, that keeping meticulous records might help somebody one day. It seemed far too little to be doing in the face of all this horror, but she clung to the hope that it was something at least. There were also the photographs. She wasn't quite sure why she'd taken them, but it was part of her instinct to record everything that happened.

Suddenly she had a thought. She got up from the desk and went through to the laboratory behind the office. The young Polish lab assistant smiled at her. She'd got talking to him yesterday. She'd immediately realised she could trust him, and he'd said he would develop the photographs for her himself in the lab for a few marks.

'I was wondering, how are the photos coming on?' she asked.

'They are ready, Nurse Weiss. I did them yesterday evening. Would you like to take them now?'

'Not all of them,' she said. 'Do you remember the one of two girls?'

He nodded. 'Of course. I made two copies of that negative. I judged that each of the children would need a copy.'

'You're a genius!' she said, genuinely impressed, and he blushed with pleasure.

'It would be better if you took all the photographs now, though,' he said. 'They will have less chance of being discovered if you have them, rather than here in my drawer. We often have inspections...'

He opened a drawer in his desk, picked up a bulging envelope and handed it to her.

'Be careful, won't you?'

'Of course,' Margarete said, 'And thank you so, so much, Marek.'

She handed him ten Reichsmarks and hastily shoved the envelope into her handbag. When she went back through into the office, the Untersturmführer was coming back through the door. She hastily went over and sat down at the desk, putting her handbag quickly beside her feet.

'You may go up to the dormitory now, Nurse Weiss,' he said.

She opened her mouth to ask him how the news had been received by the children, but then closed it again, thinking better of it. This man had no compassion, no mercy, so he probably hadn't noticed their reaction, and if he had, he was unlikely to tell her anyway.

When the officer had his back turned, she picked up her handbag and left the room, and hurried up the stairs to the dormitory with great trepidation. When she entered, Marta and Joanna were lying together on the bed, crying. Before going to them, she quickly checked on the other children who hadn't passed the tests. The little boy had no understanding of what it all meant, so was unaffected by the news, but the little girl, Lili, asked her some questions.

'What does it mean?'

'It means that you will stay in Poland for a while, that you'll not be going to Germany.'

'Does it mean I can go home?' Lili asked, sudden hope in her eyes.

Margarete shook her head and put her arm around her. 'I'm afraid not. Not yet at least. To start with, you will stay here. You might be sent somewhere else soon but at least you know where you will be for a while.'

'Will *you* be here?' she asked and, once again, Margarete had to disappoint her.

'I have to go with the others,' she said. 'Other people will look after you, though. And Joanna will be here too. And little Josef. You will be together. Try to be brave.'

The little girl sat on her bed silently, contemplating it all.

'I'll come back in a little while,' Margarete promised, then went over to Joanna and Marta and laid her hand on Joanna's back.

'I'm so sorry, Joanna,' she said, and tried to murmur some words of comfort. But everything she said seemed inadequate, and nothing she could say would stop the tears that both Marta and Joanna were shedding.

She opened her handbag and surreptitiously flicked through the bundle of photographs until she found the girls.

'Look, I've brought your photos,' she said quietly, 'I will write on them for you.'

She took her pen out of her bag and scribbled a message on the back of each photo. She knew it could get her into serious trouble, but she needed to try to alleviate the sisters' pain.

'Never give up hope,' she wrote in Polish on the back of each photograph, then she signed them and gave one to each girl. Their crying subsided momentarily as they took the photos and studied them.

She sat down on the bed and put one arm around each girl.

'I'm so, so sorry,' she said. 'If I'd known, I would have tried to stop it.'

'It's not your fault, Nurse Weiss,' Marta said through her tears.

Margarete was touched that, even in this terrible moment, Marta could be so generous.

'I will try to speak to the Untersturmführer again, but please don't count on it.'

The germ of an idea was forming in her mind. She was

supposed to have told the children to get ready for their journey, but instead, after telling Marta and Joanna that she would be back soon, she left the dormitory and hurried downstairs again. She went back through to the medical room and into the lab, where the young lab assistant still sat, peering down a microscope. She knew that in speaking to him she would be taking all sorts of risks, but she was prepared for that. Hadn't she already taken many, many risks for those in her charge?

'Marek,' she said, and he looked up.

'Is something wrong with the photos?' he asked.

She pulled up a stool and sat down beside him. She took a deep breath, trying to slow her heartbeat down.

'No, no, they are perfect. It's something else. When we spoke yesterday, I think I detected something in your manner,' she said. She moved closer to him and lowered her voice still further. 'I'm taking a risk here in asking you this, but do you have friends in the Polish resistance, by any chance?'

He stared at her, his eyes wide with fear.

'I know. I know,' she said. 'You think I'm trying to trick you but trust me, nothing could be further from the truth. I wouldn't ask, but I'm desperate. Is there any way of changing the tests on those children who failed?'

He shook his head. 'I'm sorry. There are so many tests. It's not just the blood tests, it's appearance, measurements, everything. If I were to change something now, it would be obvious. The SS have seen the results already.'

'Well then, I will ask you this,' she said, looking straight into his eyes. 'The three children who failed. Will you contact your friends in the resistance about them and try to get them out of here? They might not be able to go home at first, but they could be cared for by good people, instead of these monsters.'

The young man hesitated.

'Marek, please. They will die here, or in one of the work camps.'

He swallowed, then spoke in a whisper.

'I will try. I do know some people, as you guessed. I will ask them to try.'

'Thank you,' she said.

Margarete got her notebook out of her bag and scribbled down the names and home addresses of the three children. 'If there's any hope of getting them home,' she said, tearing out the page and handing it to Marek. His hand shook as he took it from her.

'Thank you! You are very brave,' she said. Then she got out her purse, took out all the Reichsmark notes she had and handed them to him. 'This won't be enough but it is a start.'

He stared at the money, then slipped it into his pocket.

'Now, I have to go and help the children get ready for the journey,' Margarete said. 'If I don't see you again, good luck, Marek, and thank you from the bottom of my heart.'

TEN

MARTA

Camp for Polish Children and Youth, Łódź Ghetto, Poland, 1944

Being parted from Joanna was the worst thing that had ever happened to Marta. It was even worse than when they'd been seized by the SS in the marketplace at Jasło. That had been a terrible shock, but at least they'd been together. Knowing she was going to have to leave her sister behind at the youth camp made Marta feel as though she was losing part of herself, as though her heart would never heal.

They sat together on the bed, arms entwined, contemplating the terrible situation they were in. Nurse Weiss returned to the dormitory and asked everyone, apart from the three children who were staying behind, to get ready for the journey to Bruczków.

Holding back the tears, and with an aching heart, Marta rolled her pyjamas up and put on her coat and shoes. That was all she had. Although they'd been promised new clothes at the camp, they hadn't been given any. Not that Marta really cared about new clothes right now. She would happily go about in blue pyjamas for ever if it meant she and Joanna could stay together.

She sat on the bed beside Joanna and put her arms around her again. When her sister started sobbing, Marta's tears fell too.

'We will be together again one day,' Marta said. 'Be strong, Joanna, and just concentrate on trying to get through each day. When the war is over, we will both be able to go home.'

'Are you sure?' Joanna looked up at her with wet, blotchy cheeks, a glimmer of hope in her eyes. Of course Marta wasn't sure. They both knew that. How could she be? But it was good to have something in the future to hold on to, even if it wasn't true.

'Yes,' she said, 'never lose hope.'

Nurse Weiss came over and sat down on the bed beside Joanna.

'I'm so, so sorry that this has happened, girls,' she said, and Marta saw that there were tears in her eyes too. 'If there is any way I can help you to find each other in the future, I will. In the meantime, you mustn't breathe a word of this to anyone, but I've asked a friend to help Joanna get out of this camp. He will come and see you soon, I'm sure.'

Marta looked at her with gratitude. A chink of real hope opened up in her heart. She was going to ask Margarete to explain more, but the SS officer came into the room. Nurse Weiss got to her feet and went to help other children to get ready.

'The lorry is ready to take you to the train station,' he announced, and Marta's stomach plummeted. This was it. This was the end. She turned towards Joanna and kissed her on the lips for the last time.

'Take care, my little one,' she said and tried to move away, but Joanna wouldn't let her go. She clung to Marta and started to cry and shout.

'Don't leave me. Please don't leave me here.'

Pity overwhelmed Marta and she sat down on the bed beside her sister again. The officer hurried over, seeing the commotion.

'I want to stay here with my sister,' Marta said, looking up at him, her voice shaking.

'It is not possible. You belong in the Reich,' the man said. 'And she does not.'

'Please. I don't mind staying. I'm happy to work. I'll do anything...'

'Don't talk nonsense. Now, come on,' he said. 'And you let her go,' he snapped at Joanna.

Joanna shook her head, so in a flash the man bent down and seized Marta by the waist. He started picking her up, pulling her away from Joanna. But Joanna kept holding on, digging her fingers into Marta's arms. The man prised Joanna's hands off her sister and flung her down on the boards of the dormitory. Marta was stunned into silence.

'Untersturmführer Winkler, that really isn't necessary,' Nurse Weiss said, hurrying over.

'Be quiet, Nurse. This is not your concern,' the man said.

'But, please...'

The man put Marta, who started screaming and crying again immediately, over his shoulder, and carried her out of the dormitory and down the stairs. She was kicking him and pummelling his back all the way and, when they got outside, he slapped her hard around the face and flung her in the back of the lorry.

Marta found herself face down on the boards, panting for breath, her cheek stinging. She scrambled up and found a place to sit on one of the benches. Looking up at the windows of the dormitory as the lorry drew away towards the gates of the camp, she caught her last glimpse of her sister's tear-stained face peering down at them.

.   .   .

The train journey to a remote station near Bruczków took the rest of the day. As before, the children were given their own compartment on the train. Marta stared out at the flat farmland, the stone-built farm buildings and villages that the train steamed through. She was grateful that this time the blinds weren't drawn over the windows. Trees lined the track and she saw that some of them bore the first bright green growth of springtime. Realising that the seasons were changing and that she wouldn't see the cherry blossom and spring flowers with Joanna this time brought a lump to her throat. How could she bear this?

She looked around at the other children. They all looked as sad as she felt, but on many of their faces she noticed an expression of resigned acceptance. They were two days ahead of her in terms of accepting the loss of their entire families. Having Joanna with her until now had softened the blow at first, but their traumatic parting that morning had made it an even harder transition.

She decided to think back over her memories of Joanna, to try to fix them in her mind. She recalled when she'd first seen her sister as a newborn, swaddled in shawls, taking her first breaths, then playing with her as a toddler, teaching her games and her first letters, to caring for her while Mama was sick. Since the day Joanna was born the two hadn't spent a night apart and Marta couldn't bear to think how she might feel when night-time came.

At last, with a blast of the horn and a lot of hissing of brakes, the train pulled into a remote country station. They had been travelling for several hours. None of them knew where they were. All the children were ordered to get out of the carriage and line up on the station platform.

As usual there was a truck waiting for them outside the station. They were pushed on to the back of it by soldiers, prodding them with rifle butts, shouting at them to hurry. Then, the truck took them to a large, rambling manor house on the edge of a wood. When it stopped, they were ordered out with the usual barked orders from soldiers.

As she climbed down from the back of the truck, Marta saw that this place was in the middle of nowhere. The nearest village, Bruczków, which they'd driven through on the way, was very small, only a few ancient houses and a couple of farms. It was in the middle of farmland that stretched as far as the eye could see.

'Walk in line into the house,' one of the soldiers shouted to them. So they moved off, walking tentatively, everyone looking around at their new surroundings.

Once inside, a soldier pointed them into a bare room on the ground floor. When they were all inside, he shouted, 'Sit down on the floor. All of you. Sit down.'

As she sat down on the bare boards, Marta noticed that Nurse Weiss was seated on a chair at the end of the room, looking anxious. She wondered where the other nurses were and realised that she'd seen them climbing back into the truck after the children had got out. Perhaps they weren't staying here. She hoped fervently that Nurse Weiss was.

A tall man in glasses, dressed in a white coat, strode into the room and stood in front of them. He clapped his hands for their attention, even though all the children were far too intimidated to speak, let alone make a noise. Then he gave the Nazi salute and said, 'Heil Hitler!'

'Good afternoon, children,' he said then in the same broken Polish that all the Germans used. 'I am Doctor Schiller, the director of this regional children's home here at Bruczków. We Germans call it an assimilation home, because what we do here is try to get you used to German ways and prepare you for life in the Reich. I will tell you a bit about how it works. Now, every day, in the mornings, you will all have two hours' study of the German language.'

'Doctor Schiller,' Nurse Weiss interrupted him, leaning forward in her seat, 'some of these children are only three years old.'

'Precisely, Nurse. And these are the children most ripe for assimilation. They absorb languages like sponges. They will have no trouble at all with daily language lessons, I can assure you. We do it all the time here, Nurse.'

Nurse Weiss sat back, looking troubled, and Doctor Schiller carried on speaking.

'In the afternoons, the older children will study German culture and society. I'm sure you will all find that fascinating. The younger ones will be supervised by our nursery staff. After those lessons, there will be lessons in marching, followed by physical work such as gardening. As well as all this preparation, you will receive new identities. New names and new papers, in order to make you completely German.'

Marta looked at Agata, who was sitting next to her, frowning, and Agata shrugged. Marta didn't want to receive a new name and a new identity. She was Marta Kaminsky from Floriańska Street in Jasło. She was Polish too, just like Mama and Tata, and she never wanted to forget that fact. She looked round at the other children's faces. Most seemed bewildered. The younger ones clearly didn't understand any of this and were looking around them and fidgeting.

'There are other things that we will be doing to ensure that you quickly forget your Polish ancestry and become fully German. We will explain those things as we go along. Now, most of you will only be here a few months until your language skills are sufficiently developed for you to go to Germany. Others may stay longer. If you show obedience and a willingness to learn, that will help you enormously.'

He paused and smiled down at the children for the first time.

'I must tell you, in the public parts of this building, that is in the dining room, the classrooms and the garden, from tomorrow morning, you will not be allowed to speak Polish. You may do so in the dormitory, but that is all. This is a German institution and only the German language is allowed.'

The older children all stared at him open-mouthed. Most of them hardly knew a word of German; could this really be the rule?

'But, Doctor,' Nurse Weiss spoke up again, 'none of these children speak any German at all. It means that in the public rooms they will have to be silent.'

The doctor wheeled round on his heels to glare at her.

'Precisely. It is designed to have the effect of encouraging them to learn quickly, Nurse,' he said. 'Now,' he continued turning back to the children, 'I expect you are hungry after your long journey. Let us go through to the dining room, where supper is waiting for you.'

Everyone got to their feet and trooped through to a large room with a big window overlooking a windswept garden. There were four long trestle tables in this room, two of them already occupied by children aged from three or four to six or seven years old. Marta realised that she, Maja, Agata and the other older children in their group were the oldest ones here.

Supper followed the same routine as in the reception centre and youth camp. This time it was doled out by an ample-looking kitchen lady with a red face. Once again it was soup and stale bread, but Marta didn't mind. She was very hungry; she realised that they had been taken to the train without breakfast, and all they'd had that day was water and some slices of bread that were passed around the carriage.

The dormitories were upstairs and to Marta's relief, the older girls, of whom there were six, were all together in one room, while the rest of the children were in a larger, adjoining one. Here at least the beds, although narrow, had clean sheets and pillows and two blankets each.

She slipped between the sheets and lay down, exhausted, but sleep wouldn't come. It had been bad enough during the daytime to keep her mind from its wildest imaginings about Joanna. But now she had nothing else to think about, she started running over the worst possible scenarios for her sister. Where was she now? Still in the same dormitory in the youth camp with the smelly beds, lying awake miserable and cold, missing her sister desperately, or sobbing herself to sleep? What would happen to her tomorrow? Would she be marched to work, like the poor children they had seen in the yard? Tears stung her eyes just thinking about it. And what about Nurse Weiss's plan: would that work? Would Joanna be able to escape from the camp and find her way home?

She lay awake feeling desperately miserable until the first light of dawn appeared in the sky and the birds started twittering in the trees outside. Then, finally, she slipped into a fitful sleep. But she didn't sleep for long. Woken by shouting and screaming from the adjoining dormitory, she sat up.

'What's happening?' she asked Agata in the next bed.

'I don't know.'

Marta swung her legs out of bed and ran to the door. There, she watched what was happening in horror. A nurse was standing over one of the smaller boys, who was lying face down on the bed. His pyjamas were round his ankles and the nurse was whipping him with some sort of implement. The little boy was squealing. The other children were sitting up in their beds, eyes wide with fear.

'Hey!' Marta ran forward and grabbed the nurse's apron and tried to pull her away. The woman spun round and hit her round the head with the implement, which looked like ropes tied together, something normally used to beat the dust from rugs. Marta stumbled backwards and fell on the floor and the woman resumed beating the boy.

As Marta was getting to her feet, the door opened and

Nurse Weiss hurried into the room. She rushed over to the bed where the nurse was still beating the boy.

'Stop that,' she said, seizing the woman's arm.

The nurse turned towards her angrily.

'The boy wet the bed and we've been told to beat them if they do that.'

'Not any more. I'm in charge of the nursing staff here now. The poor boy is confused and unhappy. He's been torn from his family, no wonder he's wet the bed. Now go and get a cold flannel and cool his skin down, Nurse. Then change his bed and let him have a bit more sleep. I will not tolerate cruelty to children while I'm in charge. Do you understand?'

'Yes, ma'am,' the nurse said sullenly and headed towards the washrooms.

ELEVEN

JOANNA

Camp for Polish Children and Youth, Łódź Ghetto, Poland, 1944

Joanna was too distressed to get up the day that Marta was taken away. She lay on her bed, staring up at the filthy, cobwebbed ceiling, wondering where her sister was at that moment, if they would ever see each other again, and what would become of her in this terrible place. She also wondered if she would soon start to look like the other children she'd seen in the camp – skinny, covered in sores, and unable to smile.

The hours passed. Numbed by loss, she didn't move from the bed, other than to visit the smelly washroom on the ground floor. She found it hard to walk down the stairs, her whole body was aching and her head was pounding. Had she caught one of those terrible illnesses that people got in work camps?

She wondered why no one had come to tell them what to do. Perhaps they'd been forgotten? She wondered too if the friend who Nurse Weiss had mentioned would come and find her soon. She wished Nurse Weiss had been able to tell her more about the plan. It all sounded so strange that she began to wonder if she'd dreamed it. Her dreams had been horrible since she'd been snatched from Jasło. Perhaps this was just another one of those.

The other two children who had failed the tests, Lili and Josef, were lying on their beds. Joanna felt a surge of pity for them both. They were just as unlucky as she was. More so perhaps, because they hadn't shared the first part of their ordeal with their sister. She propped herself up on her elbow.

'Hey, Josef, Lili. Why don't you come and lie on these beds next to me? We can talk.'

The two children didn't need any encouragement. They picked up their blankets and made their way over to Joanna, and settled themselves on the beds either side of hers.

'Did you have lunch?' she asked them, and they shook their heads miserably.

'I'm hungry,' Josef said, rubbing his stomach.

'Me too,' Joanna said. 'When it gets dark, the bell will ring. We must go down to the canteen for supper then and eat what we can,' she went on 'We must keep up our strength.'

Listening to herself speak, she realised that she sounded just like Marta. Those were the sort of things that her sister would say. That was a good thing. Normally she would have let Marta take charge of everything, but Marta wasn't here.

She quickly realised that, because she was the eldest of the three, the other two would look up to her and follow what she said. Knowing this stopped her feeling quite so sorry for herself. She could help these two children – all she had to do was to imagine what Marta might do or say.

She watched the sky anxiously, willing it to get dark. Her stomach was taut with hunger. When, finally, the bell rang, she got up and led the other two downstairs to the canteen. They sat at the end of one of the trestle tables. Other children, dressed in grey uniforms, joined them, almost jostling them off the bench, and supper was doled out. It was the same as the previous day: vegetable soup made with potato peelings and a slice of stale bread. While Joanna ate, she glanced at the boy who sat beside her. He looked about thirteen; his cheeks were hollow, his head shaved, and she couldn't help noticing that he smelled of sweat and filthy clothes.

'Where are you from?' she asked him, and he almost spluttered his soup out in surprise. Clearly, nobody normally made conversation at mealtimes; they were too preoccupied with eating as much as they could in the time available.

'Warsaw,' he replied, not taking his eyes off his bowl and continuing to spoon soup into his mouth.

'Why are you here?' Joanna persisted.

The boy wiped his greasy mouth with the back of his hand. 'One day, the SS came to the house and took my father and mother away to Germany to work. It's called forced labour. I was left alone in the house. That was two years ago. One day, another lorry came and picked me up and brought me here. I put up a fight, but it didn't do any good.'

Joanna stared at him. It was almost as bad as her own experience.

'What about everyone else here?' she asked.

The boy shrugged. 'I don't know everyone's story,' he said, looking around at the other pale faces at the table. 'Some people's parents were in the resistance and were executed. Some were sent to concentration camps. Some children were orphans already and having to fend for themselves on the streets.'

'And what do you have to do here?' she asked, and he stared at her with disbelief.

'Isn't it obvious?' he asked. 'We have to work, of course. Some of us are taken off to factories in the ghetto or in the city, others to workshops here in the camp, others have to look after and clean the camp buildings. We work twelve hours a day, six days a week, for no reward other than a rat-infested dormitory and this slop,' he said, gesturing at his soup.

Joanna was shocked into silence. Marta had told her about the columns of children she'd seen marching across the yard. They were being marched off to work, even though some of them were probably as young as ten years old, Joanna's own age. She looked around her at the room full of children guzzling the filthy soup as if their lives depended on it and a shudder went through her. This was what was going to happen to the three of them, she was sure of it, unless they had somehow been forgotten. It was strange that no one in authority had been to see them all day.

But that was not to be. When they left the canteen together, a woman in uniform approached them. 'You three, come with me,' she said sharply, and they followed her down a long, tiled passage to a room at the end.

Inside was a barber's chair and a mirror. A man in an overall at the end of the room was reading a newspaper. He stood up when he saw them enter and grabbed a razor.

'You first.' The woman nodded to Joanna.

Trembling, Joanna sat down in the big chair and stared into the mirror. It was the first time she'd seen her face since she'd been taken from Jasło marketplace. What she saw shocked her. Even in the space of a few days, her face had grown thinner. Her cheekbones stood out and she looked old somehow. She was incredibly pale, with bruised skin under her eyes from crying.

The man took some scissors and cut all her hair off first. Joanna loved her hair, and she watched it fall on the floor in clumps. She and Marta had prided themselves on having long plaits and had often compared the length of their hair. She'd hardly ever had it cut. With a shaved head, she would be just the same as all the other poor children in the camp.

After he'd cut her hair short, the man took the razor and

shaved off the rest of it. He didn't use shaving soap or cream and the blade felt blunt, nicking her scalp in several places, leaving tiny cuts and making her flinch. When he'd finished, she stared at herself in the mirror. How pitiful she looked with her bare head and her big, sad eyes. Even more pitiful than before.

'Get up,' the barber said, indicating impatiently, and motioned for Lili to sit down in her place. Joanna stood and watched the same process being carried out on Lili and then on Josef. The little boy cried when the barber cut him, and the man rewarded him with a slap on the cheek. He didn't cry again.

When they'd finished, the woman ushered them back along the corridor and into another room. This room seemed to be some sort of storeroom. It was lined with shelves, on which were stacked piles of grey cloth. The woman pulled a couple of piles down and handed one to Lili and one to Joanna. On a lower shelf were pairs of wooden clogs. Again, she handed a pair to Lili and a pair to Joanna.

'Put them on,' she said, and pushed Josef out into the corridor. 'Stay there,' she ordered him and shut the door. 'You can give me your blue uniforms and change into these ones,' she told the girls. 'Give me your shoes too.'

Joanna's hands didn't seem to work properly when she tried to undo the belt of her pyjamas and she realised they were shaking. She fumbled with the knot that Marta had helped her to tie that morning.

'Come here,' the woman said impatiently and pulled the knot apart. Joanna quickly kicked off her shoes and got out of the blue pyjamas, and stood shivering in her grubby pants.

'Well, put the grey one on,' the woman said, and, with clumsy hands, Joanna obeyed, the rough cloth of the grey uniform grazing her skin as she pulled it on.

'Now the clogs.'

Joanna put her feet into the hard, clumsy wooden shoes. Even before she took a step, they pinched her feet.

'Now come with me,' the woman said.

Josef was still standing outside the door. He looked up enquiringly when they emerged from the room.

'What about me?' he asked the woman.

'You are too young to work,' she said. 'There is no place for young children here. You will be sent somewhere else.'

'No!' he cried. 'I want to stay with Lili and Joanna.'

This outburst was rewarded with a slap around the head from the woman. Then she picked him up by one arm, told the girls to stay where they were and dragged him along the corridor and into another room near the end.

'Where is he?' Joanna asked when the woman returned.

'He will be taken to another camp. As I said, he is too young to stay here.'

Joanna stared at her. If he was too young to stay here, where would he be sent? To an orphanage perhaps? To a children's home?

'Can we say goodbye?' Lili asked and the woman gave her a withering look.

'Of course not. There is no need for that,' she snapped.

They walked past the closed door and could hear Josef's cries even through the thick wood. Joanna felt wretched for him. What had he done to deserve this treatment? He must be feeling terrible.

They reached the bottom of the stairs up to their dormitory.

'Now up you go. Be sure to get a good sleep. The bell will ring at six a.m. and you must get up and be down at breakfast by six thirty. Tomorrow, you will be working, like all the other children here. And after work, we will transfer you to the girls' dormitory. But tonight, you will stay in there. Now off you go.'

Joanna took Lili's hand and together they walked up the concrete stairs to the dormitory. The woman hadn't even said goodnight. How Joanna wished that Nurse Weiss was with them now.

She and Lili lay down in their beds side by side. It felt strange, just the two of them going to sleep in this enormous room. Joanna felt a sliver of fear enter her heart. She'd always been afraid of the dark, but she took some deep breaths and told herself to keep calm. She wasn't a little girl any more, she had a responsibility to herself and to Lili to be strong. Besides, what could possibly be frightening about the dark? She was already facing the most terrifying time of her life. The darkness could hold no monsters for her in comparison to the fear instilled in her by Untersturmführer Winkler, the woman who'd slapped Josef and shut him in the room, and all the other terrifying people who worked here.

TWELVE

MARGARETE

Bruczków Assimilation Home, Poland

Margarete Weiss sat in her new office that looked out over the bleak, windswept countryside. She was at her desk making coded notes in her notebook. She was recording that three of the twenty children they had brought from Kraków – Joanna, Lili and Josef – had failed the Aryan tests and had been left behind at the Camp for Polish Children and Youth in Łódź Ghetto. Somehow, at some point in the near future, she would try to find out whether the children were able to escape from the camp and record that too. She didn't want to write to Marek, the lab technician at the children's camp in Łódź, at least not at the moment, for fear of compromising him, but she would find another way of discovering the truth.

She closed her book and put it into the drawer of her desk, turned the key and slipped it into her handbag. Then she put her head in her hands and took some deep breaths. Every so often, grief would rear its head and she would be almost over-whelmed with sadness for her lost family, especially her baby daughter Tomasina, and for Tomas Müller, the father of her child. The extent of her loss would paralyse her momentarily, and in those moments she would feel as though she couldn't go on. She had learned that, if she let the feelings come to her and didn't try to resist them, they would reach a peak before subsiding, and soon she would gradually go back to her normal state, one in which she was aware of her grief, but where it didn't threaten to overwhelm her.

Losing Joanna, Lili and Josef had added to her sadness. She was angry with herself for not having predicted what might happen. Perhaps she could have fended it off, if only she'd been more aware of the consequences of failing the tests. She sighed, thinking of all the injustices and cruelty meted out by the Lebensborn programme. Each and every time she witnessed one, she blamed herself for not having been able to prevent it.

She turned her mind back to the children's home. She knew she had her work cut out to improve things here. It seemed as though, until now, it had been run along the harshest of lines. She would do her best to change that, although Doctor Schiller seemed to be a dyed-in-the-wool Nazi. He didn't appear to have an ounce of compassion. He had no children himself, and lived with his wife, a hardbitten-looking woman, in an apartment in one of the wings of the house away from the rest of the staff, like Margarete, whose rooms were on the top floor. Margarete had seen Frau Schiller about the corridors sometimes. She looked like a typical Nazi, with severe grey hair and a hard, set jaw – all she lacked was the SS uniform.

Margarete sighed. She would certainly have to fight to change things under Schiller's supervision. She would find a way, though, she was sure of that. She reminded herself of all the risks she'd taken so far – the young mothers and babies she'd helped both in Bavaria and in Norway, the records in her notebooks that she'd taken so many risks to keep. She was convinced that these notebooks would be useful at some point in the future.

There was a knock at the door and a nurse put her head round.

'You wanted to see me, Nurse Weiss?' the woman said.

'Yes, Nurse. Come in and sit down.'

Margarete had decided to speak individually to the three nurses under her supervision. She wanted to know first-hand what went on at the home and to set out how she was going to change things, although she knew that she would have to tread carefully to avoid being reported to Reich Security Main Office.

The woman who entered was middle-aged and running to fat. Her shoulders drooped and her uniform strained at the seams. She had a sullen look about her. It was the nurse whom Margarete had stopped beating the little boy early that morning.

'Good morning, Nurse Wolff,' Margarete said. 'Please sit down. I asked you in because I want to get to know a little bit about the running of this home. You have been here for... how long?'

'Three years,' the woman said proudly. 'I'm the longest-serving member of staff, apart from Doctor Schiller, of course.'

'And where did you work before?'

'In a reception centre, in Kalisz.'

'So, that was somewhere that children were brought when they'd been taken from their families?'

'Yes,' the nurse replied without a trace of emotion.

'So, you will have seen how traumatic that is for these children, especially in the first few days of separation.'

The nurse shrugged. 'I don't know about that. My job was to look after the little ones in the dormitory.'

Margarete regarded the other woman for a moment. She could barely imagine anyone less suited to that task.

'And did looking after the little ones include administering beatings to them if they wet the bed?'

The woman's face coloured and she shuffled in the chair.

'Of course. The Nazi way is to be tough on these children – softness and pandering do them no favours at all.'

Margarete sighed. How many times had she heard that line before? In Schloss Schwanburg, the Lebensborn home in Bavaria, she had gone out on a limb against all this ideology and had encouraged the young mothers to cuddle their babies and to pick them up if they cried. This was completely contrary to Nazi philosophy on childcare, which was to show babies no affection and to ignore them if they cried. It was supposedly to toughen them up to become good soldiers or citizens of the future. She drew herself up in her chair.

'I know about those teachings, Nurse Wolff,' she said, looking the older woman in the eye, 'but I'm afraid I fundamentally disagree with them, particularly in this case. These children are traumatised and confused, especially the young ones. They have just been taken from their families and have lost everything they knew and loved. They have been plunged into a confusing, new environment that is wholly unfamiliar to them. I see our duty as being to comfort them. To help them through that difficult transition.'

Nurse Wolff stared at her, her eyes slightly narrowed. It was impossible to know what she was thinking.

'I'm afraid if you don't agree with me, Nurse Wolff, it would be better all round if you were to transfer to another home elsewhere.'

'I don't think Doctor Schiller would agree with you,' Nurse Wolff replied. 'In fact, I'm sure he wouldn't.'

'Let me worry about Doctor Schiller, Nurse,' Margarete said, knowing full well that as soon as she'd left the room Nurse Wolff would be hurrying to tell Doctor Schiller everything she had said. 'Now, I would like you to tell me a bit about the routines here in the home. In particular, the discipline of the children. I'm very interested in what has been happening here up until now.'

'Well, as you've already seen, there is a strict routine here. The children are woken at six thirty in the morning. They must get dressed in their uniforms and be down in the dining room by seven o'clock. After breakfast, they must go outside for exercise for half an hour. Lessons start at eight o'clock and continue until lunchtime. In the mornings they must learn German and in the afternoons they are taught Nazi ideology, marching and PE. Then they work in the gardens.'

'And who teaches them?'

'There are two teachers, one for the older children and one for the younger ones. They live here in the school.'

'And what about this rule about not speaking Polish, how is that enforced?'

'The same way we enforce no wetting the beds,' Nurse Wolff replied stiffly.

'You mean with a beating?'

Nurse Wolff nodded, her eyes steady.

'And what else is enforced with a beating?'

'Bad behaviour, disobedience, lack of cleanliness and disagreeable conduct.'

Margarete digested this information for a moment and then said quietly, 'While I'm in charge here, Nurse Wolff, there will be no more beatings. No more at all. If a child misbehaves, please send them to speak to me. Bedwetting is to be expected amongst the younger children in such circumstances, and if they want to speak their native language outside the dormitory, I cannot see a problem with that.'

'It will take them longer to learn German with that approach and they will be here for longer,' the nurse replied.

'So be it, Nurse Wolff,' Margarete said. 'Thank you for coming to see me. I hope all this is clear. Please could you send in one of your colleagues when you go out?'

Margarete repeated the same conversation with the two other nurses, both of whom were younger and seemed a little

more flexible than Nurse Wolff. When she'd finished, she went
through to the classrooms to watch the lessons. She crept into
the back of the room where the older children were being
taught.

They were all sitting rigidly at desks while the teacher, an
earnest young man with a Hitler moustache, shouted out
German words and got the children to repeat them. Behind
him, on either side of the blackboard, two great Nazi flags were
draped.

The children were all dressed in uniform. That morning,
Margarete had been horrified to discover that the uniform here
was for the girls a stiff grey skirt and a white shirt with swastika
badges embroidered on the collar. The boys had to wear a tie
covered in swastikas. It disturbed her to see these rows of Polish
children dressed in Nazi regalia chanting German words; it all
looked and felt so unnatural.

If any of the children failed to repeat the words properly,
the teacher would rap his cane on his desk and say, 'Hey, you
there! Say that word out loud again. Yes, you!'

He spoke mainly in German and those children who had
only arrived the day before were unable to understand what he
was saying. Margarete felt deeply sorry for the children
subjected to this, especially Marta, who at one point turned to
look at her with mournful eyes.

Margarete would have dearly loved to have taken the
teacher to task for speaking so harshly to the children, but she
knew that the teaching staff were not her responsibility. They
were under the direction of Doctor Schiller. She felt as though
she had done as much as she could in one day to make her presence felt and she didn't want to tempt fate by going too far.
Instead, she left the room and went into the classroom where
the younger children were being taught. The same scenario
played out there too. The children were being taught by a
severe-looking young woman, with blonde hair and bright blue

eyes, who didn't smile once while she was speaking to them. Margarete's heart turned over with pity to observe these tiny children trying to get their tongues round strange foreign words for the first time and receiving no praise or encouragement from their teacher.

When she left the classroom, Doctor Schiller was waiting outside for her. His face was like thunder.

'Nurse Weiss, could I have a word, please?'

He led her briskly to his office across the hallway and asked her to sit down. Then he sat down behind the desk. Margarete had a terrible sense of déjà vu. This felt horribly like being in Doctor Finkel's office back at Schloss Schwanburg. Doctor Schiller seemed to have been cut from the same cloth as Doctor Finkel. They were both zealous Nazis and truly believed in their cause. Still, neither of these men frightened her. Whatever they might say, she was fully prepared to stand up for what she believed in.

'I've been hearing some very strange reports from the other nurses about some changes you want to make, Nurse Weiss,' he began.

She made no reply, just waited for him to go on. This appeared to annoy him, because he leaned forward and raised his voice further.

'I'm told that you have banned them from disciplining the children.'

'I've asked them not to beat the children. The children may be disciplined in other ways, if needed. I've asked for such children to be sent to me in the first instance. I will decide what is needed each time.'

Doctor Schiller raised his eyebrows. 'I'm surprised you have taken this stand, Nurse Weiss. After all, you came strongly recommended by the Lebensborn programme. Doctor Finkel spoke very highly of your work in Bavaria and Norway in particular.'

'I see nothing incompatible with the programme in what I've said, Doctor Schiller. Surely Lebensborn isn't built on beatings? It is far more complex and subtle than that.'

'Well...' He fumbled for words, and she realised that she had wrong-footed him. But he soon recovered.

'As you are aware,' he snapped, 'Nazi ideology states that children should be subject to tough discipline in order to grow strong. They mustn't be protected or cossetted.'

'I hardly think not beating a three-year-old child when he wets the bed is cossetting him.'

'Well, that's as maybe, but I really must insist on the enforcement of the rule about language. It has proven very successful in the past. If we want the children to learn German quickly and move on to the Reich to fulfil their duty to the Fatherland, relaxing that rule won't help in the slightest.'

'But I must insist that the nurses in my charge do not beat the children,' Margarete repeated.

'Very well, but I'm afraid I won't allow you to interfere with the teaching in this establishment, Nurse Weiss. And learning the language comes firmly within that. So, the rule will stay. However, if you won't allow your nurses to enforce it, it is going to be less effective, I can assure you.'

'Understood,' Margarete said.

As she rose to leave, she took care to suppress a smile of triumph. She'd won a partial victory, and she knew that Doctor Schiller was seething with anger, although he was doing his best not to show it.

When she came out of his office, the children were filing into the dining room for lunch. She followed them in. When they'd all taken their places and had been given their meal of soup and bread, Doctor Schiller swept into the room. Everyone fell silent and turned to look at him.

'Children,' he said, 'as I told you yesterday, at mealtimes only German may be spoken. In fact, that is the rule everywhere in this house except the dormitories. I just wanted to remind you of that. A member of staff will supervise you at all times to ensure that you observe that rule. Tomorrow, new members of auxiliary staff will be arriving to supervise you in the common parts of the building and ensure you keep to the rules. If you don't, they have my permission to discipline you with a beating.'

He smiled and turned to look at Margarete with raised eyebrows. Margarete's mouth dropped open and she stared at him with deep loathing. What a snake that man was. He must have got on the telephone to the Reich Security Main Office as soon as she'd left the room and asked for more helpers. That way he would retain control and wouldn't need the nurses to administer beatings.

She sighed and left the room. She wouldn't give up her crusade, she vowed, as she hurried up the broad staircase to her own quarters on the top floor. She flung herself on the bed, shaking. Then, she pulled a small photograph out of her handbag. It was of a good-looking man with a kind face and intelligent, dark eyes.

'Tomas,' she said, tracing the lines of his face with a finger. 'Why did you leave me?'

She put her lips to the photograph and kissed it, as she'd done so many times before. She knew he had been sent to Dachau for falsifying the tests of newborn babies at Schloss Schwanburg. As a doctor he'd done his best to save the babies, disobeying the orders of his Nazi masters. But now, she had no idea whether he was dead or alive.

'I wish you were here, Tomas,' she whispered. 'But even if you're not, you are with me in spirit. And I won't give up the fight. Even small victories are worth fighting for. Knowing you are with me, willing me on, helps me to stay strong and to carry on.'

THIRTEEN
MARTA

Bruczków Assimilation Home, Poland

'Repeat after me: *Ich bin Deutsche*. It means *I am German*. Go on, I know you can say it. You said it yesterday!'

The teacher, Herr Sturm, was standing in front of Marta, his hands on her desk. He was looming over her, glowering, growing visibly more and more impatient. For once, he had spoken to her in Polish, clearly frustrated with her lack of progress and lack of understanding of German.

She knew that the eyes of the whole class were focused on her. Everyone was waiting for her to say the words. Children who couldn't or wouldn't repeat words after the teacher were rapped hard on the knuckles with a ruler. Marta's knuckles were already bruised from the rappings she'd received over the past fortnight since her arrival at the Bruczków Assimilation Home.

Now she felt tongue-tied, as if she'd never be able to say the words properly. Herr Sturm standing there, breathing heavily, was making her more and more nervous. She could smell rotting vegetables on his breath and that was making her stomach churn, adding to her distress.

She opened her mouth. Her throat felt dry and for a second, she thought she wouldn't be able to make any sound at all.

'Go on, Marta, say it,' whispered Agata, who was sitting next to her.

'Be quiet!' the teacher snapped at Agata. 'Nobody asked you to speak.'

Marta opened her mouth again. 'Ish... issh.'

'No, *Ich...*' the teacher said, making the sound in his throat. 'Try again.'

With supreme effort, Marta repeated the sentence, but still she couldn't pronounce 'Ich' as he'd wanted her to. She closed her eyes.

'That is not good enough. You are not trying. Hold out your hand!'

She did as he'd commanded and held her breath, screwing up her eyes against the pain. He brought the wooden ruler down on her knuckles. The raps were short and sharp, but, because she'd received so many before, this time it felt more painful than ever. It was all she could do to stop herself screaming out loud. Instead, suppressing her cries, she felt tears seeping out from between her eyelids.

Without a word, the teacher moved on to Agata and asked her to repeat the same phrase. Agata had no trouble forming the words and repeated the phrase loud and clear. She seemed to have a knack for languages and was picking up German without any difficulty at all. Some of the other children were like that too, but Marta was one of those who was struggling. Part of it was because her whole being was resisting. She didn't see why she should have to learn the language of the oppressors. There were other children like her who couldn't or wouldn't learn and they all bore the bruises to prove it.

After the class had finished and the children had been dismissed, Marta hurried into the washroom and held her hand under the cold tap. The burning sensation gradually subsided, but her knuckles were still raw and painful, and this time the blows from the ruler had split the skin and drawn blood.

She sank down on the cold tiled floor of the washroom, sobbing. Where had all her strength gone? She used to be so controlled, so sure of herself. When she'd had Joanna to look after she would never have let her own emotions get out of control. Then she had a disturbing thought – if she was feeling like this, how on earth would Joanna feel, coping on her own in the youth camp? It was terrible, not knowing, and time and time again Marta would relive the moment when the truck had pulled out of the yard at the Łódź ghetto and she had seen her sister's pale face peering from the dormitory window for the last time.

She felt a gentle hand squeeze her shoulder, and looked up. It was Agata. The other girl knelt down beside her on the cold tiles and slipped her arm around her.

'Don't cry, Marta. That teacher is evil and one day he will be punished.'

'What's that you said?' Nurse Wolff, the portly one, came striding into the washroom and the girls looked up at her in fear.

'Stand up!' the nurse said and, shivering, they obeyed.

'Now, what did I hear you say?'

'Nothing, Nurse Wolff,' Agata replied.

'It wasn't nothing. I definitely heard you say something.'

Agata didn't reply and for a moment all three stood there in silence, staring at each other, while a tap dripped noisily in the sink.

'And why are you crying?' The nurse addressed Marta.

'Because... because the teacher hit me with the ruler and my hand hurts.'

Nurse Wolff put her hands on her hips, leaned forward and looked Marta straight in the eye.

'I'm not surprised he hit you. You're a disobedient, badly behaved little girl. I can see that you are not even trying to learn German or making any effort at all to fit in.'

Marta hung her head and stared at the floor, willing the telling-off to be over and for Nurse Wolff to have left the washroom.

'You both know that you are not allowed to speak Polish anywhere other than the dormitory, and yet you carry on doing it. If it were up to me, I would give you a sound beating with a strap. But unfortunately, it is no longer up to me. I can tell you, though, that if I catch you doing it again, I will ask one of Doctor Schiller's new members of staff to do it for me. They are here especially for that purpose so be warned.'

Then she turned on her heel and walked out of the washroom, and Marta breathed again. She and Agata looked at each other, but they didn't dare speak. Instead, Marta pointed to the ceiling and Agata nodded, then they both hurried out of the washroom and upstairs to their dormitory, where they could talk to each other without risking a beating.

They sat on their beds and Agata took Marta's hands in hers and stroked her hot knuckles.

'They will soon heal,' Agata said. 'Look, why don't I help you with the German? To be honest, I'm not finding it too difficult. Why don't we go over what we learn in class each day after supper, and then you will be ready for the next day?'

Marta felt touched by Agata's kindness. When she'd first met her in the dormitory at the reception centre in Kraków, she would never have guessed in a million years that they would become firm friends. But underneath her bossy exterior Agata had a heart of gold and, since they'd arrived at Bruczków, they'd grown very close.

'All right,' she agreed. 'Thank you.'

The bell went for lunch, and they trooped to the dining room to be served the same tasteless soup they were given every lunchtime. After that, they went back into the classroom for their daily dose of Nazi teachings.

During the first lesson they'd had, the day after they'd arrived, Herr Sturm had given each of them a piece of paper on which was written their new, German, name.

Marta had stared down at hers. At least her first name hadn't changed much. She was to be called Marthe instead of Marta. That wasn't too bad, but her surname had changed too. Now she was Marthe Kaplan instead of Marta Kaminsky. She didn't want to be Marthe Kaplan.

'Now you have your German names,' Herr Sturm had said, 'you must tell your classmates and they must call you by your new names. It is forbidden to use your old names from this moment on.'

Marta glanced at Agata's paper. Agata had been relatively lucky too; she could keep her first name but, like Marta's, her surname had been changed. She had been Agata Dabrowski, but now she was Agata Danner.

Later, in the dormitory, they decided that they would ignore the change of names between themselves and only use them when it was necessary to avoid a beating.

During the subsequent afternoon lessons, Herr Sturm had introduced them to Nazi racial theory. He'd told them that they belonged to the master race of Aryans, a group of superior beings who had the right to rule over others, to be served by others, and to have a better life than other racial groups. He was trying to instil in them the idea that Polish people, Slavs and, in particular, Jews, were far inferior to themselves – in fact that people of those races could hardly be regarded as human.

Marta had heard her parents discussing the racist ideas of the Nazis so she wasn't surprised at what he told them, but looking around at the other children she could see how surprised they were by what was being said. This afternoon, he was expanding on that theory still further.

'It is important that you realise that the people you lived amongst before you were found by us were not to be trusted,' Herr Sturm said, pacing round the room, warming to his theme. 'If your parents were Poles, Slavs, Slovaks or of any other inferior race, it is highly likely that they've been lying to you and trying to infect you with their ideas your whole lives. It is certain that most of them are shameful people – criminals, prostitutes or alcoholics – and they have probably been pretending to be upstanding citizens in order to gain your trust.

'You are very lucky that you have been taken away from that environment. It might have felt difficult at first, but the day the SS found you and took you from your so-called homes was in fact the luckiest day of your lives. They have saved you from a life of shame amongst undesirables.'

Marta found herself at first incredulous, then indignant, and finally seething with anger at his words. How could this man peddle such lies? And how could he say those things about people like Mama and Tata, the most honest, hardworking, generous and trustworthy people in the world? How could *they* be criminals or prostitutes? She knew they weren't. She drew in a deep breath and sat up straight. She refused to believe it. She opened her mouth to challenge him, but instantly felt Agata's hand on hers on the desk. She glanced at her friend, who was shaking her head and giving her a warning look.

Slowly, Marta relaxed and let out her breath. Perhaps Agata was right, perhaps she should just let it go. She looked around at the rest of the class. Some were frowning, puzzled at Herr Sturm's words, but others were looking at him with eager interest. Marta couldn't believe that they were taking what he was saying seriously. She decided to have a word with them in the dormitory later to set them straight.

When the lesson was over, they lined up at the door and

trooped outside into the yard. It was time for marching practice. This was again taken by Herr Sturm and consisted of learning how to march side by side in perfect formation, practising how to do a stiff Heil Hitler salute, then, to finish off, they were made to practise the goose-step. Marta had to hide a smile, seeing the other children struggling to lift their legs to the requisite height and to keep their balance while marching forward. This was something she herself could do easily – she had long legs and had always been athletic – but her whole body recoiled from the idea of it. She'd seen so many terrifying SS officers goose-stepping down the street in Jasło that learning how to emulate them was an abhorrence to her. But she didn't want to be punished again, so she went along and goose-stepped around the yard with all the others.

Afterwards, they were all given outdoor jobs for the last hour before darkness. Some children were made to sweep the yard and paths around the building, some to chop wood for the fires, others to muck out the pigs and chickens that were kept in pens behind the house.

Marta and Agata were consigned to the vegetable patch. It was their job to weed between the potato plants and dig fresh ground for a new crop. It was tough work and Marta knew Herr Sturm had only given it to them to punish her for her lack of progress in German. She felt sorry for Agata, who wasn't strong, and who struggled with the spade she'd been given to make any impression at all in the frozen earth. None of this was Agata's fault, but she just got on with the tasks. She never complained.

When the sun went down, the teacher called them inside. They washed their hands, then went back into the dining room for the usual supper of greasy stew and potatoes.

Later, up in the dormitory, Marta sat down on her bed and looked around at the other girls.

'You know what Herr Sturm told us this afternoon about our parents isn't true, don't you?' she said.

A couple of the girls murmured their agreement, but one of them, a girl who'd once been called Gita, but who was now Gisela, said, 'But why would he tell us that stuff if it wasn't true?'

'Isn't it obvious?' Marta asked. 'They want us to think that they've saved us, and they want us to think like Nazis, but I for one will never think like a Nazi.'

'Me neither,' said Agata and the three girls who occupied the beds on the other side of the room, Beate, Maja and Adelheid, murmured their agreement.

'Well, I think Herr Sturm might be right,' Gisela said. 'You know, my parents were very poor. We children were always dressed in rags. My tata worked in a factory, but he was often drunk on vodka. He was always dressed shabbily too, and he often came home with extra meat or food. Thinking about it now, how do I know he didn't steal it?'

This was too much for Marta. She got off the bed, charged at Gisela, grabbed her pyjamas and pulled the other girl's face close to hers.

'How can you speak about your poor tata like that?' she yelled. 'He looked after you and provided for you your whole life. No wonder he liked a drink if he worked in a factory! Shame on you for doubting him and shame on you for believing what these evil devils tell you!'

'Get away from me!' Gisela screamed and pushed Marta backwards. Marta wobbled and took a step back, but then she recovered herself and lunged at Gisela. Soon both girls were on the floor punching each other, biting, kicking and screaming.

'Stop!' Agata cried, pulling Marta's arm. 'Stop, before they hear you!'

But it was too late. Doctor Schiller appeared in the doorway.

'What is all this?' he shouted. 'Get up, both of you.'

They both stood up and faced him.

'What is the meaning of this? What are you fighting about?'

'She said what the teacher has been telling us is rubbish!' Gisela blurted out in a shrill voice.

'And what did the teacher tell you?'

'That our Polish families are not to be trusted, that they were probably criminals or drunkards. I said it might be true and she attacked me.'

Doctor Schiller strode towards them, his heels loud on the bare floorboards. Marta didn't take her eyes off the floor in front of her. She wondered what had become of her. She'd never fought with anyone before. She wished she was a million miles away.

'Is this true, Marthe?' he asked.

Marta forced herself to lift her head and look up at him.

'I told her that it wasn't fair to assume that her father was a thief,' she said.

'And you attacked her?'

'I didn't attack her, no. I wanted to be sure she was listening to me, so I went up close to her. She attacked me.'

'What happened?' Doctor Schiller asked, turning randomly to Beate. She looked shocked.

'I don't know, Herr Doctor. I didn't really see.'

'Did Marthe Kaplan say that she didn't believe in Herr Sturm's teachings?'

Beate shook her head. 'She didn't say that, no.'

'She didn't say exactly that, but was that what she meant?'

Beate shrugged. 'I'm not sure,' she said, tears in her eyes. 'I don't know what she meant.'

Doctor Schiller let out a great sigh. 'Can any of you girls tell me whether or not Marthe Kaplan said that what the teacher told you today wasn't true?'

All the girls remained silent. Doctor Schiller turned to Gisela.

'Is that what she said?'

Gisela nodded. 'And she attacked me because I said it was true.'

'All right. You can go and sit on your bed, Gisela. Marthe, you will come with me.'

He grabbed Marta by the shoulder and propelled her forward, his hands digging into her skin, then he pushed her towards the top of the stairs.

'Go downstairs,' he said.

There was nothing else she could do. She had to walk downstairs with his hand propelling her from behind. It was hard not to trip and fall. At the bottom, she thought he would push her towards the office, but instead he made her turn in the opposite direction and walk towards a door at the end of the hall. She knew where that door went – she'd seen the caretaker going in and out with scuttles of coal for the fires.

Doctor Schiller turned the handle and pushed the door open. The door opened onto a staircase that led downwards. This was the cellar.

'Go down,' he said.

She turned to him with pleading eyes. 'But it's dark.'

'Yes, it's dark. Now go down. Be careful not to slip.'

She put her hand out to guide herself by the wall and slowly made her way down the steps. The cold, dank air of the cellar rose to meet her and soon she was shivering. Doctor Schiller was right behind her. At the bottom, he guided her towards another door. She could smell coal dust and mould. He pushed her into a small room. Once she was inside, he slammed the door shut and locked it from the outside.

She immediately turned around and hammered on the door with her fists.

'You will stay there until you've learned some obedience,' Doctor Schiller shouted. 'There is a bed in there. Get some sleep. Someone will bring you food and water in the morning.'

'Please!' she shouted, sobbing. 'Please don't leave me here!'

But his footsteps were already retreating, and she heard him walk up the steps and slam the door at the top shut. She was alone in the cold, dark, damp cellar, and terrified. When would they let her out? Would they ever let her out? How would she ever get through this? And if she didn't get through it, how would she ever see Joanna again?

FOURTEEN

JOANNA

Camp for Polish Children and Youth, Łódź Ghetto, Poland, 1944

As the sour-faced woman had told Joanna and Lili it would the previous evening, the alarm bell sounded at six o' clock the next morning. Joanna woke with a start, looked around her, and quickly remembered where she was. Her heart sank. Beside her, in the next bed, Lili was stirring too. Seeing her there and remembering what had happened to Josef made Joanna feel even more desperate than before.

Rubbing the sleep from their eyes, the two girls went straight to the washroom for a quick wash in cold water. Then, back in the dormitory, they put on their rough, grey uniforms and heavy wooden clogs. Stifling their yawns, they went downstairs to the canteen for the usual breakfast of hard bread and acorn coffee. But even though the bread tasted stale and was tough and chewy, Joanna forced herself to eat it. She knew that it was important to get as much nutrition as she could and that she must eat everything that came her way. Looking around her, she saw that all the children were doing the same, including Lili.

Afterwards, a man dressed in grey overalls, carrying a clipboard, started shouting out names, and those children he called gathered beside the door in lines. Joanna and Lili were the last ones to be summoned. The man told them to join the final group, which consisted of young girls of about their own age.

The other groups marched out of the room, then the man turned to them.

'You will be working in one of the factories in the ghetto today,' he told them. 'They make clothes there – clothes for the Wehrmacht. It's important work. There are men and women working there on sewing machines. They are Jewish, so you are forbidden from speaking to them. A foreman will give you tasks to do when you get there. Follow me.'

Joanna slid her hand into Lili's and they walked beside each other as the group of eight girls left the canteen and went out into the freezing morning air.

It was hard to walk in those clumsy clogs and Joanna could feel more than one blister forming on her feet, but she shuffled forward, keeping up with the others. She didn't want to risk punishment by lagging behind.

They stumbled over the uneven cobbles towards the gates of the children's camp and, after a brief discussion between the orderly and the guards, the guards dragged the gates aside and let the children pass through. Then they were out in the ghetto again. Joanna was once again shocked to see how thin the inhabitants were and how shabbily dressed, how many beggars sat with their bowls against the walls of buildings, and how rundown those buildings were.

The factory was a couple of blocks away from the camp gate.

'They call this factory "the Resort",' the man told them.

When they entered through some double doors, the noise of

dozens of treadle sewing machines rattling away under a high tin roof was deafening. Lines of men and women were hard at work, their heads bowed over their tasks. No one was talking. Instead, they were working away on their machines in the dim light cast by the few electric bulbs strung from the roof. Fascinated, Joanna watched the speed with which one woman sewed the seam of a pair of trousers. She worked like lightning and her skill was astonishing.

Another man in a brown overall approached, carrying a pile of hessian sacks, and the man with the clipboard left the building.

'Your job today is to keep the factory floor clean,' the man said. 'You must go round and pick up the scraps of material that drop from around the work benches where the pattern-cutters work, over there, and put them into these sacks. You must check the floor around all the sewing machines too, because sometimes the machinists have to cut pieces off as they work. When your sack is full, bring it to my desk in that corner and I will sort it out. When all the material is cleared from the floor, you will also need to sweep it. There are brooms in that cupboard.' He pointed to a door in the opposite corner of the factory.

'There will be no lunch break as we don't have food for you children today. If you're here tomorrow, I will arrange for extra soup for you, but you can stop for ten minutes and have water when the workers have their lunch.'

He threw the pile of sacks on the floor and clapped his hands. 'Don't stand there staring, get to work!'

Joanna and Lili agreed to stay together and at first the job didn't seem too difficult. There were three long trestle tables where men stood, cutting material from patterns with long shears. Scraps of material fell from the tables and the girls scrabbled round on the floor, collecting them up and putting them into their sacks. After a while, they realised they were working far too fast because they had to wait for more scraps to appear from the cutters. Joanna's back soon began to ache, and she was coughing from all the particles of material floating in the air.

'Let's sit down for a bit,' Lili said, and they found a discreet spot beside the wall.

'I don't think we're meant to sit down,' Joanna said anxiously. 'What if that man spots us?'

'He's right over there at his desk,' Lili replied. 'Let's wait until there's a pile under the cutters' table, then start again.'

It didn't take long for the floor to be covered in scraps of material again. The girls went back to work, more slowly this time, but they had soon filled their sacks. They dragged them over to the foreman's desk and exchanged them for empty ones. The morning wore on and, by the time the bell sounded for the lunch break, Joanna was exhausted. Her back and legs were aching, her throat was dry and her eyes itching.

The workers stopped working but didn't move apart from to reach into their bags for their bowls and spoons. Soon the factory doors rumbled open and two old women appeared, pushing trolleys with great cauldrons wobbling on them. They began to dole out the soup and hunks of bread and, just as in the dormitory at the camp, the workers tucked in hungrily. When a trolley approached them, Joanna and Lili both looked up at the woman with pleading eyes, but she ignored them and trundled past to serve the man at the cutting table.

Joanna's stomach was rumbling even more than usual at the smell of the soup and the sight of others eating.

'I'm hungry, aren't you?' she said to Lili.

'Yes. It's so unfair. Why can't we have any?'

Just then there was a hissing sound from one of the men at the table and, looking up, Joanna caught the eye of one of the cutters. He beckoned her towards him with a quick movement of his head.

'Here,' he said, 'have some bread.' He dipped a slice into his soup and held it out to her.

Joanna went over to him, stooping so the foreman wouldn't see her above the desk, and the man handed her the slice of bread.

'Thank you!' she whispered, and he smiled.

'Share it with your friend,' he said.

'I will,' Joanna replied and crept back to the place where Lili was sitting, tore the moist slice in half and gave one half to her.

They'd only just finished eating and were savouring the taste when the foreman approached. Joanna looked up at him guiltily. Had he seen them eating?

'If you want a drink, go over to the table by the door. There are cups of water there,' he said gruffly, and Joanna breathed a sigh of relief that they hadn't been discovered. She didn't want to get the kind cutter punished for sharing his food with them as much as she didn't want to be punished herself.

They carried on picking up material for most of the afternoon, then the foreman came and handed them brooms.

'When you've finished this, you two can go and clean the ladies' washroom. There's a mop and bucket in there, bleach too. Make sure you do a good job. I will be in to inspect your work later.'

When he'd gone, Joanna and Lili pulled a face at each other at the thought of cleaning the washrooms. They'd already visited them that morning and knew them to be filthy and smelly, with blocked toilets and sinks. But they knew there was no getting out of it. So, when they'd finished sweeping the area where they'd been working, they put their brooms away and headed to the washroom.

When they entered, they had to cover their mouths, the stench was so bad.

'Why don't we open the window?' Joanna said. 'Look, one of us could climb on the sink.'

'I'll hold onto you if you want to climb up,' Lili said. 'I'm shorter than you.'

Joanna climbed onto one of the sinks and, while Lili held her legs steady, reached up and pushed the window open. The opening was quite large and she peered through the gap. To her surprise the window opened onto a quiet street. She'd expected some sort of factory yard with trucks rattling to and fro, but there was only a solitary old man in a shabby overcoat pushing a rag and bone trolley along at a snail's pace. It was strange to get a glimpse of the outside world by chance like that, when she was a prisoner here.

She climbed down and they set to work cleaning the washroom. To begin with, they flushed the toilets and emptied the sinks and put bleach in them all. Then they filled the mop bucket with a mixture of water and bleach and mopped the tiled floor. The whole exercise took them over half an hour and, when they'd finished, they put the cloths and mops and buckets back where they'd found them and went to report to the foreman.

When he inspected the washroom, he stood there thoughtfully, examining the newly scrubbed place.

'Good work, girls,' he said. 'You've done so well that this can be your last job of the day each time you come here.'

Joanna's heart sank. She wished they hadn't gone to so much trouble. Still, for the chance of peering out of the window again at that deserted street, perhaps she wouldn't mind cleaning out a few lavatories.

Soon after that they were marched back to the children's camp, their clogs clattering over the cobbles of the ghetto. Joanna felt exhausted. Her stomach was rumbling, craving food. She could hardly stay awake long enough to eat the portion of greasy stew dished up for dinner, though.

After the meal, the stern female orderly came to find them.

'We are moving you to the girls' dormitory now. Your things

have already been taken there. I will show you where it is,' she announced.

They followed her down a long passage towards the back of the building and up another staircase to a dormitory about twice the size of the one they'd just left. It was already full of girls of around their age and a little older. Some were sitting on the beds, some chatting beside the window. Everyone fell silent when Joanna and Lili were brought in.

The orderly showed them to two beds at the end of the room.

'Where are the blankets for these beds, girls?' the woman said sharply, looking around at the other girls. 'Come on, I know someone has taken them.'

Nobody volunteered, and she said, 'If no one comes forward in the next minute, I will have to take this to the SS officer in charge and they will come up here and do a complete search.'

There was silence and no one stirred for a few moments, then a sullen-looking girl of about fifteen rose from a bed a few rows down. She brought two blankets and threw them down on the empty beds.

'At last,' the orderly said. 'I will overlook this incident, but there is to be no more stealing. You hear me?'

The girl nodded and sidled back to her bed.

'The washroom is at the bottom of the stairs,' the orderly explained to Joanna and Lili. 'The alarm will sound at six. You will be in the clothing factory again tomorrow.' She then left the room.

Joanna sat down on her bed, but she could feel the gaze of the girl who'd taken the blankets on her back. There was something terrifying about that girl. She had a fierce, wild look about her and Joanna had no desire to cross her.

Later, when Joanna and Lili went past her bed to go to the washroom, she shouted out: 'I'll get you for that one day, you two! You just wait.'

Joanna exchanged a worried look with Lili and hurried on past without saying anything, but the older girl's words had struck fear into her.

As they entered the washroom, a man stepped out of the shadows in the corridor. He wore a white lab coat and glasses. He was quite young, and he looked anxious. He closed and locked the door.

'Are you Joanna? And Lili?' he asked, and they nodded.

'I'm Marek,' he said in a low voice. 'It's taken me a while to work out who you are, then they moved you. I promised Nurse Weiss that I would try to get you out of the camp. You know that, don't you?'

Joanna nodded, nerves coursing through her. She'd been waiting for this to happen, but now it was she suddenly realised how dangerous it would be.

'We need to find a way of taking you when there's no one else around. Are you working at the factory again tomorrow?'

'I think so,' Joanna replied.

'We might try to take you when you're on your way there, but that would probably be spotted straight away. Or perhaps at lunchtime... we haven't decided yet.'

Suddenly Joanna remembered. The perfect escape route. That was why that quiet backstreet had looked so inviting to her: it was her route to freedom.

'I think I might have an idea!' she said, beaming up at Marek.

FIFTEEN

MARGARETE

Bruczków Assimilation Home, Poland

Casting her eye over the children eating their breakfast in the dining room that morning, Margarete frowned. There was an empty chair at the older girls' table. Something was wrong. She went up to Agata and tapped her on the shoulder.

'Where is Marta?' she asked.

When Agata looked up at her with mournful eyes, Margarete could see that she'd been crying.

'I don't know,' Agata said miserably.

'Don't know?' Margarete asked, lowering her voice. 'Or don't want to say?'

Agata glanced around the room with fear in her eyes. She seemed too afraid to speak. Doctor Schiller and two of his new workers, whom Margarete thought of as his henchmen, stood near the door. Realising that she wasn't going to get any information out of Agata while they were watching, she decided to wait.

'We can talk later,' she told her quietly. She went upstairs to the older girls' dormitory and sat on Agata's bed to wait.

Marta's bed was made, and her pyjamas neatly folded on the pillow. There was nothing to suggest that anything out of the ordinary had happened, but where was she? All Margarete's instincts told her that something had happened to her, and that it wasn't good.

When the girls came back to the dormitory to get ready for lessons, Margarete was waiting by the door. She took Agata by the shoulders and hurried her out of the room.

'Come with me,' she said, and, checking round to make sure that no one was watching, took Agata up to her own bedroom on the top floor, then closed and locked the door behind her.

'Please, sit down,' she said and Agata sat down on the bed, still looking miserable.

'No one is listening here,' Margarete said, sitting down beside her and taking her hand. 'You can tell me what happened.'

Still, Agata hesitated.

'I can't help if you don't tell me,' Margarete said gently. 'I want to help, but I can't if you don't tell me what you know.'

Agata took a deep breath, and it all came out in a rush.

'Marta was fighting with Gita – I mean Gisela – in the dormitory. Marta was saying that some of the things the teacher told us weren't true, but Gisela thought they were. Gisela started talking about her father, saying he could have been a thief and that he was always drunk. Marta got angry then. She grabbed Gisela and they ended up fighting.'

'Oh no!' Margarete said, shocked. This didn't sound like Marta at all.

'Doctor Schiller came in and took Marta away. I don't know where he took her to...' Agata trailed off and stared down at the floor.

'When did this happen?'

'Yesterday, after supper. She didn't come back all night.'

Margarete was puzzled. Doctor Schiller had been known to

take children into his office for a dressing-down, and sometimes he would lock them in the boot room at the back of the house as a punishment for a few hours, making them miss a meal or two, but he'd never been known to keep them there overnight.

It had been clear from the start that Doctor Schiller was suspicious of Marta. She was too clever by half and was not afraid of challenging things he, or any of the teachers, said if she disagreed with them. It was crystal clear to everyone at the home that Marta was against everything the Nazis stood for: she was resisting every effort to Germanise her.

She was the sort of 'troublesome individual' whom Doctor Schiller referred to darkly as a 'late reject'. He'd told Margarete that they'd had a few children who refused to co-operate and who'd had to be transported to one of the concentration camps in southern Poland. She'd shuddered at his words, wondering where those poor children were now. Had they even survived? When she'd heard him say that, she decided she would do everything in her power to prevent Marta being sent away. She'd been thinking of a way of approaching Marta about it, to warn her, but hadn't done that yet – she didn't want to alienate her. But perhaps she'd left it too late?

The bell went for the start of lessons, breaking into her thoughts.

'You'd better go,' she told Agata. 'I will take you downstairs. Come on, before everyone leaves the dormitory.'

They crept downstairs and Margarete left Agata on the first floor. She waited for all the children to file into their lessons, then went straight to Doctor Schiller's room and knocked on the door. There was a long pause before the doctor called out, 'Come in.' Margarete opened the door. One of Doctor Schiller's new members of staff, a young woman called Herta, sidled out as Margarete went in.

'Come in, Nurse Weiss,' the doctor said, 'Take a seat!'

She sat down in the chair opposite his desk.

The doctor looked distracted, so Margarete came straight to the point.

'I'd like to know where Marta Kaminsky is,' she began.

He peered at her. 'Do you mean Marthe Kaplan?'

'You know who I mean,' she said, her eyes on his face, refusing to be deflected. 'Where is she?'

'I had cause to punish her. She attacked another girl.'

'Are you quite sure? That doesn't sound like Marta.'

'I am quite sure. The girl has become more and more irrational. She has a temper. I have had to confine her for her own good.'

'In the boot room?' Margarete asked.

He shook his head. 'The boot room is for mild punishment only, this required harsher measures.'

Margarete regarded him with loathing. What a despicable human being he was. Every bit as bad as Doctor Finkel at Schloss Schwanburg. The two men had embraced Nazi ideology with open arms and were only too happy to use it and their positions of power as an excuse for sadistic behaviour.

'I wish you would stop talking in riddles, Herr Doctor,' she said, finally. 'I would like to know where Marta is. The girl's health and wellbeing are my concern.'

Doctor Schiller sat back in his chair and put his fingertips together. A cruel smile spread across his face.

'Her health and wellbeing won't be your concern for much longer. I believe that she is fast becoming a late reject. She is showing no aptitude for her studies here. She refuses to learn German and she doesn't take the other lessons seriously, according to Herr Sturm.'

'No, Doctor Schiller, that's simply not true. She struggles with the language, it is true, but she is a good, obedient girl. The separation from her sister has been hard for her to take. I'm sure, with help, she will settle down very soon.'

'Ah, since you mention her sister, I have been looking into

the records and I see that she was rejected because of her dark colouring and Slavic blood. It is possible that Marthe too is tainted that way. I intend to speak to Reich Main Office about sending her away.'

'No!' Margarete said, appalled, imagining Marta crammed into a crowded cattle wagon on a train bound for a concentration camp. 'Leave her to me, I will take her under my personal care. I will give you my word that she will learn German and work hard during her lessons. Just give me that chance, please, Herr Doctor.'

'Do you really have time to lavish such care on one disobedient girl? You have been appointed to your post to care for all of the children here.'

'I will make time, Doctor. Now, please tell me where she is, and I will go and speak to her.'

The doctor let out an exaggerated sigh. 'She is in the cellar, in one of the back rooms.' He looked in his desk drawer and took out a key, handing it to Margarete.

'I warn you, Nurse, this is her last chance. You have one week to turn her behaviour round. If there's no improvement, I will have no hesitation in getting in touch with the Reich Main Office and recommending her deportation.'

Margarete took the key and left the doctor's office without a further word. She hurried along the hall to the cellar door. As she opened it, a blast of cold air came up to meet her and she shivered. It was as cold down there as it was outside, and there had been a thick frost on the ground that morning. There was no electric light, so Margarete left the door open so she could see to go down the steps. At the bottom she wondered which way to turn. In front of her was a coal cellar; beside that, a log store. Beyond that was the door to another room.

As she put the key in the lock, she thought she heard a sound. She put her ear to the door and could hear sobbing. Turning the key quickly, she pushed the door open.

Marta was sitting there on a low, wooden bed in the half-darkness. The only light came from a narrow window up near the ceiling. The room smelled of urine and Margarete noticed the bucket in the corner. On the floor was an empty tin cup and plate.

'Marta!' She held out her arms and Marta ran to her and buried her face in Margarete's chest. 'I'm so sorry this happened to you. If I'd known, I would have come before.'

Marta was sobbing uncontrollably. She tried to say something but the words got jumbled.

'Don't talk, Marta. There is plenty of time for that. Now let me take you upstairs and get you cleaned up. The other children are in lessons, so there is no one about at the moment.'

Marta hesitated, clearly afraid to go upstairs and face whoever might be up there, but Margarete put her arm around her and persuaded her to take some steps out of the room. They walked slowly up the cellar steps and emerged into the hall. Looking at Marta in the light, Margarete was shocked at how blotchy her face looked. She'd been rubbing her eyes so much that she'd bruised the skin under them too. When she put her hand up to wipe her eyes, Margarete saw the cuts and bruises on her knuckles.

'Let's go to the washroom,' Margarete said, taking Marta's hand.

In the washroom, Margarete helped Marta to take her dirty uniform off. She had spilled her food down it in the dark and it smelled of sweat and dampness.

'I will get you another one from the storeroom,' she said. 'And clean underwear too. Wait there.'

Margarete went to fetch fresh clothes from the cupboard and her own towel from her bedroom. The washroom ones were grey with the filth of twenty girls and still wet from their morning ablutions. When she got back, Marta was sitting on the side of one of the baths looking listless. At least she had stopped crying.

Margarete ran the bath and tested the temperature.

'Get in, Marta. You'll feel much better afterwards.'

Marta obeyed silently. Margarete handed her the soap and Marta washed herself listlessly.

'I'm so sorry, Marta. Whatever happened?' Margarete asked, kneeling down beside the bath.

'He locked me in a dark cellar,' Marta said. 'I could hear rats running about in the night. I didn't go to sleep at all in case they ran over me. I didn't dare lie down.'

'How terrible for you. I promise you I'll not let that happen again.'

'But how can you stop it? Doctor Schiller is in control here.'

'He won't do it again. I've already spoken to him and I'll speak to him again.'

'I want to leave this place,' Marta said.

'If you run away, they will come after you with dogs. They are bound to catch you.'

'You asked someone to help Joanna to escape from the ghetto at Łódź,' Marta said. 'What's different here?'

Margarete thought for a moment. She understood why Marta might ask that question, but to her, the answer was clear.

'Well, there are people in the resistance in Łódź who will help her get out and help her get away from there. They have done so many times for others in the past. There is no one like that here, Marta – we are in the middle of nowhere. If you were to run away, your absence would be quickly noticed and Doctor Schiller would call the SS, who would bring dogs. I couldn't bear that.'

'I don't know how I can bear it here a moment longer,' Marta said. 'I thought I was strong, but they are trying to break me with their Germanisation. I don't want to be Germanised, I am Polish.'

'I know, my dear,' Margarete said. 'But you must be careful. Doctor Schiller has been talking about sending you away.'

'Well, why doesn't he? I hate it here.'

'Because where he would send you is far, far worse than here. His intention would be to send you to a concentration camp.'

Marta's eyes widened in fear.

'As you know, people don't leave those places – they are starved, used as slave labour. They are overcrowded and disease runs rife. Don't give him an excuse to send you to one of those places, please Marta.'

Marta was visibly shocked at Margarete's words.

'I've told him I will work with you to help you, and he is giving you one more chance so don't let's waste that chance. I can help you with your German, and I will also help you with your lessons, but in return, you will have to promise me to at least pretend that you are willing to learn. I know that you aren't really, but you must play the game in order to survive. Can you do that for me?'

Marta nodded. 'Thank you, Nurse,' she said.

'Now, let's get you out of the bath and into your clean uniform. I think it's all right to have this morning off, but this afternoon you must go to class as usual.'

'All right,' Marta agreed and hauled herself out of the bath.

Margarete held the towel out for her. She heaved a sigh of relief as she did so. Perhaps she would be able to save Marta after all if the girl was willing to co-operate, but they would have a long, hard road ahead of them to bring Doctor Schiller round.

SIXTEEN

JOANNA

Camp for Polish Children and Youth, Łódź Ghetto, Poland, 1944

It was the third morning that the girls had worked at the factory. When she stepped out of the dormitory building into the chilly morning air just after dawn, Joanna felt the chill of fear mingled with the excitement of anticipation. She'd been feeling the same way ever since their conversation with Marek in the washroom the evening before last, but now it was getting more intense.

Today was the day! She took Lili's hand and smiled at her friend. This time tomorrow who knew where they would be? On their way home perhaps, although after all the stories she'd heard, she was terrified that Tata and Mama wouldn't be there when she arrived in Jasło. She wasn't going to think about that now though; she had to get through today and whatever dangers it might bring.

When they passed through the gates of the Camp for Polish Children and Youth, and they clanged shut behind them, she crossed her fingers. If all went to plan, she and Lili would never have to go back to that terrible place. But her heart still squeezed with pity for all the other children who wouldn't have the chance they'd been given to get away.

When they arrived at the factory, the foreman met them as usual. They were given the same familiar tasks they'd been doing for the past two days; they now knew how to pace themselves while they collected the scraps of material so they didn't get too tired. The morning passed quickly. Too quickly perhaps. In some ways Joanna was dreading the afternoon. What if things went wrong? She drew in a deep breath – she mustn't think like that.

A trestle table was brought in for the children to sit at for lunch and, as on the previous day, they were given a small bowl of soup each and a slice of bread. Joanna was getting thoroughly sick of the taste of vegetable soup, but she was so hungry she had no choice but to gulp it down.

After lunch, the foreman came up to Joanna and Lili as they picked up their sacks and prepared to go back to work.

'Ah, my two little cleaners,' he said, smiling down at them. 'You've done a good job on the toilets these past two days. So good in fact that I was thinking I might give the washroom to someone else for a change today. It doesn't seem fair for you two to have to do it every day.'

Joanna stared at him. Her heart began to hammer against her ribs and her mouth went dry.

'We don't mind doing it,' she said quickly, feeling her cheeks growing hot. 'In fact, we like the work.'

He stared at her and frowned. 'You *like* the work?'

Joanna lifted her head and looked him in the eye.

'Yes. We like making the washrooms look good, it makes us feel proud.'

The man carried on staring at her for a moment, then suddenly began to roar with laughter. He reached out and ruffled her bald head as if she had hair.

'All right, little one. You can carry on if you like. I just thought you might like a change, but be my guest...'

He walked away, shaking his head, still laughing. Joanna looked at Lili wide-eyed and they both sighed with relief.

The next couple of hours dragged and Joanna kept a firm eye on the clock on the factory wall. The hands seemed to crawl round until at last it was twenty minutes to four and time to go.

She and Lili walked quickly to the washrooms. Her heart was pounding even harder now, her palms sweaty with fear. They collected the mops and buckets in silence; they were far too tense for words. The appointed time they'd agreed with Marek was ten past four, so for the next ten minutes or so they mopped the floor and cleaned the lavatories just as if it was a normal afternoon. At about four o' clock a woman, one of the seamstresses, came into the washroom. She smiled at the girls, went into one of the cubicles and locked the door.

Joanna and Lili exchange worried looks. On previous days they had put a broom across the door to warn people not to enter while they cleaned. In their panic today, they had somehow forgotten to do that.

The woman took her time in the cubicle. Joanna stared at the door, willing her to come out. She knew they were going to be late. When the woman came out, she washed her hands carefully in the sink, then left, smiling once again at the two girls.

When she'd finally gone, Joanna hurried and put a broom across the doorway and shut the inner door.

'Come on, we'll have to hurry now. You go first.'

She helped Lili to climb up onto the washbasin, pushing her from behind. Then, Lili leaned forward and put her head and shoulders out of the window. She took her clogs off and threw them down outside, then Joanna helped her to squeeze out through the gap. It took a lot of effort, but finally she was out. Joanna heard her land with a thud on the road on the other side of the window.

Then it was Joanna's turn. She would have no one to help her, but she was taller and stronger than Lili. She climbed up onto the sink, then stood up and put her hands on the windowsill. Like Lili, she took her clogs off and threw them out through the window. She heard them land on the road with a clatter. She put her right knee up onto the windowsill first, then, with a lot of effort, managed to get the other knee up, then hauled her whole body up so she was crouching on the windowsill. Panting with the effort, she managed to turn round and put both legs out through the window. They were dangling on the other side, and she had no idea what was underneath her.

'It's all right, Joanna. You can jump,' Lili said.

Joanna did as she said, and landed in a heap on the road. As she landed, she felt her ankle twist underneath her. She got up instantly and dusted herself down then took a step forward to test her ankle. To her relief she could walk, but it would definitely slow her down.

'Come on,' she said, tucking her arm into Lili's, trying not to sound as nervous as she felt. 'We need to walk to the end of the road.'

They set off quickly down the deserted road, looking anxiously about them. There was no one around, not even the rag and bone man who'd been there on the first day. They turned a corner in the road and were now on a busier street. Horse-drawn carts trotted to and fro, men hauled handcarts and sack barrows in either direction, a tram rattled past, full of passengers. Some ragged children played in a doorway opposite. As instructed, they turned left, keeping to the right-hand side of the street beside the buildings. Joanna was just beginning to wonder if anyone was coming to meet them when a young man with dark hair and glasses, dressed in ragged trousers and a waistcoat, stepped out of a doorway.

'Come this way,' he said quietly, and they followed him the length of the buildings and into an alleyway. About halfway along the alley, the young man pushed a door open and went inside a building.

'Follow me,' he said and went up a bare, wooden staircase inside. At the top, he opened a door and beckoned them into a small apartment. A young woman was sitting at a table reading a newspaper. When they entered, she got up to greet them.

'Joanna! Lili! Thank goodness you've made it,' she said, coming forward and hugging them both. 'I am Ilona and this is Jan, my husband. We work for the Polish resistance. Our friend Marek asked us to help you.

'You will stay with us tonight and tomorrow,' she went on. 'I will take you on the train as far as Kraków and there, others will meet us and take you on trains directly to your home towns. Does that sound all right?'

The girls nodded gratefully, and Joanna felt relief surging through her. Ilona was young and pretty with wavy blonde hair tucked up into a messy bun. She had a kind face. And the small, simply furnished apartment felt warm and homely, with colourful rugs on the floor, cushions on the chairs and posters on the walls.

'Come, I'll show you where you will sleep tonight,' Ilona said.

She took them to the bottom of a ladder that stretched up through a trapdoor in the ceiling.

'Come on up,' she said.

They followed her up the steep ladder and into the roof. When Joanna clambered into the room under the eaves, she saw that two mattresses were laid out on the boards, complete with pillows and plenty of blankets.

'I hope this is all right for you,' Ilona said. 'I've put some clothes out on the beds for you too. They belong to my young cousins. You won't want to be wearing those camp uniforms when we go to the train station tomorrow morning.'

'Thank you,' both girls said in unison.

'I'll leave you to try your clothes on while I prepare supper. It is only kapusta, and we don't have much meat, I'm afraid, but I will pad it out with vegetables.'

'We've been eating potato-peel soup for the past few days. Kapusta sounds lovely,' Joanna said, her mouth watering at the prospect of sauerkraut stew.

When Ilona had gone, the two girls quickly changed out of their grey uniforms and put the new clothes on. They had both been given sweaters, pinafore dresses and woollen tights. Ilona had even left a pair of shoes out for each of them. They pulled them on and tied the laces. Joanna's were a bit small and pinched her toes. Still, they felt better than the awful factory clogs.

Ilona's head appeared through the trapdoor.

'Pass me your uniforms,' she said, holding out her hand. 'Jan will burn them in the stove. We don't want any trace of that place to be left in the apartment.'

The girls handed her the uniforms and she disappeared back down the ladder.

'You look nice,' Joanna said to Lili, who was transformed from a colourless waif by the warm red sweater and check woollen dress. She even had some colour in her pale cheeks now.

'You too.' Lili smiled.

Joanna sniffed the air. 'Hmm, I can smell the stew. I can't wait for supper time,' she said. She sat down on her bed, hugged her knees and closed her eyes. That smell transported her home to the family kitchen in Jasło. She and Marta would sit at the kitchen table reading or writing while Mutti cooked, when she was well enough to. The smell of the supper to come would make their stomachs rumble with anticipation, making it hard to concentrate on what they were doing.

Poor Marta. Wherever was she now? The sight of her

looking up from the back of the truck as it had rumbled over the cobbles and out of the yard had haunted Joanna since that terrible morning. Where had she been taken? Was she in Germany now? Would they ever find their way back to each other? And what would happen to her and Lili? Would they find their way home eventually? That seemed like far too much to hope for. And if she did manage to get home, what might she find there?

'Don't worry, Joanna,' Lili said. 'We're out of the camp at least. Surely the next bit can't be any worse than that?'

Joanna looked at her friend. How innocent she was. Didn't she know that what they'd just done was only the beginning? Tomorrow they would be on the streets of the city, patrolled by SS guards with their Alsatian dogs. No, today was the easy part. The worst was yet to come.

'Supper is ready!' Ilona's voice came from below and the two girls scrambled to the trapdoor, but Ilona appeared at the top of the ladder, carrying a tray.

'You'd better not come down. They will have discovered you're missing, so if anyone comes to the door you'd better be out of sight.'

The girls thanked her and took the plates. Ilona climbed into the loft and sat with them. While they ate, she talked, telling them how she and Jan were both teachers, but how they hated Nazi rule and had worked with the Polish resistance ever since the occupation in 1939. Since then, they had mostly focused on helping Jews escape from the ghetto, or to go into hiding.

'We haven't helped children from the camp before,' Ilona said. 'Not because we haven't wanted to, but because nobody has asked us. Most of the children don't have anyone to help them. We can see that what goes on there is terrible – starving children being used as forced labour – but no one has asked us to help a child escape before. You must have been helped by some very brave people.'

'Yes,' Joanna agreed. 'We were lucky.'

Her mind went to Nurse Weiss, who never hesitated to go out of her way to help those in her care. She didn't seem to worry about saying something controversial or about putting herself in danger. Knowing Nurse Weiss had made Joanna realise that not all Germans were as brutal as the ones they had encountered in Jasło.

Everyone fell silent as they ate their stew. Joanna tried not to gobble hers down, but it was so delicious, and she was so hungry, that it took an effort not to. Ilona even gave them second helpings.

After they'd finished, Jan appeared to collect their dishes.

'You two girls need to go to bed and get plenty of sleep,' he said. 'You have a big day ahead of you tomorrow, but if all goes to plan then this time tomorrow you should be at home with your families. They might need to hide you for a while, as the SS might come looking for you, but at least you will be at home.'

Joanna stared at him. This was something she'd hardly dared to dream of.

'The first difficult thing will be to get you into the railway station. The SS usually check papers as people go into the concourse. We have managed to obtain some false ID papers for you two, stating that you are our children, so we're just hoping that that part will go smoothly.'

Prickles of fear coursed through Joanna's body. She hadn't thought that simply going to the station would be so difficult, but then she recalled that there had always been guards at the station in Jasło, which itself was a big interchange connecting trains from many different parts of the country. Mama had always just shown the guards their papers and they had never had any problems entering. Joanna tried to console herself with that thought. Why should it be any different tomorrow?

Later, she lay awake under the eaves, staring up at the wooden beams of the old house. It was warm up there in the roof; the heat from the stove in the apartment rose up through the hatch, and she had plenty of blankets too. She should be tired – it had been an exhausting day and she'd been up since six o' clock in the morning. But the stress of escaping from the factory had left her wide awake, buzzing with adrenaline. She could hear Lili's gentle snores a little way away and envied her the ability to drop off to sleep in an instant. But finally, her mind settled down, and she drifted off into a restless sleep.

Ilona held Joanna's and Lili's hands tightly as they walked through the city streets to the station. None of them spoke; they were all too tense for words. In Joanna's other hand, she carried a little suitcase that Ilona had given her. It contained more of Ilona's cousins' clothes.

'You might not need the clothes,' Ilona had said, 'but it will make our story more believable.'

Ilona had also given a small suitcase to Lili, and she carried one herself. They were all dressed in coats and hats, as if they were off on a long journey. The hats were partly to hide the girls' shaven heads.

The station was only a few streets away from the apartment. Joanna looked around her as they walked along, noticing how different things were here from the streets in the ghetto. There were still queues of people waiting outside food shops, but the buildings were well maintained, the people reasonably dressed, and there were no beggars. Of course there were SS men standing on the steps of buildings scanning the crowds, or patrolling the pavement, rifles slung over their shoulders. But compared to the ghetto, this place felt normal, and it was hard to believe that the poverty and suffering of the ghetto existed within such a short distance of these thriving streets.

The station loomed ahead of them. It was an imposing building. The swastika flags fluttered down from above the entrance. Beneath the central one, underneath one of the arches, stood two guards in long grey overcoats and leather boots, with Alsatians straining on leashes. They were checking the papers of the passengers entering the station.

'Don't be afraid, girls. Just pretend this is perfectly normal,' Ilona said, but Joanna could hear the nerves in her voice.

They joined the back of the queue. It was moving forward relatively quickly, up the front steps of the station building towards the guards. At one point, a dark man with a long beard was pulled out of the line and made to stand and wait beside the officers. Joanna tried her best not to stare at him. What had he done to deserve such treatment?

When it was their turn, Ilona held the papers out to the officer. Snatching them from her, he seemed to spend an age reading them. He turned them over and over, peering down at them, examining them closely.

Joanna's heart was thumping against her ribs. She tried to keep her head down, her eyes focused on the flagstones. *If I can stay like this for a few minutes longer, it will soon be over*, she kept telling herself.

'Where are you travelling to, Frau Ryczek?' he asked finally.

'To Kraków, to visit relatives,' Ilona replied.

The man turned to his colleague and raised his eyebrows in an exaggerated gesture and his colleague shrugged.

'Very well. Be careful, please,' the officer said, handing back the papers.

'Thank you.'

There was a pause while Ilona put the papers back into her bag, then they left the queue and hurried into the station. Joanna breathed again, but her heart was still pounding.

'We must get to the ticket office,' said Ilona. 'That took longer than I thought. We need to hurry.'

They ran across the busy concourse. To Joanna's dismay, she noticed many SS guards patrolling with dogs amongst the crowds. Was this usual?

'Don't worry about them. Just act normally,' Ilona said.

They approached the ticket office, where there was a long queue, and Joanna heard Ilona take a sharp intake of breath. They joined the back of the slow-moving line and began to shuffle towards the kiosk. As they edged forward, Joanna happened to look to the right of her, and shock washed through her at what she saw.

There was the foreman from the clothing factory, just a few metres away from her, walking between two SS officers. He was shading his eyes and scanning the crowds, searching for something, or someone. In that split second, before Joanna had time to turn away, the foreman's eyes alighted on her. She saw them widen in surprise and the next second, he pointed to her and shouted something to the officers. Paralysed with shock, she still managed to tug at Ilona's arm. But just as Ilona turned to look, the officers started running towards them.

'Hey! You with the children! Stop!'

'Run!' Ilona said, tugging Joanna with one hand and Lili with the other.

They pushed their way across the concourse, bumping into people as they went. Joanna felt sick and her stomach was doing somersaults. They didn't get far. In the next second a shot rang out and Joanna heard Ilona cry out. She went tense, then let go of Joanna's hand, and with horror Joanna saw her stumble and fall to the ground.

Joanna stopped and stared down at Ilona, sprawled out face down on the marble floor of the station, blood spreading from a wound in her head. Sickening panic washed through her, but before she could do anything, she felt a rough hand grab her arm. She looked up to see the face of one of the SS officers glaring down at her.

'You're coming with me,' he said.

She knew it was the end. The end of any hope of getting away from that place.

SEVENTEEN

MARTA

Bruczków Assimilation Home, Poland, 1944

'I'm so pleased you've agreed to let me help you with your German language,' Margarete said, opening a book on her lap.

'It's very kind of you to offer,' Marta replied. 'But I'd prefer it if you would help me get away from here.'

She didn't want to sound ungrateful, and she understood the reasons why Margarete thought that escaping wasn't an option, but learning German seemed to be a step further away from getting back to Jasło and Mama and Tata, rather than a step closer.

They were sitting side by side on Margarete's bed on the top floor of the old house. It felt good to be here, away from the dormitory and the noise of the other girls.

'You know, one day, when this terrible war is over,' Margarete went on with a sigh, 'it will be much easier for you to return home. I've kept all your details for you, so that if you need them in the future—'

'I won't need them in the future. I know my address in Jasło. That's all there is to know, isn't it?'

Margarete's face fell and Marta instantly felt guilty for being rude.

'I'm sorry, Nurse Weiss. I know you're trying to help me. I just wish things were different, that's all.'

'Don't worry, Marta,' Margarete said with a sympathetic smile. 'I know it's very hard for you, but one day, all this effort will pay off, I'm sure. Getting better at German will help you get out of this place, at least.'

'I don't want to stay here a moment longer. The only things keeping me going are you and Agata,' Marta replied.

Nurse Weiss had told Marta how she'd managed to persuade Doctor Schiller to give her another chance, otherwise he had threatened to put her on a train to one of the work camps in southern Poland. Marta had shivered, knowing how close she'd come to such a terrible punishment, and she knew she had Margarete to thank for saving her from that fate.

'Doctor Schiller really meant it, Marta. Only one more chance. So, you need to be very careful from now on. No more fighting with other girls, not matter how much they annoy you, and you must try your best not to give the teachers any cause to send you to Schiller's office again.'

Marta had agreed, and from that moment on she had done her best to comply with the rules, although it felt wrong giving the appearance of going along with the teachings on Nazi ideology. She didn't agree with any of it, and it rankled with her not to be able to speak her mind. She had to bite her tongue in the dormitory when Gisela and her friends discussed that day's lessons in approving tones.

Now, Margarete opened the German textbook on the first page and started to show Marta how to speak simple sentences. It made so much more sense the way Margarete taught it. Soon Marta was repeating words after her without difficulty.

After half an hour, Margarete closed the book.

'Well done, Marta. If we do this every evening, you will be fluent in no time. Now you'd better go back to the dormitory. It will be bedtime soon.'

Marta thanked her and went back downstairs to the dormitory.

'It's good that Nurse Weiss is helping you,' Agata said. 'I think she will do it far better than I could.'

'It was kind of you to offer though, Agata,' Marta said, giving her friend a hug.

Life in the assimilation home fell into a regular routine and the weeks passed quickly. Marta made good progress with her German with Margarete's help; she also learned all the marches and salutes to the satisfaction of Herr Sturm. Agata excelled at German and was an exemplary student in every way. The best in the class.

One day, after lessons, Agata was called in to see Doctor Schiller. Marta went out to the yard with the other children and walked over to tend the vegetable patch alone. No longer a bed of weeds on hard, unyielding earth, now it was a large square of soft, tilled soil, where vegetables were sprouting their first shoots.

How hard she and Agata had worked on it. Once they had broken some of the ground, Herr Sturm had sent other children to help them and the patch had expanded quickly. They had planted it out with beans, potatoes, onions, carrots and swede. Marta was proud of it. But looking at it now, she realised that it represented several months of hard toil. Several months during which she'd been away from Mama and Tata and Joanna. That thought left a hollow feeling in her chest that obliterated the pride she'd felt looking at the fruits of her efforts.

Shading her eyes, she stared into the distance at the rolling farmland that stretched away from the old manor house grounds for many kilometres in every direction. There was the odd spinney and village, but the view mainly consisted of enormous fields, bounded by hedgerows and planted with crops, now sprouting in the sunshine.

A train puffed along the distant horizon, sun glinting on its windows. It left a trail of white steam in its wake. She watched it for a moment. It was the only moving thing in her vision. It was heading south, towards Kraków, towards her home. She wasn't quite sure whereabouts in Poland Bruczków was, but she knew it was a long way north of Kraków. If only she was on board that train, heading home. Her heart yearned to be there, for the comfort of her mother's arms around her, to bask in her father's smile and feel his hand ruffling her hair. To sit in front of the fire and read, to lie in bed listening to the birds in the trees outside the window.

The station wasn't far from the assimilation home. It had only taken ten minutes or so in the truck. If she left now, she could walk there... She clenched her fists and let out a stifled scream. She had no money, no papers; she was trapped here.

She saw Agata approaching across the yard. Agata's head was bowed, she was dragging her feet, and when she got closer, Marta could see that she was crying.

'What's the matter? What's happened?'

'They're sending me away,' Agata said. 'Doctor Schiller said I was ready to go to a family in Germany.'

Marta's mouth dropped open. She was dumbstruck – she hadn't foreseen this.

'If only I hadn't worked so hard,' Agata said. 'I just wanted to do well. To be top of the class like at home. If only I'd stopped and thought for a moment...'

'Oh, Agata,' Marta said, through tears, stepping forward and embracing her friend. 'I can't believe it. When are you leaving?'

'In a few days' time,' she said miserably.

Marta stared at her. 'Oh, Agata,' she said again, 'I don't know how I'll be able to bear it.'

Yet again, she was to be forcibly separated from someone she loved. She and Agata had forged a close bond over the past months. Now she couldn't envisage life without her.

'Come on, we'd better do some weeding before Sturm catches us,' she said, and they collected hand-forks and trowels and a wheelbarrow from the shed.

As they walked back to the vegetable patch, Marta realised something. The train she'd seen powering across the horizon, and Agata's news, were both signs. They were telling her that it was time for her to leave this place. If only she could find some money from somewhere, and work out where the station was, she could do it. She could just walk away during gardening hour or in the middle of the night. And if Agata was no longer there by her side, there was very little reason for her to stay.

The days that followed were bittersweet for Marta. She still had the pleasure of Agata's company, but the day her friend would have to leave was drawing closer every second. Soon all this would be at an end. They would probably never see each other again. How she would miss Agata when she'd gone. She knew that Agata's departure would bring all her feelings of loss to the fore.

'I'll try to write to you,' Agata said, 'but I'm not sure it will get to you. If I just put Children's Home, Bruczków, Poland, the letter should get here.'

'But they probably won't allow me to read it,' Marta said miserably.

They were sitting on Agata's bed, the day before she was due to leave. She was packing her meagre belongings into a holdall given to her by Doctor Schiller, although she didn't have much to take with her.

'I expect I'll get some new clothes when I'm there,' she said. 'I can hardly go round in this dreadful uniform all the time.'

Listening to Agata talk, Marta realised that, although her friend was as sad as she was at the forthcoming parting, a part of her was looking forward to her next chapter. Living with a family, even if they were Nazis, might be more comfortable than it was here, with the poor food, rigorous discipline and lack of comfort and privacy.

She turned away to hide her sadness.

The next day, after breakfast, a black SS vehicle came to collect Agata and two other children who had been selected to go to Germany. Every child in the home was encouraged to go out onto the front steps of the old manor house to wave.

'Wish them well on their journey and with their new lives in Germany, children,' Doctor Schiller said, standing on the steps himself. 'This is a moment of triumph for our Lebensborn programme and we should celebrate it.'

Marta and Agata had said their goodbyes upstairs in the dormitory, hugging and clinging to each other. Now, before she got into the back of the limousine, Agata turned and sought Marta out with her eyes, and waved a last, sad wave just for Marta before she got into the car and the officer who had been holding the door open shut it with a slam. Then he got into the front, the engine started up and the car drew away, Agata's little face peering out of the back window.

Marta went back inside with a heavy heart, but before she crossed the hall she felt a hand on her shoulder.

'Try not to be too sad, Marta,' Nurse Weiss said gently. 'We must redouble our efforts to get you away from this place too now. I'll see you in my room after supper as usual for some language practice.'

There was still half an hour to go until the lessons started.

Marta couldn't face going into the dormitory and listening to Gisela and her acolytes discuss Nazi ideas in excited, reverential tones. Instead, she went and shut herself in one of the toilet cubicles, put her hands over her face and sobbed quietly for everything and everyone she'd lost.

The bell rang for lessons. Marta wiped her eyes and left the washroom, quickly checking her reflection in the cracked mirror as she went. On the landing, she noticed that the door to the staff cloakroom was ajar. This was where the members of staff who came in daily would leave their coats. She could see a row of them hanging there. Her heartbeat sped up. This was too good an opportunity to miss.

Looking around to check there was no one watching, her heart pounding, she slipped inside the cloakroom and began to rummage through the pockets of the coats. There was loose change in some of the coats, which she quickly slipped into her own pocket, and in one of them there were two five-Reichsmark notes, scrunched up in the bottom. This was surely enough to pay for the journey to Jasło? Looking around warily again, she slipped out of the cloakroom and made her way to the top of the stairs, about to go down to the schoolroom. Then she changed her mind. It would be better to hide the money in the dormitory than to carry it on her. She turned to go back into the dormitory, but her way was barred by Nurse Wolff.

'What are you coming back in here for?' she asked, arms folded.

'I... er... forgot my cardigan.'

'Well, quickly then,' the nurse said, letting her through.

Marta went over to her bed. She wanted to slip the money under the mattress, but with Nurse Wolff's eyes upon her, she had no choice but to pick up her cardigan and walk back to the door. On her way downstairs, she took care to go slowly, acutely conscious of the slight bulge in her pocket and the chink of the coins as she moved. She prayed fervently that no one would notice.

She went into the classroom and sat in her usual place quietly. The empty place beside her reminded her once more of the loss of Agata.

Herr Sturm stood at the front of the class and clapped his hands.

'Guten Morgen, children,' he began, then proceeded to speak in Polish.

'This morning, we have much to celebrate, with a select little band of our best pupils having departed for lives in the Fatherland. It is a proud moment for us all. Let us take their success as our inspiration and work as hard as we can so that more of you will soon be setting forth on journeys of your own.'

Then, the lesson began. Herr Sturm asked pupils to repeat various phrases after him and to answer simple questions that he wrote on the blackboard.

Marta found it hard to concentrate. Half her mind was on Agata, wondering where she was, where she would end up, and the other half on her own escape. Now she had enough money, she needed to figure out a few more things. How would she obtain ID papers, and how would she find her way to the station? She guessed that, if she were able to get into Doctor Schiller's office at night somehow, she might find some papers there that she could use. She might also be able to find a map from somewhere, or discreetly ask one of the staff about the whereabouts of the station without arousing suspicion.

She was just musing on this when the classroom door opened and Doctor Schiller entered the room flanked by two of his henchmen. Herr Sturm stopped speaking.

'Herr Doctor,' he said. 'What a surprise! Welcome to the class.'

The doctor strode to the front of the classroom.

'I am here, children, because there has been an unfortunate

incident this morning. Money has been stolen from the staff cloakroom.'

Shock washed through Marta. How did they find out so quickly? Had someone seen her?

'Considerable sums of money have been taken,' the doctor went on. 'We have already searched the younger children in the other classroom and found nothing. We are here to conduct a complete search of this class. You must come forward one by one so we can search through your pockets. Now, come forward, please. Starting in the front row.'

Marta's place was on the front row. She watched, her heart in her mouth, while the three children to her left went to the front and were patted down by one of the men. Their pockets were turned out, fingers were run around their collars and inside their shoes.

'If we don't find anything, we may have to do a strip search,' Doctor Schiller warned.

Marta went alternately hot and cold. Could she take the money out and conceal it in the desk somehow? It was impossible. She could feel the doctor's eyes on her constantly. What could she do? Her heart was hammering, and her breaths were coming quick and shallow. Her palms were sweating, and she knew her cheeks were red. She felt trapped. There was no way out.

'Marthe Kaplan,' Doctor Schiller called out. 'Come forward, please.'

Marta stood up and shuffled her way to the front, where Doctor Schiller stood.

'Go ahead, check her,' Doctor Schiller said to one of the men.

It took him roughly five seconds to reach in her pocket and take the money out.

'Here!' He held it out to Doctor Schiller, who stared at

Marta, his eyes popping, his face full of fury. But at the same time, she noticed that he looked triumphant too.

'So, it was you!' he said. 'I knew it! I knew you couldn't be trusted, but Nurse Weiss persuaded me otherwise. How wrong I was to believe her. Come with me, Marthe. You can go back to the cellar again while I make arrangements for your departure. And you certainly will not be going to the Fatherland, let me tell you that!'

EIGHTEEN

JOANNA

Poland, 1944

Joanna and Lili were dragged from the station concourse by SS guards and returned to the children's camp on the back of a truck. When they arrived, an SS officer with cruel, narrow eyes stood waiting for them in front of the dormitory building.

The guards dragged them off the truck and into the building, marching them along the corridor and into an office on the ground floor. When she entered the room, Joanna noticed that it was the same room that poor little Josef had been locked in that terrible night he had disappeared. Would the same thing happen to her and Lili? She almost cried at the thought.

The officer, who'd been waiting for them outside, swaggered into the room and sat behind the desk.

'Stand there,' he said, pointing to a spot in front of the desk.

The girls shuffled forward so they were standing side by side in front of him. He leaned back in his chair, put his booted feet up on the desk and smiled a thin-lipped smile.

'So, you were trying to get away from here, weren't you?' he said.

Joanna hung her head. She didn't want to look at him.

'I don't blame you,' he said. 'Life here is hard. You showed great ingenuity to get as far as you did, but you had help, that is for certain.'

He paused, letting his words sink in. Joanna looked up at the man, trying not to let the fear show on her face.

'The young woman you were with,' the officer went on, 'what is her name? Or rather, what *was* her name?'

Joanna glanced at Lili, whose face was white. She was visibly shaking.

'We don't know her name,' Joanna said. 'We just called her Panna.'

Panna was the Polish word for Miss. She thought then of poor Ilona, of her pretty face, her smile, her kindness, shot down, lying in a pool of blood on the station floor. A lump rose in her throat.

'Interesting. And I know she wasn't the only one who helped you. There were others too, weren't there? Perhaps somebody here in the camp?'

Both girls shook their heads.

'There was nobody else. It was just her,' Joanna said, keeping her face expressionless.

'That's right,' Lili said. 'It was only her.'

'So, how did you meet this young lady? You see, to my mind, all this had been prepared in advance. She had false identities for you both. She couldn't have arranged that within the space of just a few hours.'

'We just met her on the street,' Joanna said, keeping her voice steady, her eyes on his face. 'When we got out of the factory. She said she would help us.'

'And she took you home to her place to stay the night, didn't she?'

Joanna glanced at Lili. She didn't want to say any more. Perhaps she'd said too much already. Neither of them answered.

'Let me repeat my question,' said the man, irritation in his voice now. 'The young woman took you home to stay the night at her place, didn't she?'

Joanna shook her head.

'So, where did you sleep, then?' the officer asked.

'In a warehouse.' It was Lili who spoke. There were dozens of disused warehouses and old factories in the area; it sounded plausible.

The man leaned forward and banged on the desk with his fists, making the two girls jump.

'I do not believe you!' he yelled, his face growing red. 'You did not sleep in a warehouse, you slept in that young woman's apartment. I know it! Now we need to find the people who helped you and you are going to help us do that. To jog your memories, I am going to shut you away in separate rooms for a few hours. The rooms are not heated. You will get no food, only water. When you are hungry enough, you will be only too happy to tell me what I want to know. Trust me, I've done this many, many times before.'

Joanna felt someone approaching from behind. Her arms were seized by one of the soldiers who had brought them into the room. She and Lili were dragged out into the passageway, then all the way along it to the end. There, the soldier opened a door and threw Joanna into a room. He pushed her in with such force that she found herself sprawling on the floor. She heard a key turn in the lock.

She sat up and looked around her. There was little light in the room that was not much bigger than a cubicle. There was only a small window in the back wall, and the sky outside was gloomy and overcast. The room contained no furniture – just a wooden bench and a bucket in the corner.

Joanna sat down on the bench and waited. She wasn't hungry – she'd eaten plenty of breakfast and she knew she could last for hours without food. She made a silent vow to herself that she wouldn't tell the officer anything more than she had already, and she would stick to the story that they had slept in a warehouse. If she stayed silent, Jan and Marek and Nurse Weiss would be safe. But how would Lili cope with being locked in alone? She was two years younger than Joanna and not as strong, either physically or mentally.

Joanna went over to the wall that separated her room from Lili's and put her ear to it: she could just hear Lili's sobs through the partition. She knocked on the wall with her fist, but there was no response. She sat back on the bench and waited. It was all she could do. But it was hard to sit still and she found herself getting up and pacing up and down the room. She was worried about Lili. What if she gave in to the pressure and started to talk? How could Joanna possibly prevent that from happening?

The hours crawled by. When she was tired of walking up and down, Joanna lay down on the bench and closed her eyes. She must have drifted off, because when she woke, the sky outside the window was dark, and someone was turning the key in the door. She sat up and rubbed her eyes. The sour-faced woman who had taken Josef away the other night entered the room and closed the door. She handed Joanna a tin cup.

'There's some water for you,' she said. 'Get yourself ready for a journey, you are leaving tonight.'

Joanna stared at her. Leaving tonight? So, she wasn't to be questioned any further? Did that mean that Lili had broken down and told them what they wanted to know? She refused to believe it. Lili couldn't even be hungry yet, so why would she have talked?

The door slammed behind the woman and the lock was turned, but soon it opened again and the officer who'd questioned them earlier entered the room. He strode about, watching her with his narrow eyes.

'Well, we've got what we wanted,' he told her. 'No thanks to either of you. We found a name tag on some clothes in the suitcases. That should be enough for us – it will enable us to find those who helped you.'

Joanna didn't reply, but rivulets of fear trickled through her body. Of course. It must have been those clothes belonging to Ilona's cousins. She hadn't noticed any name tags, but perhaps they'd been folded up inside the clothes. If only she'd checked them, she could have warned Ilona. What would become of Jan and Marek now if they did manage to track them down? She shuddered to think what might happen to them.

'We are going to send you girls away,' the man went on. 'To another place. A long way south of here. It is a whole day's journey on the train, but there is a transport tonight and you will be on it. It will take all night.'

She stared up at him. He stood looking down at her, smiling a smile of triumph.

'Where are we going?' she asked.

'You will find out soon enough,' he said, laughing. 'Get ready. You will be leaving here in approximately half an hour.'

They were taken by truck to the station, but the journey from the camp was very short. They stared at each other wide-eyed all the way, neither daring to speak. As they pulled into the forecourt, Joanna realised that this was a different station from the one they'd walked to with Ilona that morning with so much hope in their hearts. When the truck stopped outside the station entrance, Joanna saw that this one was called Radegast station.

A guard came round, undid the tailgate bolts and pulled it down.

'Get out,' he ordered, and the girls climbed down onto the cobbled forecourt.

The place was busy. Crowds of people were being herded into the station by SS guards wielding guns. Some of them held dogs straining at their leashes. From their clothes and the yellow stars they wore on their arms, she could tell that these people were Jewish. Joanna had heard about Jews being transported to camps, but she'd never seen it herself before. It was a terrifying sight, but most of all she was shocked at the brutality of the guards. They were shouting and yelling at people to hurry up, prodding them with their rifles, sometimes aiming a kick at an old man or woman who was too slow.

The guard behind Joanna was pushing her forward now with the butt of his gun and soon she was walking right behind the last crowd of Jews. She could see that there were whole families amongst them, tiny children and babies, men and women, grandparents. They were huddling together and shuffling forward into the crowded station, clutching their luggage.

'You will travel on a truck with these people, but when you reach the camp, give this paper to the doctor in charge,' the guard told them and handed them each an official-looking document. Joanna glanced down at hers: it had the swastika emblazoned at the top, and it was written in German. She had no idea what it said.

They were swept across the station towards the platform with the crowd. The soldiers were still behind them, though. More than once, Joanna felt the prod of a rifle between her shoulder blades. As they got closer to the train, she was surprised to see that there were no carriages waiting on the platform, only cattle trucks. She wondered if animals were being transported on this train as well as people, then she was stunned to see people being pushed onto the cattle trucks by the guards. The truck doors were high up above the platform and there were no steps. Some of the older people and smaller children were struggling to climb into the wagon and had to be helped by others. The guards showed no mercy, pushing and shoving people as if they were animals.

Joanna and Lili moved forward with the crowd and soon it was their turn to board the truck. Joanna scrambled up easily, then turned round and held out her hand for Lili to follow. Inside, the truck stank of animal dung and there was straw scattered around on the floor. In one corner was a bucket. Joanna found a space for them to sit on the opposite side of the truck – she didn't want to be near the bucket – and they sat down together on the floor. But the wagon was quickly filling up with people and there was no longer room for them to sit.

The people around them urged them to get up and make more space, so they scrambled to their feet and soon found themselves crammed against the wall, penned in by the bodies as more and more poured into the truck. Pressed against Joanna was a young woman and her three children, a baby, a toddler and a little girl who must have been about four or five years old. The baby was crying, and the woman was trying to comfort him, rocking him to and fro and singing lullabies, but to no avail. The two other children clung to their mother's skirts, looking terrified.

When the cattle truck was packed as tightly as it could be, the door was slid shut from the outside, and then came the ominous sound of a bolt being pulled across. Everyone gasped as it was clicked into place. They were locked in, pressed together like sardines in a tin, unable to get out and unable to move. It was already hot and airless inside the truck, the only ventilation being a slit high up on one side, covered in barbed wire. People were already sweating. Joanna covered her mouth and nose against the smell. If it was like that now, before they'd even started on their journey, what would it be like by the morning?

Whistles shrilled on the platform, accompanied by German voices shouting orders, then came the blast of a horn and the train jerked forward. Everyone toppled together at the first lurch, grabbing each other to avoid falling over. There were a few more jerks as the train gathered pace, and soon it was rattling along steadily, if slowly. Joanna wondered how she would last all night standing here in this airless spot, breathing in the sweat and breath of over a hundred other bodies. She and Lili had no water, but she saw that many of her fellow travellers had brought their own supplies of food and water for the journey. Perhaps she would be able to beg some water from them if her thirst became unbearable.

It was pitch dark in the cattle truck, but sometimes a flicker of light from outside would penetrate the slit at the top or the cracks in the boards and dance on the passengers for a second. It frightened Joanna to see their faces lit up like that, frozen in time. On every one was etched a look of terror, of dread at what the end of the journey might bring.

The journey wore on. The baby didn't stop crying and soon the toddler joined in. Other children were crying too, their parents trying to comfort them with soothing words. Joanna felt like crying herself, but she knew she must be strong for Lili's sake. She squeezed Lili's hand, and Lili squeezed hers back. At least they were still together, whatever the morning might bring.

Her mind went back over the past twenty-four hours, during which they had come full circle. They had started the day full of hope, thinking they could soon be on their way home. Then there had been the horror of Ilona's death and their recapture, the fear of solitary confinement followed by the terror and discomfort of the cattle truck. How foolish she had been to even hope. She should have known those hopes would be dashed. She should have guarded herself against hope at all costs.

The hours crawled by. A kind woman standing beside Lili offered the girls some water and they drank gratefully. Sometimes the train sped up for a few kilometres, sometimes it crawled, sometimes it stopped for a long time for seemingly no reason. Sometimes it rattled over bridges and a welcome waft of fresh river air made its way through the cracks in the truck wall; sometimes it went through towns, with the smell of smoke from factories and fires.

There was constant movement in the sea of bodies. Every time someone needed to go to the bucket, they had to push their way through the press of the crowd. Joanna hung on for as long as she could, but when she felt as if her bladder would burst she asked the woman with the children if she could squeeze past to get to the bucket.

People did their best to move aside to let her squeeze through and everyone was very patient with her. When she finally reached the corner, she felt self-conscious pulling down her underwear and sitting on the wobbling bucket that was already half full. But it was pitch dark, she reminded herself. No one could see her. She didn't envy those who had ended up standing in the immediate vicinity. It must be difficult not to trip over the bucket, which had filled up during the journey, especially when the train went over bumps or ground to a halt as it often did.

Once she was back beside Lili, she squeezed in next to her with relief.

'I don't want to go,' Lili said. 'It's too much trouble. I can wait until we get there.'

Joanna leaned against the wall and closed her eyes. The heat of the truck and the rocking motion of the train soon lulled her into a fitful sleep. She had no idea how many hours she stood there, drifting in and out of sleep, but at one point she woke and saw that the light through the slit in the wall was daylight. It must be after dawn, so their journey must soon be at an end.

The train moved forward even more slowly now, and a new smell entered the truck through the cracks and mingled with the rank smell of bodies. Joanna sniffed the air. It was the smell of smoke, but not the familiar smoke of woodfires; it was foul-smelling, with a stench such as she'd never smelled before. It turned her stomach. She held her hand over her mouth, and saw that many others were doing the same.

Finally, the train ground under a great brick-built archway and came to a halt. Everyone looked at each other, wondering if it would start up again, but after a few minutes came the sound of wagon doors being opened, of voices shouting. This must be the end of the journey. They had reached their destination.

The bolts were pulled back and the doors slid open. One on either side of the truck. A blast of stinking air wafted into the truck. From where she stood, Joanna could just about see the platform outside, and beyond that a fence topped with barbed wire. SS men in helmets with guns and dogs stood beside the truck.

'Everybody out! Quickly now! Form a line opposite. Leave your belongings on the platform.'

People at the edge of the truck began to climb down, slowly at first but then more quickly, prodded on by the guards. Some people helped others, some virtually fell down and were picked up by their companions. Joanna and Lili moved nearer to the edge and soon it was their turn.

Joanna climbed down first, then turned to help Lili down.

'Hurry,' said one of the guards. 'Form two lines on that side. Young men and women on one side, older people and women with children on the other side. Leave your belongings on the platform. Don't worry, they will all be returned to you later.'

Joanna held Lili's hand and they joined the line that was forming on the other side of the platform where women with children had been directed to queue. People were putting their luggage down on the platform and it was being collected by camp inmates, pitifully thin people dressed in striped uniforms. These people kept their eyes down, fixed on their tasks. They didn't once look up or even glance at the new arrivals.

'What is this place?' a woman asked one of the guards.

'This is your final destination,' the guard replied. 'You've arrived at Auschwitz.'

NINETEEN
MARGARETE

Bruczków Assimilation Home, Poland, 1944

Margarete was walking past the senior classroom when she heard Doctor Schiller's voice in the room, booming out in anger.

'I knew it was you, Marthe Kaplan!'

Margarete frowned, puzzled. She stopped and listened. Whatever had happened now? She'd really thought that Marta was making good progress and that she had decided to at least give the appearance of having settled down, but she seemed to have done something else to anger Doctor Schiller now. Perhaps Agata's departure had shaken her and dampened her resolve. Margarete knew how close the two girls had grown. It would have been hard for Marta to cope with another separation, having been taken from her parents only a few months ago and brutally separated from Joanna a few days afterwards.

Margarete couldn't hear everything that was being said, but she did hear Doctor Schiller's threat to send Marta away. The door opened abruptly and the doctor pushed Marta out into the hallway, following close behind.

'What's the problem, Doctor?' Margarete asked.

'It's this girl again, Nurse. Marthe Kaplan. She's the problem. This time she's really done it. She's been stealing from the staff. Someone reported it to me this morning when they went to get their coat after the night shift. We conducted a search of the pupils and found the money in Kaplan's pocket. She has no need of money of her own here, so no doubt she was planning to run away... So much for your promise, Nurse Weiss.'

He peered at her accusingly, his face red and flustered.

'I'm sure there's a good explanation, Doctor,' Margarete said, trying to give Marta a reassuring look, but Marta wasn't looking at her; she was staring down at her feet, her shoulders drooping in defeat and despair.

'The time for explanations has long gone, Nurse. I was foolish to give the girl a second chance. I shouldn't have listened to you. No, this girl is rotten to the core. We cannot have her infecting the minds of the other pupils here for a moment longer.'

'Please, Doctor. Let me have a word with you in private,' Margarete said, beginning to panic. She knew how harmful it was to Marta to hear herself spoken about in this way. Like all Nazis, the doctor had no compassion or mercy and would relish denigrating the girl within her hearing. He seemed to have made up his mind now, though. She dreaded to think what he had in store for poor Marta.

'Not now, Nurse,' he said. 'I will speak to you later. I need to take this girl down to the cellar again. I should never have let her out in the first place.'

With that, he pushed Marta forward towards the cellar door in the corner of the hallway. Marta was looking back at Margarete with wide, terrified eyes.

'But surely, Doctor. If she has to be locked up for a time, the boot room is far more appropriate?'

'Keep your ideas to yourself, thank you, Nurse,' he muttered over his shoulder, pushing Marta towards the cellar door. 'I have decided upon the cellar, so the cellar it is. You can wait for me in my office and we can speak there.'

Margarete turned away, her thoughts jumbled. What could she do to get Marta out of this situation? Doctor Schiller was never going to give her a second chance. His mind was dead set against her now.

Margarete wandered towards the doctor's office deep in thought, wondering what had led Marta to the decision to steal money. It was so unlike the good, kind, thoughtful girl she'd met in the old hospital in Kraków, so anxious to care for her sister, always putting her own needs second. She'd changed so much since then. It must have been the shock of her loss and the terrible situation she was confronting daily that had altered her irrevocably.

Margarete opened the door to Doctor Schiller's office, went inside and shut the door behind her, but then stopped with a start. Herta, the woman she'd seen in Doctor Schiller's office once before, was already in the room. She was seated on an easy chair in the corner, leaning back, her legs crossed in front of her, flicking through a magazine. This was one of the members of staff Doctor Schiller had recruited to help with disciplining the children. The rest were all young men. She had luxuriant blonde hair and her face was heavily made up, with long false eyelashes and bright red lipstick. When she saw Margarete her face fell, and she sat forward rigidly.

'What are you doing here, Herta?' Margarete said coldly. She had no time for this young woman. She'd never seen her doing any useful work and she'd once caught her smacking some of the younger ones for speaking Polish in the corridors.

'I'm here to speak to Doctor Schiller,' Herta replied in a haughty tone.

'I see you were making yourself comfortable,' Margarete replied with a raised eyebrow.

Herta didn't reply. She stood up and smoothed her tight skirt down.

'Actually, the doctor asked me to wait in his office,' Margarete said. 'So, he clearly wasn't aware that you were here. Perhaps you should come back later. The doctor and I have something important to discuss.'

Without replying, Herta stalked past Margarete, leaving a waft of heady, cheap perfume in her wake, and left the room, banging the door behind her.

Margarete sat down in front of the doctor's desk. Her mind was on Marta, but she couldn't help wondering what Herta had been doing, looking so relaxed in the doctor's room. She couldn't think about that now, she decided. Her mind was too frazzled trying to work out what to do about Marta. She would think about Herta later.

A few minutes later, the door opened and Doctor Schiller came in.

'Ah, Nurse Weiss,' he said, striding to his desk. 'I really don't think there is anything to discuss. The girl is downstairs now. I am going to telephone Reich Main Office and arrange transport for her to one of the work camps as soon as possible. We are done with her here.'

'But Herr Doctor, she has passed all the Aryan tests...'

'I'm aware of her record, Nurse, but I really think there must have been a mistake somewhere down the line. She is showing so many undesirable traits, I believe she must have Slavic blood after all, just like her sister.'

'Someone once told me that the tests are never wrong, Doctor,' Margarete said, grasping at straws. 'Have you ever known them to be inaccurate in the past?'

He shook his head. 'Not generally, no. But there's always a first time.'

'Please, please reconsider, Doctor,' Margarete said, leaning forward, looking him in the eye. 'Let me work with Marta. She has a good heart. I think she must have stolen the money because she was upset about Agata leaving. The two of them were very close.'

She saw him hesitate for a moment and thought that he was going to relent, but then he frowned deeply and said, 'Such close friendships amongst the pupils should be discouraged. They lead to weakness and inefficiency. Now, Nurse Weiss, please leave the room so I can make my phone calls – the sooner that girl is off these premises, the better.'

Margarete got to her feet. 'I will just go and check that she is all right,' she said, and immediately regretted it.

Doctor Schiller banged on the desk, making her jump.

'You will do nothing of the sort, Nurse! I have locked the door from the hall and I have the key, so no one but me can go down there. You don't need to trouble yourself with that girl any more. I instruct you to put her out of your mind and return to your duties immediately.'

He reached for his telephone and Margarete had no choice but to leave the room. Herta was standing in the hallway and looked up when Margarete appeared, her eyes full of hope.

'He's on the telephone now, Herta. I would come back later if I were you,' Margarete said and watched the girl's smile vanish.

Margarete crossed the hallway and tried the door to the cellar. Doctor Schiller was right: the door was locked and no amount of rattling it made any difference. She hurried to the cloakroom, found her coat, went outside and took the path that led all the way round the edge of the old manor house. At the back of the house were a couple of gratings that she knew ventilated the cellar. She crouched down on the flowerbed beside the first one and spoke through it.

'Marta! Marta, it's me, Nurse Weiss. Are you all right?'

There was silence and Margarete wondered if she was

speaking into the wrong grating. She tried again: 'Marta! If you can hear me, please say so.'

After a few seconds, she heard Marta clear her throat, then say, 'There's nothing you can do. He's going to send me away, to one of the camps. I'm sorry I've let you down, Nurse Weiss.'

'Please don't talk like that, Marta. You haven't let me down at all. I just wanted to let you know that I'm going to do everything in my power to change Doctor Schiller's mind, so please don't give up hope.'

'Thank you, but he will never change his mind. I'm sorry I stole the money, I just wanted to run away. I thought I would be able to get the train home if I could find some papers.'

'I know. You must be very upset that Agata left. I can understand why you did it. And I'm going to do my best to get you out of this mess.'

'You're so kind to me,' Marta said. 'I don't deserve it.'

'Of course you deserve it, Marta. And I won't give up on you, whatever happens, so try not to worry too much.'

'Thank you.'

'I need to go back inside now, but I'll come and let you know how I get on later.'

'Goodbye,' Marta said in a resigned voice and Margarete went away feeling that at least Marta was talking to her and sounded reasonably robust. The last thing she wanted was for the girl to give up hope.

For the rest of the day Margarete went about her duties in the normal way, making sure the dormitories were clean, that the children had enough to eat, tending to minor ailments and illnesses amongst the younger ones, checking there were enough clean uniforms and clean sheets in the store. By the end of the day, after the children had gone to bed, she was tired, but she was still thinking about Marta and how she might be coping in her underground prison. She would go to her as soon as she could, but there were too many staff milling about near the back door for her to slip out of the building at that point.

Instead, she went up to her room, changed out of her uniform and lay down on the bed, resting her aching limbs. She thought back over the disturbing events of the day, the sadness at the departure of Agata, the cruelty of Doctor Schiller. Then she remembered Herta and her strange behaviour. She had no idea what the young woman was up to, but she decided to look at Herta's staff record as soon as she had an opportunity.

Margarete sat up then, stretched and pulled on a cardigan. She must go to Marta again. The poor girl would be feeling terrible now. It would be very dark in the cellar. She just hoped that there wouldn't be anyone in the hall by now, so she could slip out of the back door unnoticed again.

She crept downstairs to the first floor, along the landing, then down the wide staircase to the main hall. When she was halfway down, she saw something that made her gasp in surprise: Herta was knocking on Doctor Schiller's door. When he opened it, she stepped inside. Then, to Margarete's surprise, Doctor Schiller took Herta in his arms before shutting the door.

So that was it! That was why Herta had been waiting in his room and had looked so disappointed when it wasn't Doctor Schiller who entered. The two of them were having an affair. Perhaps that was why he'd recruited the girl? Maybe they knew each other already? Herta certainly wasn't any good at the work, and showed no interest at all in the children.

Suddenly Margarete had an idea. If she crept around the outside of the building, she might be able to look through the office window and confirm what she thought was happening inside. Her flesh crawled at the thought of spying like that, but if she did confirm her suspicions, she might be able to use the information to her advantage. She rushed back upstairs and fetched her camera, the one Tomas had given her before she left Schloss Schwanburg. She'd photographed Marta and Joanna with it and she'd always loved it. It brought her luck. Now, she slipped it into her handbag and hurried down again. She thought about Doctor Schiller's wife, austere and humourless, strutting about the corridors with an air of authority. She looked to be a cold woman but even so, she didn't deserve for her husband to be carrying on with a young member of staff right under her nose.

When Margarete got down into the hall, there was no one about. She slipped out of the back door and, heart thumping, hurried round the side of the house, taking care to duck underneath the windows, until she came to Doctor Schiller's window. It was open a crack, but all she could hear were indistinct voices. Although she strained her ears, she couldn't hear what was being said.

Slowly, she raised her head above the windowsill and looked inside: Herta was sitting on the desk and Doctor Schiller was standing in front of her. They were locked in a passionate embrace, Herta's legs entwined around the doctor's back.

Now was the time to act. They were both so engrossed in what they were doing, they surely wouldn't notice a camera at the window. Margarete knew that to be certain of a result she should really use a flashbulb, but they would surely see if she did so, instead, she held the camera against the pane, focused the viewfinder and snapped the picture.

At that moment, Doctor Schiller looked up.

'Hey, what was that?' Margarete heard him say. 'Someone's outside.' He started striding towards the window.

Shocked, Margarete rushed away from the window and hurried back along the side of the house and in through the back door again. She tore across the hall and up the stairs and didn't stop until she was in front of her room. After locking herself in, she threw herself down on the bed, panting with the effort. Gradually her heartbeat slowed and she sat up and looked at the camera. There was nowhere around here to get the photo-graph developed, but perhaps that might not matter, she thought.

In the morning, the first thing Margarete did when she was dressed was to go outside and creep round the house to the cellar grating. She'd been again the evening before, before going to bed, but Marta had sounded sleepy so she didn't stay long.

Now, she crouched beside the grating in her overcoat. It was raining and a strong wind was blowing. Margarete shivered. It must be almost as cold down in the cellar and poor Marta didn't have a coat.

'Marta, Marta,' she called in a whisper. 'Are you all right?'

There was a pause. Then she heard footsteps as Marta walked over to beneath the grating.

'I'm all right,' she said in a small voice.

'Have you had any breakfast?'

'Yes. Just some bread and coffee.'

'Did you get some sleep?'

'Not much. It's cold down here,' came the reply. 'The doctor came to see me this morning. He said he's arranged trans-port for me – a car will come to collect me this afternoon.'

Dread coursed through Margarete. 'I will go and see him straight away. I will try to persuade him against it.'

'It won't do any good,' Marta said, sounding resigned. 'He's going to send me away whatever you say to him.'

Margarete didn't want to raise Marta's hopes, so she simply said, 'Well, I'm still going to try. Now, I'll come and see you again as soon as I've spoken to him.'

She went back into the building, where the children were trooping into the dining room for their breakfast, under the supervision of the other nurses and the watchful eye of Doctor

Schiller's henchmen. No one was speaking because they were all so afraid of being beaten for speaking their mother tongue. Margarete stood and watched them for a moment. How unnatural it was to see thirty or so children silent like that, subdued by the threat of violence.

She crossed the hall and knocked on Doctor Schiller's door.

'Come in,' he said, and she went inside. He looked up expectantly and his face fell when he saw it was her. Margarete suppressed a smile. It was exactly the same look that she'd seen on Herta's face almost twenty-four hours before.

'Don't tell me you've come to talk about the Kaplan girl again, Nurse. It really is getting tiresome.'

Margarete took a seat in front of the desk.

'Yes, Doctor Schiller. I have come to talk about her. I want to appeal to your better nature. Sending her to a work camp will surely kill her. How can you be responsible for that? You don't want that on your conscience, do you?'

He shrugged. 'I've sent children away before and it hasn't troubled me unduly. Now, please stop wasting my time. An SS officer is coming to collect her after lunch. He will take her to Kraków, where she will join one of the Jewish transports bound for one of the camps in the south. So, you see, it's all settled, Nurse Weiss, and there is nothing you can do to stop it.'

Margarete leaned forward. This was the moment. She took a deep breath – she needed all her courage for this.

'Oh, I think there is, Herr Doctor,' she said quietly, not flinching once from his gaze. 'Because if you don't stop this, there will be some unfortunate consequences for you. I happen to know that you are engaged in an improper relationship with a young member of staff. And I think Frau Schiller would be very interested to hear about it, don't you?'

Doctor Schiller's eyes opened wide in shock. His face grew very red, and he started to splutter.

'How dare you! How dare you! This is blackmail. That's what it is... I shall have you dismissed. I shall have you punished. And your family.'

'My family are all dead, Doctor, so I have nothing to lose. And what do I care if I'm dismissed, anyway? You would have to explain why to Reich Main Office and I wouldn't hesitate to tell them the truth. How do you think they would take that?'

The doctor was lost for words. He sat, glaring at her for a moment, then he said, 'I shall deny everything. You have no proof. It would be my word against yours.'

'Actually, Doctor, I do have proof. I took a photograph. Yesterday evening, through your window. Once that is developed, there will be no denying it.'

He stood up and yelled at her. 'You did what?! You filthy, conniving little bitch! And now you see fit to blackmail me?'

'I'm not blackmailing you, Doctor,' she said, keeping her cool. 'I'm just reminding you of the rules of the establishment and I'm asking you to do what any decent human being would do. That is, cancel that car and the transport for Marta, let her out of the cellar and give her another chance.'

He looked at her for a moment, clearly weighing up his options. Then he said, 'But at the moment you have no proof, and I could ask my men to search your room and confiscate your camera.'

Margarete kept her eyes on him, trying to remain calm. She needed something else. Something more to incriminate him. She scanned the desk desperately. Then she saw it, and before he could stop her, she leaned forward and grabbed it. A hair slide, bright red, threaded with ribbons. She held it up and stood up.

'Here,' she said. 'I think Frau Schiller might wonder what this was doing on your desk, don't you? Especially when I tell her what I saw?'

He stared at her for a long time, then, with a sigh, he reached out and picked up the telephone and spoke to the operator.

'Put me through to Reich Main Office in Berlin, operator. Straight away, please. It's very urgent.'

TWENTY

JOANNA

Auschwitz-Birkenau, Poland, 1944

Joanna shuffled along the station platform towards the end, moving forward with the press of people at a snail's pace, everyone jostling each other. Looking at the pale faces that surrounded her, she could see that everyone was tense and nervous, just as she was, wondering what would happen next, what this was all about.

As she drew closer to the front, between the bodies, she caught a glimpse of two SS officers standing there at the head of the queue with guns trained on the people, Alsatian dogs straining at the leash. Between them stood a man in a white coat. He was speaking briefly to every person who came before him, asking them some quick questions, then directing them with a flick of his hand either to the left or to the right. Often whole families were torn apart and separated by him. They cried out and clung together before being pulled apart by the guards. Some screamed, some yelled, but all were treated brutally; there was no reprieve.

The man in the white coat, with dark hair and a moustache,

must be the doctor that the guard at Łódź had mentioned. He did his job dispassionately but efficiently, his face expressionless, completely devoid of emotion.

As she moved forward, clutching Lili's hand, Joanna began to get a clearer view of what was happening. She tried to study who was put into each queue – trying to work out which side she and Lili would be consigned to. Older boys, men of working age and a few young, single women were sent to the right. On the left-hand side were women, children and old people, and those men and boys who looked sick or weak.

Up ahead, beyond the tracks and the confusion on the platform, behind wire fences topped with loops of barbed wire, loomed a forbidding-looking building with a single, tall chimney. It was belting out the foul-smelling smoke that had permeated the cattle truck for the last few kilometres of the journey. Close up, this smoke was so pungent it caught the back of Joanna's throat and caused nausea to rise in her stomach. Like many others around her, she held her hand over her mouth and nose, but still the foul stench got through.

Joanna and Lili were nearing the top of the queue now. The family in front of them, mother and father, three children – an older boy and two younger sisters – were being questioned by the doctor. He frowned and considered for a moment, wrote something on a clipboard, then directed them in opposite directions. The mother and two girls were pointed to the left-hand side and the father and older boy to the right. Joanna saw the look of devastation on all their faces as they joined their separate queues. They all had tears streaming down their faces and the mother and father held each other briefly before the SS officers pulled them apart, but no one cried out or screamed as others had done.

What did this mean? What did it mean to be put in the left-hand queue and what did it mean to be put in the right-hand one?

'Do you have your paper, Lili?' she whispered. 'The one the guard gave you in Łódź?'

'Yes, it's in my pocket.'

'Get it out. You'll need to show it to the doctor.'

They moved forward side by side and soon they were standing at the head of the queue, right in front of the doctor and the two SS guards.

'We have papers,' Joanna said bravely, holding hers out in a trembling hand. The doctor snatched it from her and scanned it quickly. Then he took Lili's paper and skimmed that one too. He then leaned forward and peered at the two girls with his cold, blue eyes. There was not a trace of a smile on his lips.

'You!' he said pointing at Lili. 'What is your name?'

'Lili Borucki,' she said, her voice cracking.

'I'm looking for little girls exactly like you to help me in my work,' the man said. 'You will go to a special block to stay where there are many other children – you will be safe and well fed.'

One of the guards flanking the doctor grabbed Lili by the shoulders and pushed her towards another guard who was standing nearby. Lili cried out in alarm, turned and looked at Joanna with desperate eyes, her face crumbling with fear.

'Take her to Block 16A!' the first guard shouted.

'Lili!' Joanna yelled.

She lunged forward and tried to grab her friend, but one of the guards stepped in front of her and pushed her back.

'Not you!' he yelled, and his dog barked and jumped up at Joanna, clawing at her skin, but she barely noticed in the panic of the moment.

'Please! Can I go with her?' she asked the guard, her voice shaking. 'We are together.'

But he just laughed and turned away.

'Please!' she called again, this time to the doctor, who was still looking at the paper she'd been given at Łódź station. Then he looked up at her briefly before speaking to the guard.

'To the left side for her,' he said, then his eyes slid away to the next person in the queue.

Joanna was distraught, and puzzled too. What did that mean? Why couldn't she go with Lili?

The guard took her by the shoulders and pushed her towards the gaggle of women, children and sick old men that crowded the left side of the ramp that led from the station into the camp. There were far more people on this side of the ramp than on the other side. Perhaps they were to be housed in separate barracks, Joanna thought.

The huddle of desperate people gradually moved forward off the ramp and towards the buildings. Soon they were crossing a great, paved courtyard. The terrible stench of the smoke was even worse here than on the platform. Looking up, Joanna realised with a shock that they were slowly walking nearer and nearer to the building with the great chimney. Suddenly she knew where she'd smelled that smell before: it was identical to the stench that lingered around the knacker's yard behind the slaughterhouse in Jasło where they burned the remains of animals that couldn't be sold for meat. She looked up at the tiny white flakes floating down from the chimney, like snow. She was mystified. Was that what they were doing here, burning animals?

SS soldiers with guns and dogs stood either side of the queue, shouting orders, making sure nobody stepped out of line and that the crowd moved towards the building at a steady pace. Now they were walking towards some great metal double doors in the building with the chimney, which gradually swallowed them up, one by one. Soon it was Joanna's turn to go in through the doors.

An SS man who was standing inside the door said, 'Carry on along the passage. You are going to take a warm shower after your journey.'

Joanna felt a little reassured by that, although she was still reeling from the shock of Lili being dragged away like that. Where had she been taken? Would Joanna ever be able to find her again? Feeling numb, she moved along a passage with the other women and children, who had relaxed a little now the soldier had spoken about a shower and were talking normally.

At the end of the passage was another doorway, this time into a great hall with white walls and a low ceiling. There were benches along the walls and pegs for clothes. A female guard stood inside.

'Everyone must undress for the shower. You will be able to come back for your clothes afterwards,' she was saying.

Joanna stared at her. This woman had a pretty face and wavy blonde hair, but, like the male guards, was expressionless, her blue eyes cold. Joanna had never seen a female member of the SS before. How could a woman bear to do this hateful work?

It was cold in the hall, but Joanna had no choice but to take off her clothes, fold them neatly and leave them in a pile on the bench. She didn't care any longer about being naked. In the context of the fear she was feeling, it barely seemed to matter. She looked around at the other people. Most were white and skinny, their ribs showing, arms and legs bony. They had all come from the Łódź ghetto, she reminded herself, where they had been starved for a long time. Perhaps her own body was like that too, she thought, and looking down, she saw that it was.

'Go through that door at the back of the hall and down the steps,' the guard ordered, and everyone formed a line and trooped through the great door and down some steps, along another passage and through a further set of doors, these ones made of iron. They found themselves inside a low-ceilinged room. It was spotlessly clean in there and smelled of disinfectant. Looking up, Joanna was reassured to see spouts in the ceiling – the water would be turned on soon.

More and more people poured into the room and soon it

was as crowded as the train carriage, but still they kept coming in. Surely they would shut the doors soon? There would be no room to wash, she thought, and the shower would be wasted. The smell of unwashed bodies pressed together like that was becoming unbearable.

Eventually there came the sound of the metal doors being slid across their runners, then the clang of them shutting, and the screech of bolts being pulled across on the outside. Then everyone waited, staring anxiously up at the shower heads. But no water came. People began to get restless, looking each other, puzzled. Where was the water? Surely there was something wrong? How long would they be left here like this? They waited and waited, fidgeting against each other, getting more and more restless.

After ten minutes or so came the sound of the bolts being pulled back on the door, and then it was slid open by two guards.

'There is a malfunction,' one shouted. 'There will be no showers today. File out and go upstairs. Do not collect your clothes. Go left at the top of the stairs and you will each be given a camp uniform.'

Shrugging and muttering in confusion, everyone climbed back up the long staircase, turned left at the top of the stairs and along to another large room where clothes were laid out on trestle tables. The clothes didn't look new, or even clean. It was a free-for-all. People picked up shirts, jackets and trousers and held them against themselves to see if they fitted. Joanna stood in front of a table wondering if she would find anything to fit her and, after rummaging through all the items on the table, eventually found some ragged underwear, trousers that were baggy and a little too long, a shirt with only two buttons and a jacket that just about fitted her.

On another table was a pile of shoes – uncomfortable-looking wooden clogs that had obviously been worn before.

Joanna tried on several pairs until she found a pair that vaguely fitted her, but she knew from experience that they were bound to rub and chafe.

Guards ushered everyone out of the room, across the windy courtyard again and into another room, where once again there was an interminable wait.

'What's happening here?' Joanna asked a woman in front of her.

The woman shrugged. 'We have to wait and see,' she replied.

When she neared the front of the queue, Joanna saw that this was the queue for the barber: everyone's head was to be shaved. When she entered the barber's hut, she sat down in the chair and the barber stood back and looked at her head.

'You've been done before, but I will do you again,' he said.

He was quicker and more expert than the barber in the children's ghetto in Łódź and he didn't nick her skin once. She bowed her head, willing it to be over.

She left the chair and was directed by guards to join a queue outside another hut.

'What is this one for?' she asked a woman in front of her.

'Someone said we have to get tattooed. With a camp number.'

'Tattooed?' Joanna didn't like the sound of that, and rivulets of fear ran through her at the thought. She'd heard that tattoos were painful and that they were permanent too. But there seemed to be no choice. The queue for the tattooist snaked around a yard where yet more guards with dogs patrolled. There was no way out.

Shuffling to the door of the tattooing hut, Joanna's legs felt weak and she was suddenly hit by a wave of exhaustion. She realised she had had no proper sleep since the night she and Lili had spent in Ilona's flat. The journey itself had been exhausting, standing up in that stuffy cattle wagon, crammed in with so many others, filled with terror about what the end of the journey would bring. She had been right to be worried. This place, with its brutality, its fierce guards, its barbed wire and its foul smoke that permeated everywhere, was the most terrifying place she'd ever been.

In the tattooist's hut she was lined up with five other women and an inmate in the familiar blue striped pyjamas of the camp approached each with a long, sharp tool.

'Name?' he asked when it was Joanna's turn. She told him and he wrote it down on a piece of paper beside a number.

'Hold out your left arm,' he told her.

She did as he asked and he applied the tool to the inside of her wrist.

The pain was short and sharp. She wanted to scream out and pull her arm away but she knew that would lead to trouble, so she screwed her eyes shut and held her breath and bore the pain without flinching. When it was over, there was a long number tattooed on her arm in dark blue ink, the skin around it red and angry-looking.

'You will need to show that number to get food and clothes. In fact, everything here,' the man told them, and then they were out of the hut and in another yard, where once more they were told to wait.

Joanna went to the edge of the yard and sat down beside a wall. She felt as though her legs wouldn't carry her a step further. There was a glint of sunshine in the pale sky and she held her face up to it. How good that felt, the feeling of warmth on her skin. She closed her eyes for a moment and the next second felt herself slip into a dreamless sleep.

She was woken by someone shaking her arm violently.

'Get up! You are not allowed to sleep here!' It was a female guard with a clipboard. 'Do it again and you will be beaten. Get to your feet.'

Joanna did as she was told, her heart hammering with the shock of being woken like that.

'How old are you?' the woman asked. In that split-second Joanna hesitated. Her mind was spinning. Something was telling her that it would be better to exaggerate her age by a couple of years. She wasn't sure why, but she had gathered that it was mainly the young children who were sent to the left-hand side at selection. If she pretended she was older, perhaps things might be better for her.

'Fourteen,' she replied, looking at the guard with an unflinching gaze. She was tall for her age, but she knew this was a stretch.

'You look quite healthy. Are you strong?'

'Yes,' Joanna answered automatically.

'Let me look at your hands. Are your fingers small and nimble?'

'Yes,' Joanna answered, although she wasn't sure this was quite true.

'We need more people to help in the Kanada warehouses. That is where I'm assigning you to work. What is your number?'

'Number?' Joanna stared at her and the woman rewarded the stare with a slap round the cheek.

'Show me your arm, you imbecile.'

How could she have forgotten the number, which was already stinging and itching beneath the rough sleeve of her jacket? She held out her arm and the woman grabbed it and held her wrist up to her face. Then, muttering under her breath, she noted the number down.

'Follow me,' she said, turning on her heel.

Joanna shuffled after her as best she could in the clumsy wooden clogs that were even more uncomfortable than the ones she'd been forced to wear in the children's camp. It wasn't far to walk to the long hut where the guard told Joanna she would be staying.

'These are the Kanada barracks,' the woman said. 'They are near to the warehouses so that the workers don't have too far to walk.'

They paused in front of a door.

'Now go on into the barracks,' she told her. 'The woman in charge, the Blockälteste, will find you a bunk to sleep on. Someone will give you the things you need – bowl, spoon, mug and blanket. Make sure you take care of them.'

'What is Kanada?' Joanna asked.

'You don't know? Oh, you'll find out soon enough,' the guard said with a cynical laugh as she pushed her inside the hut.

TWENTY-ONE

MARTA

Bruczków Assimilation Home, Poland, 1944

Marta was surprised that it was Margarete who opened the door to her cellar prison later that morning. She'd had a sleepless night, thinking over what the forthcoming journey would bring the next day. By the morning, though, she'd resigned herself to being sent away to a work camp, but had been expecting to wait until the afternoon for the SS car to collect her. She'd also been expecting Doctor Schiller to put his head round the door and give her one of his supercilious, triumphant smiles.

Instead, it was Margarete's face that appeared in the doorway, and Marta was shocked to see that she was smiling. What was there to smile about today? Marta's fate was sealed; she was to be sent on a long journey to a place where she was unlikely to survive.

Margarete came into the room.

'You can come back up to the dormitory now, Marta. You won't be going on the transport this afternoon after all. Doctor Schiller has called Reich Main Office and cancelled it. You are going to be staying here in Bruczków.'

Marta stared at her, uncomprehending.

'But why? Why would he do that? After everything he said about me yesterday.'

'I managed to talk him into giving you another chance.'

Marta was incredulous. She stared up at Margarete. It was difficult to process the information. She'd spent the past twelve hours coming to terms with the fact that she was going to be sent to a work camp, but now, in a flash, everything had changed. She knew that she should have been elated, or at least relieved, but she just felt numb. And she didn't quite believe what was being said.

She sat down on the bed and put her head in her hands. Margarete sat down next to her and put her arm around her.

'You've been lucky this time, Marta,' she said gently. 'Doctor Schiller certainly won't give you another chance after this. Please don't try to steal again. And try at least to pretend that you're working hard in class. Can you promise me that? I don't want to see you sent to a work camp.'

'I promise,' Marta said.

She would have to resign herself to the fact that she couldn't get away from this place, that she wouldn't see her home again for a long, long time and that she might never see her parents or her sister again. She needed to focus on her own survival. And if that meant knuckling down and pretending to take this ridiculous Germanisation programme seriously, then that was what she would have to do.

'Come on then,' Margarete said, getting up and holding out her hand for Marta to take. 'Let's go upstairs and face the music.'

Marta took Margarete's hand and got up off the bed. They went up to the dormitory, where Margarete gave her a fresh uniform, and she changed into it beside the bed.

'Lessons have just started, Marta. Why don't you go and join your class straight away?'

Marta was silent for a while. The thought of walking into the classroom after what had happened the day before made her stomach churn.

'I don't really want to,' she replied. 'They'll all have been talking about me. They will all laugh when I go in.'

'It doesn't matter. You need to be tough. The sooner you face it, the easier it will be,' Margarete said.

Marta knew Margarete was right. She'd had a lucky reprieve and she needed to show her gratitude by doing as Margarete asked. She did need to be strong. But where had all her strength gone? She used to be strong for Joanna, then for Agata, but now she had no one to be strong for.

As if reading her thoughts, Margarete said, 'Be strong for yourself, Marta. You owe it to yourself to do this.'

'All right,' Marta said, taking a deep breath. 'I'll go.'

She'd been right. The rest of the class did turn round and stared at her, and a ripple of surprise went through the room when she entered, but she tried to ignore it and made her way to her desk at the front, beside the empty one that Agata had occupied.

'Good morning, Marthe,' Herr Sturm said as she sat down. 'We were just practising the verb "go". Do you think you could stand up and recite something for me, in German, of course?'

This was something Marta could do. She and Margarete had practised this only a few evenings before and she knew she was word perfect. She stood up, looked Herr Sturm straight in the eye and began, 'Ich gehe, du gehst, er, sie, es geht, wir gehen.'

Herr Sturm's eyes widened in surprise as she went on, and when she'd finished and sat down again, he gave her a round of applause. Marta couldn't work out whether it was sarcastic or genuine, but decided to take it at face value.

That was the turning point for her at the assimilation home. From that moment on, she decided to repay Margarete's faith in her and work as hard as she could at the lessons. She'd been a model pupil back at school in Jasło, of course before schooling was banned in Poland, and she decided to see if she could go back to that form. It didn't take her long once she'd made that decision. Soon, she was coming top of the class in every lesson – even in German – thanks to Margarete's continued help during their secret evening sessions.

Despite her misgivings about learning German and about everything she learned in the culture lessons in the afternoon, she decided it was the only thing to do if she was going to survive. She owed that to her parents and to Joanna. She needed to stay alive for them, and if staying alive meant going along with this Germanisation programme, she would gladly do it.

She thought of her family constantly, wondering where they were, what they were doing. Her heart yearned for them, especially Joanna. Was she still there in Łódź, forced to work like those poor shadows of children they'd seen, shuffling past dressed in those baggy grey uniforms? Or was she somewhere else? Somewhere even worse perhaps? Marta tried to suppress those thoughts, but sometimes they rose in her mind unbidden to torture her, and refused to go away.

Marta sometimes thought about what she might be doing if Margarete hadn't intervened with Doctor Schiller on her behalf. She would be sick, starved and worked to death in one of the camps, she was sure. She also wondered what tactics Margarete had used in order to change Doctor Schiller's mind, but no matter how much she pressed Margarete, she would never be drawn.

A few months after Marta's return to the classroom, in September 1944, Doctor Schiller called her into his office. He glared at her as she entered. Since that terrible day when he'd locked her in the cellar, he'd not spoken to her once. If she met him in the corridor, he would walk past as if she wasn't there. And from the expression on his face now, she could see he was still angry with her.

'Fräulein Kaplan,' he began, motioning her to take a seat opposite him, 'as you know, I would have preferred to send you away from here as a punishment when you were caught stealing, but I was persuaded otherwise. It seems though, you took your discipline very seriously, and that you have been making a sincere effort with your studies since that day. Herr Sturm sings your praises on a regular basis.

'The time has come for you to leave the assimilation home here in Bruczków and go to begin your new life in the Reich. Some girls of your age are sent to boarding school there for further assimilation, but, like Agata before you, you have made such strides that I don't think that will be necessary. You will be able to go straight to your new family.'

Marta's mouth dropped open. She had known this would happen, but she hadn't thought it would happen quite so soon. Nerves rushed through her at the thought of what was to come.

'Reich Main Office has found a suitable family for you. A mature couple who have no children themselves but who have come forward to adopt an older child. You fit perfectly. They live in Munich and the husband is a well-respected, senior member of the SS. He works in the Brown House, the Nazi HQ, which I'm sure you will be familiar with from your lessons on Nazi culture and ideals. Your new parents are exemplary Nazis, I have to tell you, and I can't think of a better home for you.'

Marta shuddered. Exemplary Nazis? They sounded terrifying. They were clearly everything her father and mother stood against. Everything her father had risked his life working for the Polish resistance to fight against. She had known that she would be sent to live with a German family, but she hadn't known that they would be prominent members of the SS. Perhaps it would have been better to stay here in Bruczków after all. Perhaps she shouldn't have been so diligent at her lessons.

'Is something wrong, Fräulein?'

She shook her head hastily – she didn't want to get into any sort of confrontation with Doctor Schiller.

'No, Doctor. Nothing at all. When am I to leave?'

'Next week. A car will come and collect you on Sunday and take you to the nearest station. Someone will accompany you to your new home. It is a long and complicated journey and we wouldn't want you to lose your way,' he finished in a very pointed manner.

She swallowed. Next week seemed very soon – she wasn't sure she was ready.

'And let me add a warning and a word of advice,' Doctor Schiller went on. 'This is a great opportunity for you. One that I for one don't think you deserve. If, once you're at your new home in Munich, you try to run away, or to do anything that might suggest that you're not fully committed to the Fatherland, your new father has instructions to report the matter to the Reich Main Office. Needless to say, punishment of the severest kind would follow.'

She hung her head, not knowing how to respond, or even if a reply was needed or expected. She hated those words 'your new father'. Was she going to be expected to call these Nazis Mother and Father, when her own mother and father, from whom she'd been cruelly snatched, were still alive and well?

'Do you understand me, Fräulein Kaplan?' the doctor's hectoring voice bored into her thoughts.

She nodded her head slowly. 'Perfectly, Herr Doctor,' she replied. 'You don't need to worry about me.'

. . .

Marta's final week flew by, and Sunday came round all too quickly. She had hoped that Margarete would be the one to accompany her on the train journey to the Reich, but she quickly realised that would be too much to hope for. She wasn't surprised when she was told that Doctor Schiller had asked Herta, one of the new members of staff and the only woman amongst them, to accompany her to Munich. They would be taken to Poznań by car, a journey of about three hours, from where they would take a train to Berlin. There, they would change trains to go to Leipzig and from Leipzig, they would take a train on to Munich. The journey would take at least a whole day.

As the time drew closer, Marta began to dread the trip. She had never been out of Poland before and the thought of being so far away from Jasło, and in another country, the heart of Nazi Germany, made the prospect of getting home even more remote than ever.

On the morning of her departure, she woke with a feeling of dread in her heart. She had packed the small leather suitcase that had been issued to her, but she had so few clothes, only her uniform, some trousers, a shirt and sweater that she wore to work outside in the garden, and some underwear. The suitcase was standing beside her bed as a stark reminder of what was to come when she woke.

When she was getting dressed, Margarete came to see her.

'Let's go for a walk,' Margarete said and, ignoring the stares of the other girls, they went down the stairs and outside into the garden, where they walked along the stone path that skirted the edge of the lawn.

'I'm so sorry to see you go, Marta,' Margarete said. 'I will miss you so much. But it is far better that you are going to live with a family rather than being sent to a work camp.'

'I'm not sure that it is. You know I'm being adopted by a senior official in the SS, don't you?'

Margarete's eyes widened in surprise.

'I hadn't realised that, but I suppose most of the families who come forward to adopt are at least Nazi Party members. They have to be to be accepted onto the programme. But you should be able to distance yourself from that. You don't need to have anything to do with that side of things. You will go to school and meet other girls your own age. I'm hoping your life will be far less precarious than it has been for the past few months. No one will try to deport you to a camp from there.'

'That's not what Doctor Schiller said,' Marta replied miserably. 'He said that my new father has instructions to report on me if I step out of line.'

'Oh.' Margarete sounded surprised. 'That doesn't sound very fair. But if that is the case, he won't have any cause to report on you, will he?'

Marta shook her head and stared down at the stone path.

'I still think you'll be safer there than here,' Margarete repeated. 'Here, there is a constant threat from Schiller. It's unfortunate that he's found a senior SS officer to take you though – I hadn't expected that, I must admit.'

They carried on in silence for a while. When they turned a corner in the path that took them out of sight of the windows of the old manor house, Margarete stopped and opened her handbag.

'I've noted down all the information I've managed to find about you and Joanna,' she said and handed Marta a piece of paper. 'Keep this safe, in case you ever need it in the future.'

Marta looked down at the paper. In Margarete's neat handwriting, it listed their address in Jasło, the date they were abducted by the SS, the address of the hospital in Kraków, the dates they were in the Camp for Polish Children and Youth in Łódź ghetto and the date Marta was brought to Bruczków. Beside that entry was a note to say that Joanna had remained behind at the camp in Łódź.

Marta looked up at Margarete. 'Thank you, but this doesn't really tell me anything new. I know my old address and when and where we were taken.'

'One day, years from now, you might need this information. You might forget where you were taken and the dates you were sent there. It might help you to find your way home, one day, when this terrible war is over.'

Marta looked up into Margarete's kind eyes. 'Thank you, Margarete. But you haven't put anything about Joanna escaping from the camp in Łódź. You said you were going to try to find out. Have you had any news?'

She shook her head. 'I'm sorry, Marta. I would have told you if I had. I will try to find out when the time is right, but at the moment I think it's too dangerous for me to ask. They would be suspicious of my own involvement if I were to ask about someone who escaped from the camp. I will try to get word to you, once I find out,' she added. 'I know your new address, of course.'

Marta looked up at Margarete. 'Thank you. You are so kind, Nurse Weiss. But why? Why do you take such risks to help people?'

Margarete laughed.

'Why do I do it? Because I know that what is happening all around us is evil, and I refuse to go along with something I know in my heart to be wrong. Many people do go along with it, not because they believe in it, but because they are afraid, and because they want an easy life. My father said something to me when the Nazis first came to power and I've always remembered it. He said, "Be careful what you say, yes. But we all must remember one thing. Whatever happens, be true to yourself and to your own principles." And that is what I'm trying to do: to honour my father's memory.'

Marta understood completely. Her father had said similar things about the Nazis and she'd wanted to live up to his memory too. She wasn't sure that he would have approved of her stealing from the staff at the home, but everything around that time had got very confusing for her. She would try to put that time behind her and move on.

'Shall we go inside?' Margarete asked. 'I expect you need to have breakfast and get ready, but I wanted to speak to you alone, to say goodbye and good luck personally.'

'Thank you, Nurse Weiss. I will always remember you,' Marta said.

They hugged briefly, then walked back to the door. Marta's heart was heavy. She wished that Margarete was taking her to Munich and not hard-faced Herta with the cruel eyes.

As they parted, Margarete said, 'If I have news of Joanna I will write to you, but only if I have news. And I'll try to find a way of telling you without saying it directly. It could get us both in trouble otherwise.'

Marta thanked her again and they went inside, Marta to the dining room to have her last breakfast at Bruczków.

Later, as she got into the back seat of the black SS Mercedes, most of her classmates and some of the staff were gathered on the front step to see her off. She was sad to say goodbye to some of the girls, particularly Maja, but she was saddest of all to say goodbye to Nurse Weiss, who stood there waving with tears in her eyes. As the car drew away and Marta stared out through the back window, it was Nurse Weiss who she picked out in the crowd and to whom she waved until they had rounded the bend and the old manor house had disappeared from view.

Herta wasn't much of a companion on the long journey from Bruczków to Munich. On the train she spent her time filing her nails, touching up her make-up in a compact mirror, smoking cigarettes and flicking through fashion magazines. Whenever a member of the Gestapo or an SS officer boarded the train to check IDs, which was an all-too-frequent occurrence, Herta would flutter her eyelashes at him when she showed him the papers. She appeared to have no interest in Marta at all and barely spoke to her. Once, after an ID inspection, when Herta had shown the SS officer their papers, then put them back in her bag, Marta asked if she could see her ID.

'I was told to give it to your new parents, not you,' Herta replied.

'I don't want to keep it, I just want to have a look at it,' Marta said.

Herta shrugged, fished in her bag and handed the official-looking document to her. Marta had known for months that her name had been changed but it was still a shock to see it set out on an official document in black and white. The document gave her date of birth correctly, but then it stated that she had been born in Łódź, Poland, her name was Marthe Kaplan and that both her parents were dead.

'This isn't true!' she said. 'My parents aren't dead. I was taken from them. Stolen.'

'Be quiet,' Herta hissed. 'You mustn't talk like that here. All that information is highly confidential.'

'But it's wrong!' Marta insisted.

'Look, as far as you know, your parents could well be dead. If they were members of the Polish resistance they would certainly have been executed long ago. The fact is, they're not your parents any more. Once you were removed from your home, the Lebensborn programme became your legal guardian, and still is. That is, until you get to your new home and your adoption is finalised.'

Marta stared at Herta. What she'd said echoed what other children had told her about their parents being arrested and executed. She wanted to ask the woman more, but knew it was no use. Herta wasn't going to give her any more information and she knew it was no use arguing with her either about any of this. Herta was a Nazi through and through. To her it wasn't wrong to lie and falsify papers if it was in the name of the Fatherland. Perhaps she was one of those whom Margarete had referred to as going along with things for an easy life. Or perhaps she was even more than that, embracing the evil, racist ideology of the Nazis with enthusiasm, like so many others.

Marta handed the paper back to her with a sigh.

'Doctor Schiller warned me about you,' Herta said stiffly. 'He said you weren't to be trusted and that I was to watch you like a hawk. Now if you try any of your tricks with me, I won't hesitate to call one of the SS officers on the train to arrest you. You're on thin ice, Marthe Kaplan, so let's not have any more talk about your Polish parents.'

Marta was silent for the rest of the journey, staring out as the flat, rolling farmland, the pretty farms nestled amongst low hills and stone-built villages slid past the window.

When the train finally rolled into Munich Hauptbahnhof, she looked around her with trepidation. Here she was in the heart of the Reich. This city was the birthplace of the Nazi Party and it was to be her home for the foreseeable future. Even the station itself looked forbidding; the concourse was patrolled by SS officers and red swastika banners hung from every façade.

'Come on,' Herta said, ushering her through the crowds of smartly dressed people. 'There should be a car waiting for us on the forecourt.'

They walked out through the grand, arched entrance and there, on the cobbled forecourt, another black SS car was waiting for them.

People stared as they slid into the back seat. The car set off along the streets of Munich, which seemed grand and forbidding to Marta: tall, austere buildings, draped in red and black banners. Occasionally they passed a bombsite, where in place of a building was a pile of rubble where children played and dogs rooted in the dust.

Soon they left the city centre behind and were travelling through suburban streets, lined with trees and neat houses, but still there were bombsites, even here, where in places whole streets appeared to have been flattened and reduced to rubble. At one point they passed a huge, elaborate building, set behind a lake in rolling parkland.

'What is that place?' she asked Herta.

'It's Nymphenburg Palace,' came the reply. 'The Party uses it for meetings and rallies.'

It looked beautiful to Marta until they drew closer and she saw the swastikas on the front wall. She shivered and turned away.

It was only half an hour's drive to the suburb that would be Marta's new home. Obermenzing, it was called. She'd seen the address on one of the papers Herta had held out for the inspections on the train. As they drove through the tree-lined streets she could see that this was a wealthy place; rambling houses behind tall walls or hedges, set in their own large gardens.

'You are lucky to have come here,' Herta said. 'Your new parents clearly have money and influence.'

Marta remained silent. She didn't feel lucky at all. How she would have loved to be back in her humble, warm home in Floriańska Street, surrounded by love and laughter. How her heart ached for it. This place felt so intimidating and alien to her.

The car pulled in through some high wrought-iron gates and drew up on a gravel drive in front of an imposing, white-painted house. It had diamond-paned windows and a Dutch-style roof.

'I will take you inside, then go back to the station in the car,' Herta said.

They got out of the car and Herta pulled a bell-pull beside

the dark wooden front door. A bell echoed inside, followed by quick footsteps. A woman with short hair wearing a black dress opened the door.

'Frau Fiehler?' Herta asked.

The woman smiled and shook her head. 'I am the maid, but Frau Fiehler is at home. Who shall I say is calling?'

'Herta Hess and Marthe Kaplan. Frau Fiehler is expecting us.'

'Come inside,' the maid said, drawing the door aside.

They stepped into a gloomy hallway with polished oak floorboards and a grand oak staircase opposite the front door.

'Do take a seat, please.' The maid pointed to a hard, polished bench under a high window, then disappeared.

Marta sat down beside Herta and waited in silence. She could hear the maid talking to someone in a distant room and then a tall, heavily built woman with grey hair piled on top of her head appeared along the passage. She stopped in front of Marta and looked her up and down.

'So, you are our new girl?' she said, her appraising, unsmiling eyes on Marta's face. 'I must say you look the part. Blonde hair, blue eyes, fine features. Schiller was true to his word. And are you her chaperone?' she asked, turning to Herta.

'Yes, I brought her from Poland.'

'Would you like any refreshment?'

'No, it's all right, thank you The car is waiting to take me back to the station. Goodbye, Marta,' Herta said. 'Goodbye, Frau Fiehler.'

Marta said goodbye to Herta. She watched her leave and, even though Herta was her last link with Bruczków, which if not a happy place had at least been familiar to her, Marta felt no emotion at all.

When she'd gone and the sound of the SS car had faded away down the road, Frau Fiehler said, 'Well, welcome to Munich, Marthe. That is your name, isn't it?'

Marta opened her mouth to correct Frau Fiehler but then thought better of it. She didn't want to make trouble for herself, especially not in the first few minutes she was there.

'Yes, it is,' she replied.

'Good. Well, my husband will be home in a couple of hours. We normally take supper early. Tomorrow, you will be going to school, so your uniform is waiting for you upstairs. I've put out some other clothes for you too. I will show you to your room. Come, bring your bag.'

'Thank you, Frau Fiehler,' Marta said, playing the game.

Marta followed Frau Fiehler up the wide staircase. At the top of the first flight, on the half-landing, she was shocked to see a huge swastika flag draped from the ceiling. It covered the whole wall and at the top of the stairs hung a portrait of the Führer. Portraits of other prominent Nazis in uniform were ranged at regular intervals along the walls of the landing.

Frau Fiehler opened a door.

'Here it is,' she said, and Marta went inside her new room. It was large and square with white-painted furniture and a bed with a flowered bedspread.

'I didn't know what you'd like, so I put some books out for you,' Frau Fiehler said. Marta's heart sank when she looked at the bookcase. There was *Mein Kampf* by Adolf Hitler in pride of place, beside a range of other books that all looked as though they were textbooks promoting Nazi ideals.

'I've put your school uniform in the cupboard, a bag with your sports clothes, and your BDM uniform next to it.'

'BDM?' Marta asked.

'The Society for German Girls,' Frau Fiehler explained. 'The female equivalent of the Nazi Youth. You will be expected to attend meetings in the evenings twice a week. It is compulsory here,' she added.

'Oh,' Marta said, her spirits plummeting even further.

'Well, I will leave you to settle in. Supper will be at six

o'clock. There's plenty of food here and you won't go hungry. You look a little on the thin side to me, Marthe. Didn't they feed you properly at the Lebensborn home?'

'Food is short in Poland,' Marta replied.

'We need to build you up, I can see that,' Frau Fiehler said. 'There's a washbasin over there in the corner and a bathroom at the end of the passage. I hope you will be happy with us,' she finished, but still without the trace of a smile.

When she'd gone, Marta sat down on the bed with a deep sigh and contemplated her new situation. Although she knew she would never want for anything material here, she felt a great sadness welling up inside her, threatening to stifle her with its intensity. How could she live amongst these cold people in this huge house with its Nazi memorabilia, devoid of love, devoid of emotion? How could she live without Mama and Tata and Joanna and not even knowing if they were dead or alive? For a moment despair threatened to engulf her, but then she remembered her conversation with Nurse Weiss in the garden the day before. She owed it to herself and her family to get through this. The war wouldn't last for ever. One day it would be over, and she would be free. Until that day she would just have to hunker down and get through the days one by one.

TWENTY-TWO

JOANNA

Auschwitz-Birkenau, Poland, 1944

Joanna stepped through the doorway into the low building and looked around her in the semi-darkness, wondering what this place was for. It was a long, single-storey hut, stretching almost as far as the eye could see, with one narrow passage along the middle, a raised brick step running all the way along the centre of it. On either side of the passage were what looked like shelves, but when she drew closer she realised they were bunk beds because there were thin blankets stretched out on them. It was gloomy inside the hut, the only light coming from a line of narrow skylights in the roof.

Wondering what to do, she started to walk tentatively down the centre of the hut. There was nobody about and in the silence she sensed that there was something eerie about this place, something strange that made shivers run down her spine.

But then someone stepped into the passage at the far end of the building and she realised she wasn't alone.

'Who is there?' came a sharp, female voice speaking Polish. 'Why aren't you at work?'

'I'm new,' Joanna said. 'I've just arrived.'

'Come here, girl. Let me look at you.'

Joanna walked nervously towards the dark figure standing at the end of the hut. The woman was tall and thin and dressed in a shapeless grey dress, not the blue striped pyjamas that most of the inmates of the camp appeared to wear.

'Quickly now. I haven't got all day.'

It was difficult to walk quickly in those clumsy clogs, but Joanna attempted to speed up. The end of the hut opened up into a wider space where there were several long trestle tables and benches set out in rows.

'What is your name?' the woman demanded.

'Joanna,' she replied.

'And how old are you?'

'Fourteen.'

The woman bent forward and peered at Joanna's face with narrowed eyes.

'You look far younger, but no matter, we need everyone we can get at the moment with so many transportations coming in from Hungary these past few months. We've quite a backlog to deal with.'

The woman was thin, but not as thin as some other inmates Joanna had already seen in the camp. She had taut white skin, stretched over her skull-like cheekbones, but around her eyes the skin was darker and more wrinkled, almost like crepe paper. Her head wasn't shaved but her short, colourless hair was thinning at the temples. To Joanna, she looked very old.

'I am the Blockälteste of this hut,' the woman announced. 'That means that I am in charge here. I make the rules and you need to obey me or there will be consequences. There are almost two hundred women and girls living here. We are on top of each other, literally. There needs to be order, or no one can function, and the SS will be on to us in a flash. Do you understand?'

Joanna nodded.

'All the other women are at work in the Kanada warehouses at the moment. And you will be going there tomorrow. It is hard work, but conditions here are far better than the rest of the camp. You are very lucky.'

Joanna swallowed. Lucky? Looking around her, she would hardly describe it as that.

'What is Kanada?' she asked.

'Come and sit down. I will tell you.'

She beckoned Joanna over to one of the tables and they sat down side by side on the bench.

'You look thirsty. Have some water.'

She poured Joanna some water in a tin mug and as Joanna gulped it down gratefully, the woman began to speak.

'When people come into this camp from all over Europe on the trains, they leave their luggage on the platform. In Kanada-kommando, we sort through their belongings, classify them, pack them all up. It is then stored in the warehouses here until it can be sent back to the Reich.'

Joanna recalled that, when the people got off her train that morning, they had been told to leave their suitcases beside the train. 'You will be able to fetch it later,' the workers on the plat-form had assured them. Clearly that wasn't true.

'But why?' she asked. 'Don't the people need their luggage themselves?'

The woman shook her head. 'They will have no further need of their belongings,' she replied with a note of sadness in her voice.

'But why not?'

The woman eyed her carefully, frowning.

'You mean you don't know?'

Joanna shook her head.

'If they are selected for work, they are given camp uniforms. They have no need of their own belongings. If not... well, they have no further need of them then either.' Her voice cracked at the end and in her eyes was an unhappy, faraway look.

'What happens to those people?' Joanna asked, half afraid of the answer, but she wanted to know. She wanted to know what went on here; there were already so many mysteries surrounding this place.

The woman extended a bony hand and gave Joanna's a brief squeeze on the table.

'You're not Jewish, are you, my dear?' she asked, and Joanna shook her head.

'We don't have many non-Jews working in Kanada. Some, but not many. Why are you here?'

Joanna shrugged.

'I was taken by the SS from the marketplace in our town when we were out shopping for food. My sister was too. We were taken to a camp in Łódź, where they made us take some tests. My sister passed the tests but I didn't. They said I had Slavic blood. Then my sister was taken away and I was sent to work in a factory. I tried to escape from the camp with my friend and we were caught by the SS. That's why we were sent here.'

The woman stared at her.

'I've heard that they were stealing pretty children to take them to the Reich, but I've never seen proof of it before. Where is your friend now?'

'She was sent to another block when we got off the train.'

'Which block?' the woman asked sharply.

'Block 16A, I think. Yes, I'm almost sure that was the number.'

'16A?' The woman's eyes widened.

Joanna nodded and watched the woman's face fall. She shook her head again. 'I'm so sorry, my child. That's very unlucky. Very unlucky indeed.'

Prickles of alarm ran through Joanna. She'd thought Lili was going somewhere better than she was, that she'd been lucky to be selected for that block.

'Why?' she asked.

'You don't want to know, my child. You don't want to know.'

'Please...'

'You will find out soon enough. You need to understand how Auschwitz-Birkenau functions first. The camp operates on the fuel of pure evil. It takes people quite a while to understand that completely and even when they understand it, most find it hard to accept. If you find out too much too soon, it will be too much for you to take in, young as you are.'

Joanna wondered what she meant by that but did understand that the woman wasn't going to give her any more information. She would just have to find out about Block 16A from somebody else.

'My name is Ianina,' the woman volunteered finally. 'I am a Jew. I come from Warsaw, from the ghetto there. I have been here a long time. Almost since the camp began. Things have changed a lot here since then.'

Joanna sipped her water in silence. Ianina seemed kinder than she'd first thought, but she wished she'd tell her more about the work and about what happened to the women, children and old men who weren't fit for work, and about block 16A. She thought of poor Lili. What was happening to her now? Joanna couldn't even begin to imagine.

Ianina got to her feet. 'Let us go and find you somewhere to sleep. In this hut, we have two to a bunk. We are lucky. In some barracks there are three or more. At first it seems cramped but you'll get used to it. Come with me.'

Ianina began to walk down the central passageway between the lines of crudely constructed bunks.

'Be careful of this,' she said, pointing to the brick column that ran down the middle of the corridor. 'In the winter it is very hot. It is a chimney for heating the hut. Don't sit on it, or touch it, whatever you do. For the time being it is not lit, but we may get no warning of it, so be on your guard for that.'

They were in the centre of the hut now and Ianina stopped beside one of the bunks.

'You are young and strong, you can sleep on the top bunk. You will be sharing with Eva. Her last sleeping partner had to go to the medical hut and we haven't seen her since. I doubt she'll be back.'

'What was wrong with her?' Joanna asked in alarm.

'Typhus, something like that. There is a lot of disease here. You need to keep clean and keep strong. Eat as much as you can, whenever you can. It isn't so bad for us here in Kanada. We find food in the suitcases we search, and nobody minds if we eat it... So, this is your bunk.' She patted one of the top bunks. 'I will give you an extra blanket and, if you come back to the end of the hut, I will give you a mug, bowl and spoon. Without those you will quickly starve here. Hold on to them with your life.'

They began to walk back down the hut towards the end.

'What does Kanada mean?' Joanna asked.

Ianina smiled for the first time, a thin smile, her lips stretched over rotten teeth.

'People think of Kanada in North America as the land of plenty,' she said. 'And amongst all the belongings that arrive here, there are untold riches in some of those suitcases. Jewellery, gold, foreign currency, champagne, whisky, precious ornaments, beautiful clothes. Everyone tries to pack their most prized possessions when they are told they can bring luggage to the camp. These warehouses are just like the land of plenty – that is why this place is called Kanada.'

Joanna stared at her. She still couldn't understand why the people who weren't selected for work wouldn't need their belongings. Why didn't they complain? She guessed, as Ianina had said, it would take her a long time to understand exactly what went on in the camp.

'Do you want some lunch?' Ianina's voice broke into her thoughts. 'I am going over to the kitchens now to fetch my soup – I always go at this time. I can get you some too.'

'Yes, please.' Joanna nodded gratefully. She hadn't eaten since breakfast the day before in Ilona's apartment. How long ago that seemed now, like another lifetime.

Ianina got up from the table stiffly. 'You can keep that mug you had your water in. I will find you a bowl and spoon.'

She rummaged in a cupboard in the corner and laid a metal bowl and spoon on the table in front of Joanna. Then she picked up a black cauldron with a handle.

'I will be back soon. The kitchens are not far away,' she said, and Joanna watched her walk away through the centre of the hut.

Joanna sat alone at the table until Ianina returned fifteen minutes or so later. She didn't want to move about in the hut, she didn't like being alone there. As soon as Ianina had left that feeling returned, that this was a place to be feared, where people were starved and beaten, where terrible things could happen.

The soup when it arrived was virtually inedible. It was watery and thin, with pieces of vegetable floating in it. Joanna recognised a piece of potato and some green leaves, possibly cabbage, but she didn't recognise anything else it contained. It tasted foul, but from her recent experience in Łódź, she knew she must eat it – there was no knowing when the next meal would be. So, she forced it down and scraped her bowl clean.

When Ianina saw her scraping the bottom of the bowl with her spoon she looked at her approvingly.

'I can see you learn quickly. You are right to eat every drop. Even if it tastes bad, it is the only food you're going to get for hours and you need to force it down. I've seen newcomers unable to eat and they soon regret that.'

Ianina took their bowls to wash in a bucket outside the hut. Then she said, 'I need to go and speak to another Blockälteste. Why don't you get some rest on your bunk? Tonight you will have to share it. It is a rare privilege to have it to yourself.'

Joanna went to the bunk, climbed up to the third level and sat on the hard, wooden boards under the ceiling. There was no mattress or pillows and the bed was quite narrow. She couldn't imagine sharing this space with someone else – it was barely big enough for one person. But she took Ianina's advice and lay down and pulled the blanket over her. Although she closed her eyes, sleep wouldn't come. It was difficult to get comfortable, but she was plagued with images from the past twenty-four hours, of people crammed together on the train, the clickety-clack of the wheels over the sleepers, the swaying motion of the cattle car, the stench of the sweat and foul breath of over one hundred people breathing the same air. And when she managed to stop thinking about that, she couldn't stop thinking about the sight of that great chimney, belting out foul-smelling smoke. Then she relived the fear of walking down the stairs in that great building, completely naked and into a room where the people kept on being forced in until it was impossible to move and difficult even to breathe. She knew she would never forget it; it was the most terrifying thing that had ever happened to her.

How would she cope here in this strange place with its desperate people and its many, complicated rules? If only Marta was here to help her, to tell her what to do to get by. But her sister was miles away, either in Bruczków or perhaps even some-where in Germany by now. Then she got to thinking about Mama and Tata. What were they doing now? Were they still at home in Floriańska Street? Were they still looking for her? Would she ever see them again? And finally, when she'd wrung her heart out with thoughts of Mama and Tata, her mind turned to Lili. Why had Ianina looked so shocked at the mention of Block 16A? What was that place? What happened there? She couldn't begin to imagine, but if there was any way of going there and finding out, Joanna made a promise to herself that she would try to do so.

TWENTY-THREE

JOANNA

Auschwitz-Birkenau, Poland, 1944

It was early evening when the rest of the women returned to the hut from their day's work. They came in quietly, each one walking slowly to their bunk and throwing themselves down gratefully. Stress and exhaustion were etched on every face, and were evident in every movement of their bodies. Joanna felt the bunk move as the women on the first and second tiers below hers lay down. Then there was more movement and a face appeared at the end of her own bunk.

'Who are you?' a voice asked.

'I'm Joanna.'

'I'm Eva,' the woman said, hauling her frame up onto the top bunk. 'You'll have to move over if we're going to share.'

Joanna noticed that Eva wasn't as thin as many prisoners she'd seen, and she wasn't wearing the blue and white striped uniform that most prisoners were forced to wear. Nor were the other women who'd arrived with her. Instead, they were dressed in shapeless grey dresses, with different-coloured kerchiefs around their necks, but they all wore the same shoes – the wooden clogs that Joanna herself had been given. They left them on the floor when they climbed into their bunks.

Joanna shuffled herself to one side of the bunk. 'You'll soon get used to it,' Eva said more kindly and sat down beside her. Then she put her feet under the blanket, pulled it up around her and lay down.

'I need to sleep for a while, then we can talk,' she said. Then she turned her face away from Joanna and towards the boards that separated their bunk from the top bunk next door.

Joanna lay down again in the narrow space that was hers. She found that if she lay on her side and crooked her body into the same shape as Eva's she could just about squeeze in. She realised, though, that she wasn't sleepy. She would have liked to get down and stretch her legs a little, but gentle snores were already coming from Eva's side of the bunk and she didn't want to disturb her. So, she lay quietly beside her for the next hour, until the sound of a spoon banging on something metal disturbed the peace of the hut and everyone began to stir, to sit up, as far as they were able in the confined space, and to stretch and yawn.

Eva sat up and shook herself awake. Up close, Joanna could see that her face was lined with worry. Eva was no longer young, and Joanna guessed she must be in her mid-thirties. She looked at Joanna blankly for a moment, then her face cleared.

'I'd forgotten about you,' she said. 'Joanna, isn't it?'

'That's right.'

'You're new here, aren't you?'

Joanna nodded.

'I can tell. Don't worry, I'll help you. It's time for supper. That's what that racket means. You might have been told this already, but even though the food here is normally terrible, it's really important to eat everything you are offered.'

'Yes, Ianina told me earlier,' Joanna replied.

'Everyone will tell you that. Now let's get down there and eat before it's all gone.'

Eva climbed down from the bunk first. Then Joanna climbed after her, putting one foot on the second bunk and one on the first, then dropping to the floor. They joined the throng of women making their way towards the tables at the end of the hut. Ianina and another woman were doling out food into the women's bowls from two great cauldrons. Joanna squeezed herself onto the end of a row and, when Ianina came round, she spooned out a few slices of meat that looked like some sort of sausage into Joanna's bowl. The other woman handed her a couple of slices of hard, black bread.

'One of those is for your breakfast,' explained Eva, who had slid onto the bench beside her, 'so you should try to keep it until morning. You won't be given anything else for breakfast. Only tea or coffee.'

'Most of us are too hungry to wait until morning,' the woman on the other side of Joanna said, 'but save it if you can.'

When the meal was over, everyone went to the barrel of water outside and washed their bowl and mug, then Eva said to Joanna, 'Come, I'll show you to the washhouse.'

They walked the length of three huts before they came to a low, brick building, dimly lit with bare electric light bulbs. On one wall was a row of washbasins filled with filthy water. On the other side were rows of latrines, which were simply crude holes cut in long planks of wood. Joanna had to cover her mouth: the smell was sickening, unlike anything she'd smelled before.

'There is running water in the mornings,' Eva told her. 'A lot of people come over here and wash before work. Most of us shower once a week, although the water is cold. Those are the latrines, but if you need to go in the night there is a bucket in the hut beside the door.'

'I will go now,' said Joanna. She held her nose and sat on one of the holes in the wood, while Eva waited for her.

On their way back to the hut, Eva asked her where she came from, and she repeated what she'd told Ianina earlier in the day.

'What about you?' she asked Eva. 'You're Polish, aren't you?'

'Yes. I come from Sosnowiec. It's in Upper Silesia. I lived there my whole life. In 1942 all Jews were forced into a ghetto in the centre of the town, and the following year they began transporting us away, to Auschwitz and to other camps.'

'Did you come here alone?' Joanna asked.

Eva went silent for a few steps, then she said, 'No, I travelled here with my mother, my father, my husband and my two children.'

'Where are they now?' Joanna asked and she heard Eva draw in a sharp breath.

'My husband is still here, in one of the other camps in Auschwitz called Buna, working in a chemical factory. But the others... the others... I'm afraid they are no more.'

Joanna was puzzled. Did Eva mean they were dead, or that they'd been sent away? Even her children? But she didn't want to ask her any more questions. Perhaps she would find out in time. It was obviously upsetting for Eva to speak about her family.

Back inside the hut, people were getting ready for bed.

'We go to bed early here,' Eva explained. 'There is nothing to do in the evenings, and we are woken before dawn. We don't have roll call any more, which is a good thing.'

'What is roll call?' Joanna asked.

'Everyone used to have to line up in the square outside to be inspected by the SS. It was to make sure no one had escaped and that everyone was present for the day's work. It would often take a long time. As I say, they abolished it a few months ago so that there would be more time for work.'

They climbed onto the bunk and lay down. Within a few minutes, a gong sounded somewhere outside and the lights in the hut went out abruptly, cloaking the place in darkness.

Joanna turned onto her side, wriggled about and tried to mould her body around Eva's. Although it felt a little strange to have to share like this, the presence of another body so close to hers was strangely comforting. It reminded her of Marta. Her sister would always come and cuddle her in the night if she was feeling sad for some reason or afraid of the dark. It had been especially comforting to have Marta beside her during those terrible nights in Kraków and Łódź.

Joanna was exhausted, but it still took a long time for sleep to come. She'd never slept amongst so many people before and the sound of some two hundred other women breathing, snoring, coughing and sighing was hard to get used to and kept her awake. And just as in the afternoon when she'd tried to rest, as soon as she closed her eyes the worries she had for her family and longings for her home instantly returned to her mind. But eventually she must have drifted off to sleep, because the next thing she heard was the booming sound of another gong.

'Wake up! It's four thirty!' Ianina called as she walked up and down the corridor, banging a spoon against a saucepan.

It was still dark outside and the lights in the hut had been turned on. Joanna felt as if she'd barely slept. Beside her, Eva sat up and stretched, rubbed her eyes.

'Come, we need to get up quickly,' she said. 'If you're late, you'll be punished.'

They slid off the bunk and joined the other women, who were jostling through the hut towards the doors. Outside, everyone hurried straight to the washrooms. There, Joanna joined a long queue for the latrines, where once again she had to hold her breath when she sat down. It was odd, relieving herself in front of so many other people, but since everyone had to, she decided that it was pointless being embarrassed. Then she joined another queue for a basin and, when she reached the front, washed her hands and splashed her face with cold water. There was nothing to dry herself on apart from her uniform. Then, seeing other women from her hut returning between the lines of other barracks, she followed them back.

Back at the bunk, Eva, like all the other women around, was tidying the bed, spreading the blankets out on it neatly. Someone else was sweeping the corridor between the bunks.

'We have to keep the hut tidy,' Eva told Joanna. 'There are often SS inspections during the day and the place has to look well kept, otherwise there are punishments.'

Joanna wondered what sort of punishments they might be, but there was no time to ask. Eva jumped down and said, 'Come on, let's go and have breakfast now. Did you save some bread from last night?'

Joanna nodded and they both walked to the dining area at the front of the hut. Once again, they sat down on the benches drawn up the long tables and this time Ianina and the other woman came round with great kettles and poured brown liquid into each cup. There was a choice of coffee or tea. Joanna had never liked coffee, so opted for tea, which was like no tea she'd ever drunk before. It was earthy and tasted of some sort of herb, but at least it was hot, so she drank it down. She also ate her crust of black bread, which was tasteless and even more stale than on the previous evening, but she forced it down.

She was just finishing that when another gong sounded outside and, reluctantly, everyone got up from the tables and started filing outside again.

'Stick with me,' Eva said to Joanna. 'I'll show you the ropes.'

Everyone was making for an open area in the middle of the rows of barracks, where people were lining up in groups of ten, overseen by SS guards with their guns and dogs. On one side of the square a band was playing marching songs. Once groups had formed, they went marching off in different directions, in step with the music of the band.

'Where are they going?' Joanna asked.

'They are going to work,' Eva replied. 'These are the labour details for the day. Stay with me and I'll help you.'

Joanna shot her a grateful look. Without Eva's help she was sure she would already be in trouble. She had no idea what was happening, or what she should be doing so she stayed beside Eva and they joined a group of women who were all dressed in the same uniform. When there were ten of them lined up, they started marching quickly out of the square and through the lines of huts. They had to pass two officers who were standing at the exit, watching all the groups leave.

'Swing your arms and try to keep in time to the music,' Eva told Joanna, and she did her best to follow that advice but found it hard in her clogs to walk rhythmically. Luckily, she was on the far side of the group, Eva was marching on the side that passed the SS officers, so she hoped and prayed that they wouldn't notice her clumsy attempts at marching.

They marched for ten minutes between the rows of barracks as the sun rose over the distant forest. Joanna shivered in the cold morning light. All the time they were marching, they were drawing closer and closer to the chimneys that were still belting out foul air, even at this time in the morning. Joanna had to bite back the nausea that rose in her throat at every breath she took. She wondered if she might get used to it in time, but noticed others covering their noses too as they got closer.

They arrived outside some huge wooden warehouses that were built right beside one of the buildings with a chimney. Trucks were drawn up in front of the warehouses and some male prisoners were throwing belongings down from the backs of the trucks: suitcases, rolls of bedding, packs of clothes, rucksacks, handbags.

A female prisoner approached. She had dark features and brooding dark eyes. To Joanna, she looked very fierce.

'That's Kazia. She's our kapo,' Eva told Joanna.

'Kapo?'

'It means leader – she leads our kommando. She's tough, so mind you do as she says.'

Kazia stood in front of the group and started speaking.

'This morning you must sort through the belongings from this truck. Put everything into piles. Clothes in piles here,' she said, pointing at the ground. 'Women's here, men's there, but if the clothes aren't good-quality or look old, put them in a second pile. Then shoes here, alcohol here, cigarettes here, jewellery here. Come forward, you...' she said suddenly, pointing at Joanna.

Joanna froze. Did she really mean her? Why? What had she done wrong?

'You are new, aren't you? You look young, as though you have nimble fingers. Let me see your hands.'

Joanna stepped forward and held out her hands. The woman took hold of them and scrutinised them, turning them over, checking the length of Joanna's fingers.

'Good. They are small enough. What I want you to do is to go through all the clothes in the first piles – women's and men's. You must feel every seam and every hem and every lining. People often sew their valuables into their clothes before they come here, and we need to find everything. If you find anything, bring it straight to me. Understood?'

Joanna nodded.

'I will ensure you have the correct uniform tomorrow.'

'Thank you,' Joanna said.

'And by the way, we are always searched by the SS when we go back to the barracks, so don't think you can steal anything from here and smuggle it back. Apart from food, of course. No one minds if you eat what you find here, or if you take it back to your quarters. It's what keeps us all alive in this terrible place. Do you understand me, girl?'

'Yes,' said Joanna.

'All right. Everyone get to work now. There are more transports coming in today and there will be more trucks coming back to Kanada later, so you need to work quickly to keep on top of it.'

Joanna waited until there were a few garments in the 'good' pile, then picked up a woman's green velvet jacket and began to feel her way along the seams, the lining, the cuffs and through the pockets as she'd been instructed. It was a lovely jacket, beautifully cut and expertly sewed. While she worked, she thought about the woman who'd owned it. Where was she now? Had the jacket been bought for a special occasion? Getting carried away, she held it up and looked at it admiringly, thinking of the tailor whose skill had produced such a beautiful garment.

'Whatever are you doing, girl?'

Joanna jumped. Kazia was right behind her and must have been watching her. 'You're not here to admire the clothes, you're here for a purpose. Don't make me have to tell you again.'

'Sorry,' Joanna muttered and laid the jacket aside on a new pile. Then she picked up a black evening dress and ran her hands over the seams. This time she tried not to think about who had owned it and why they had bought it. She tried to concentrate on the job.

Halfway through the morning, she was examining a man's outdoor coat with a fur collar when she felt something in the lining. Small and square, it felt like a box. She hesitated. Should she unpick the seams and get whatever it was out, or should she take the whole garment to Kazia just as it was? She wasn't sure, but she decided to take it to Kazia.

Kazia was at the far end of the great pile of clothing, folding a shirt, when Joanna approached. Joanna handed her the coat and showed her what she'd found. Kazia produced some scissors from her pocket and unpicked the stitching, and a small box dropped out. She picked it up from the ground and opened it. Joanna gasped. It was a ring, gold set with shimmering diamonds.

Kazia laughed. 'Well done! Your first find. It looks expensive. I will take it to the office to be entered into the ledger. Go and put the coat back on the pile.'

Just then, an SS officer appeared as if from nowhere.

'What have you got there, Kapo?' he asked, and Joanna saw Kazia closing her fist around the box.

'Show me,' the man demanded and grabbed Kazia's hand. He took the box from her and opened it. His eyes widened with greed at the sight of the diamond ring.

'It has to be taken to the office and entered into the ledger,' Kazia said.

'I know that, Kapo. I will take it myself.' And he put the box into his pocket and walked away.

'Damn him!' Kazia said. 'Greedy pig! They're all on the take, these officers. And no one does anything about it. Next time you find something, let me know quietly and we will go behind one of the lorries to look at it.'

Joanna went back to work and carried on sorting through the garments. Sometimes she looked up to see what was happening around her. Still the chimneys were belting out their foul-smelling smoke. Two of them were close to where the women were working. Joanna wasn't getting used to that smell – it caught the back of her throat every time she breathed.

She longed to breathe clear air; she wanted to take deep breaths, but that only made it worse. She wished she had something to tie around her mouth and nose to keep the smell out. She glanced at the girl working next to her, going through a leather suitcase, sorting clothing into piles, separating the shoes. She was young, only a few years older than Joanna, her blonde hair tied back from her face. Joanna straightened up and spoke to her.

'Do you know what that terrible smell is?' she asked.

The girl looked at her, pity in her gaze.

'You mean you don't know?'

Joanna shook her head. She'd heard that answer before, and she was tired of being kept in the dark about what happened in the camp. Why wouldn't anyone tell her the truth?

'I wish someone would tell me,' she said. 'I'm not a child. I'm fourteen years old.'

'Really?' The young woman eyed her sceptically. 'What's your name?'

'Joanna.'

'I'm Zofia,' said the girl, wiping her brow with the back of her hand.

'Do you know what the smell is, Zofia?' Joanna asked again.

'I will tell you, but this will come as a shock to you, so prepare yourself.'

Joanna didn't know how to prepare herself, but stood up straight and said, 'All right.'

'That smell is the smell of burning bodies,' Zofia told her.

Shock washed through Joanna and her mouth dropped open. She thought she might be sick.

'When people, mainly Jews, arrive here by train, they are divided into two groups.'

'I know. I came yesterday. It happened to me.'

'One group are judged fit to work as slaves in the camp, the other group is not, so they are sent to their deaths in those buildings.'

'No!'

'Yes. There are gas chambers in the basement of those buildings and that is where the Nazis send them to be killed. Then their bodies are burned in the crematoria. That's what the smell is that we are forced to breathe day and night – those crematoria never, ever stop burning.'

'Oh.' With another wave of nausea, Joanna sank to her knees. Her mind had gone into panic mode and it was impossible to think straight. But then she remembered.

'It happened to me!' she said. 'Yesterday. Hundreds of us were crammed into an underground chamber. We were told we were having a shower. The doors were sealed and we waited, but nothing happened. A guard said there was something wrong and we were let out. We were given clothes and let out into the yard.'

'Are you sure?'

Joanna nodded. 'Quite sure. I didn't know what was going on. No one knew.'

'You were very, very lucky,' Zofia said. 'God must have been watching over you.'

Then her eyes strayed towards something in the middle distance, beyond the crematorium.

'Look, another train's coming in now. We have to watch this happening over and over again, many times a day, and it tears our hearts out.'

Joanna followed her gaze. A train was pulling in to the platform, belting out black smoke and hissing steam onto the platform. As soon as it came to a halt, guards and some prisoners beat on the doors of the trucks with sticks, then slid them open. People came pouring out onto the platform. Men, women and children and all their luggage. They were quickly sorted into two lines by the guards: men in one line and women and children in the other. They left their luggage on the platform. Then the lines moved forward towards the doctor for the selection. Joanna could see it all plainly from where she stood. It was exactly what had happened to her and her travelling companions the day before.

Those poor, unsuspecting people. She wanted to warn

them, to run over and shout to them to run away, to do anything to avoid what was coming. But she knew it was impossible; she would have been shot and her body ripped to shreds by the dogs before she'd gone ten metres.

She tried to get up, but her legs failed her. The shock of learning about the horror that she'd so narrowly escaped was so great that her whole body had turned to jelly. However had she managed to escape death? How had she been so lucky? She thought of all those who hadn't been so lucky and of all those walking innocently to their deaths right now. It was almost impossible to believe, but it was happening right there in front of her. She watched women carrying babies and shepherding children, old men and women with sticks shuffling innocently towards the front of the queue where they would be selected for certain death, and her eyes filled with tears.

TWENTY-FOUR

MARGARETE

Bruczków Assimilation Home, Poland, 1944

When Marta left the assimilation home in Bruczków to travel to her new home in the Reich, she left a great void in Margarete's days. Margarete hadn't realised how attached she'd grown to the girl and how much she'd looked forward to her company. She'd really enjoyed the closeness they'd had when she had taught Marta German in the evenings. Marta had been such an easy pupil, and, once she'd got over her initial antipathy towards learning the language, she'd picked it up quickly and easily. Now, Margarete spent her evenings alone in her room. She had no desire to spend them in the staffroom with Herta, Nurse Wolff or any of the other staff, with whom she had very little in common.

Reflecting on her sadness at Marta's departure, Margarete realised that in Marta she'd found a substitute for her own family and that the feeling was probably mutual. They'd each lost everyone they loved and were both feeling raw and grief-stricken. And now that Margarete had lost Marta too, the grief had returned to haunt her. In every unoccupied moment her mind would go back to thoughts of Tomas, her lost love, to baby Tomasina, and to her mother and sister. How she longed for them. How hard it was, knowing she would never get to see them again, to put her arms around them, to laugh with them, to love them.

A few days after Marta's departure, Doctor Schiller called Margarete into his office. As usual, she took a seat opposite him at his desk. He put his fingers together and leaned back in his chair, regarding her coolly.

'Nurse Weiss,' he began, 'now that that unfortunate child, Marthe Kaplan, has left the home, I think we can draw a line under our little charade, don't you agree?'

Margarete frowned. 'I don't know what you mean, Herr Doctor,' she replied, genuinely mystified by his words.

'Oh, I think you do. You and I have never seen eye to eye. Right from the beginning it was clear that we think very differently. At first, I was prepared to give you some latitude, but after you saw fit to blackmail me, to undermine my own authority, I'm afraid I was prepared to do that no longer.'

'It wasn't blackmail,' Margarete said steadily, her eyes on his face. 'You knew that what you were doing was wrong and against the rules of the programme. I was simply reminding you of that. And in the process, I was doing my best to ensure that Marthe was treated fairly, and not deported to a labour camp as you'd proposed.'

'Once again, Nurse Weiss, I have to say, you and I see things very differently.'

Margarete didn't answer and the doctor went on.

'So, I asked you in here to let you know that I've been in touch with Reich Main Office and asked for you to be transferred away from here. They have agreed with my request. You are to leave for Berlin tomorrow.'

'Oh?'

'I'm afraid so, yes. A car will collect you to take you to

Poznań at eight o'clock tomorrow morning. It will drop you at the train station in time for the Leipzig train. From there, you can go direct to Berlin.'

Margarete was surprised, but quickly realised that she shouldn't have been. Schiller had always been suspicious of her, so it wasn't surprising that he would want to get rid of her as soon as he could. Especially because she knew about Herta. But at the same time, she realised that she wouldn't mind leaving the assimilation home, although she wondered what Reich Security Main Office might have in store for her after this. She'd done her best to ensure that the children in the home were treated properly, but because the doctor had brought in new staff to enforce discipline for the precise purpose of undermining her, she felt as though she had only partially succeeded. If she were able to stay, she might, in time, be able to get over that, but she knew that while Doctor Schiller was there, she would always be fighting against an immovable force.

'Very well, Doctor, I will go and pack,' she said, getting up from the chair.

'Before you go, Nurse Weiss, let me give you a piece of advice.'

Margarete sighed and sat down again, although she wasn't sure why he had any right to be advising her about anything, or why she needed to be polite enough to listen to him.

'You are a talented nurse, and you clearly have a lot of empathy with the children in your care,' he began, then leaned forward and looked straight into her eyes, 'but I also see a subversive streak in you, Nurse Weiss, which prevents you from fully embracing Nazi ideology. To me, this must be regarded as dangerous, and I've reported that fact to Reich Main Office.'

He sat back in his chair, putting his fingertips together with a triumphant smile, but Margarete refused to react. She was sure that she'd been the subject of reports to Reich Security Main Office before, so it didn't trouble her too much. She'd always known that she had to tread carefully if she wanted to do what she knew was right and to stay true to her ideals.

'I understand from what they told me,' the doctor went on, 'that you were very close to a known subversive while you were working at Schloss Schwanburg maternity home. A Doctor Tomas Müller, apparently, who has since been sent to Dachau for his treachery. I believe his mistaken and dangerous ideas may have rubbed off on you.'

She thought of poor, brave, good Tomas. How he'd suffered for his actions. He was either dead or rotting away in Dachau because he'd tried to do what was right. A lump came into her throat and she swallowed hard, still keeping her eyes on Doctor Schiller, still trying not to react.

'So, my advice to you, Nurse Weiss,' the doctor said, 'is to watch your step very carefully in the future. Wherever you are posted next, make no mistake, your card is marked; people in the Party will be watching you very closely.'

Margarete got up from her chair. 'Is that all? If so, I will go and get ready to leave.'

She went upstairs to her bedroom and began to pack the few belongings she'd brought in her suitcase. It was only six months since she'd come to Bruczków, but it seemed like an age. She sat on the bed and contemplated her return to Berlin, the city where she'd lost her entire family to the bombings. How would it feel, going back there? It was bound to open up old wounds that were only just beginning to heal.

She knew she would never again be able to go to the square where her old apartment building had once stood. It was just too painful to even think about. If she closed her eyes, she could hear baby Tomasina's happy gurgles and feel the weight of her little body on her lap. What she would give to hold her one more time, to bury her face in Tomasina's fluffy hair, to breathe in the scent of her skin.

She took the photograph of Mutti, Alicia and Tomasina out

of her suitcase and looked at it, smiling through the tears. There they were, looking out at her, all smiling for the camera. That's how she wanted to remember them, happy and carefree. She didn't want to torture herself by thinking about how they might have suffered when the bombs came down.

With a deep sigh, she slipped the photograph away in her suitcase again and finished her packing. The last thing she put in were her precious notebooks, the ones in which she'd noted down as many details of the children she'd cared for as she could – their dates of birth, their original names and addresses, their destinations. She slipped the notebooks into the lining in the bottom of the suitcase. She'd made an opening specifically for this purpose. The last entry she'd made was for Marta. She'd discovered Marta's new address in Munich from some records she'd seen on Doctor Schiller's desk soon after the girl's departure. She'd copied it out on a slip of paper, then inserted it into the notebook she'd kept for the children in the code she'd developed especially for that purpose.

Handling the notebooks made her think of the children for whom she hadn't been able to complete entries, particularly Joanna, Lili and little Josef, left behind at the Camp for Polish Children and Youth in the Łódź ghetto. She thought of them now. Had Marek been able to help them get out of there? If so, where were they now? Could they be in the care of the Polish resistance, or back at home with their families? If so, they would have had to be hidden for a time, but at least they would be at home and safe amongst their loved ones and not starved of love and nourishment and forced to work in that brutal environment. She hardly dared hope that her plan for them had come to fruition.

In the morning, Margarete went to say goodbye to the children in the dormitories. Many of them cried and clung to her, bringing tears to her own eyes.

Maja asked, 'Can we come and wave you goodbye, like the others?'

It had become a tradition, after Agata left, for all the staff and children to go out onto the front steps to wave goodbye when one of the children set off for their new home in the Reich.

'I'm sorry, but I don't think so, Maja. That's only for the children.'

She was sure that Doctor Schiller wanted her departure to be as low-key as possible.

Maja's bottom lip wobbled. 'I will miss you, Nurse Weiss.'

'I will miss you too. Keep on with your studies and keep your head down. You will soon be going to your new home.'

'But I want to go to my *real* home,' Maja said, tears welling in her eyes.

Margarete patted her hand. 'I know you do, my darling. And one day, when this war is over, I'm hoping that dream will come true.'

When she left the dormitory Margarete felt heavy with guilt. She'd done her best to help the children here, preventing the worst abuses against them, trying to show them that they were loved and cared for. But she knew that she'd been unable to tackle the root of the problem. She knew that this home shouldn't exist at all. That no child should be ripped from their home, transported to a strange environment and forced to learn a new language and culture alien to their own.

Alone as she was, she'd been unable to prevent it. She'd done what she could, but she still had a niggling worry. Had her presence and actions amounted to some sort of collusion with the Lebensborn programme? She desperately hoped that it did not and tried not to blame herself. She'd done her best, but deep in her heart she knew it hadn't been enough.

As she headed across the hall with her suitcase to the waiting SS vehicle, she realised with a bolt of shock that the photographs of the children she'd taken in Łódź were still where she'd hidden them under a loose floorboard in her room. How could she have forgotten them? She'd been so preoccupied, so distressed and panicked. She dropped her suitcase, turned, and ran back upstairs. Doctor Schiller was standing at the top, staring down at her.

'Nurse Weiss, your vehicle is waiting. You will miss your train,' he said coldly.

'I... I left something in my room. A... a... book,' she managed to stutter.

'The room will be thoroughly cleaned, and I will ensure that anything we find of yours will be sent on to you in Berlin.'

She stood there, blinking at him, not knowing what to do. Outside the front door the driver sounded his horn.

'Nurse Weiss! You must go now, or you'll miss your train. You don't want to risk that just for a book, now do you?'

She had no choice but to turn around and retreat down the stairs, her nerves in turmoil, hoping fervently that no-one would think to prise up the loose floorboard and find the hidden photographs.

There was no one to wave her goodbye on the steps of the old manor house when she was driven away, sitting in the back of the black SS Mercedes, but she was so preoccupied, worrying about the photographs, she barely noticed. As the countryside flashed by, she gradually calmed down. She still had the note-books, she reminded herself. She thought about the children she'd left behind and hoped that the home wouldn't revert to what it had been before, and that her influence, at least on some of the younger staff, had been beneficial and might last. But she knew that Doctor Schiller and Nurse Wolff and some of the other staff were so entrenched in their thinking that it might be a vain hope.

The journey was long and exhausting. Some of the train lines in Germany had been destroyed by Allied bombings, so the Berlin trains had to be diverted. Margarete tried not to get frustrated when her train trundled through village stations on a branch line instead of powering along on the mainline towards Berlin. She was pleased, in a way, that the Allies were making so much headway. Perhaps it would mean that this terrible war and the evil regime that had started it might at last be coming to an end.

When they finally arrived at Anhalter Bahnhof station in Berlin, things were a little less chaotic than Margarete had expected and out on the forecourt she managed to find a taxi to take her to Reich Security Main Office. The trams were full to bursting and the roads were gridlocked, but she couldn't face the walk there with her suitcase. Once again, as the taxi crawled through the traffic, she looked out at buildings that had suffered bomb damage with holes in their walls or roofs, others reduced to rubble, bombsites full of mud and debris, a city brought to its knees by war.

She felt a terrible sense of déjà vu when she entered the austere building of the Reich Security Main Office between the black marble pillars of the portico, under the red and black swastika flags. The same receptionist was on the desk as had been there before, with her blonde hair scraped back in a severe bun, her bright red lipstick to match her nails, and her ice-blue, unsmiling eyes. Just walking into the main hall reminded Margarete of the last time she'd been here and of the devastating news she'd discovered that day.

She asked to see Fräulein Koch.

'Ah yes, Margarete Weiss,' the receptionist replied. 'Fräulein Koch has been expecting you. Just go on up to her office.'

Margarete thought about leaving her suitcase behind at the desk, but was wary of doing so, given its contents so she carried it discreetly with her when she went up the stairs, worrying all the time that in doing so, she could be arousing suspicion too.

On the first-floor landing she knocked on Fräulein Koch's door.

'Come in... ah, Nurse Weiss. Come in and sit down. I've been expecting you. How was your journey from Poland? I hear train travel isn't what it once was in this country.'

'Thank you, Fräulein Koch. The journey was rather disrupted.'

She sat down and tucked her suitcase discreetly behind her chair.

Fräulein Koch fixed Margarete with her steely gaze.

'Let me come straight to the point, Nurse Weiss. Doctor Schiller praises your work very highly. However, he did note a certain reluctance on your part to embrace Nazi ideology. Both you and I know that he isn't the first person to have raised concerns like this.'

Margarete remained silent. So, Schiller had carried out his threat. He was taking a risk, relying on the fact that Margarete was a decent human being and was unlikely to tell Fräulein Koch about his affair. Still, she had that up her sleeve if she really needed it.

'I put it down to that sister of yours,' Fräulein Koch went on. 'She worked for the resistance, didn't she? We had her followed on numerous occasions, but she was too clever, even for the SS. We could never prove anything.'

Margarete shuddered inwardly. She'd known this before, when Fräulein Koch had been able to tell her exactly what had happened to her family during the bombing. She'd known then that they must have been watching Alicia. However, to have it out in the open like this was still a shock.

'Well? She did work for the resistance, didn't she, Nurse Weiss?'

'I don't know. She didn't tell me anything. And what does it matter now anyway? She was dead and gone months ago.'

Fräulein Koch shuffled some papers on her desk.

'You are a difficult case, Nurse Weiss. In some ways you are very valuable to the programme, but time and time again you've proved yourself to be less than trustworthy. We've always had our suspicions about you, which is why I've arranged for your next position to be here in Berlin. Here, we can keep a close eye on you. You must report to me weekly and I will install someone in your office who can report back to me on your activities.'

'Really, Fräulein Koch, that isn't necessary.'

'Let me be the judge of that, please. We are opening up a Germanisation home for children under six here in the city. We would like you to run it. The children will have been brought here from Poland, Ukraine, Slovakia, Hungary. They will have passed the initial tests but you will need to carry out further screening on them. Those who fail will, naturally, be deported, those who pass will need to undertake a Germanisation programme. Your experience in Bruczków will be invaluable for that job.'

Margarete looked at Fräulein Koch, at her severe face, her zealous gaze. How different the two of them were. Then she wondered how she would be able to bear this job. It would involve yet more little children orphaned by the Nazis or ripped from their parents and everything they'd ever known. It would tear her heart out to hear them crying for their mothers at night, to know they would never go home again. But at the same time, she was torn. She knew she could help them. She could try to show them love and care, to help them come to terms with their loss. Perhaps she could also find a way of ensuring that none of them got deported...

'So, Nurse Weiss, your orders are to report to your new workplace in Luisenhof tomorrow. I'm not asking if this is acceptable to you, it is what you are required to do for the good of the Fatherland. And once a week, you will come and see me here, in Reich Main Office, and we will discuss your conduct. Now, do you have any questions?'

Margarete took a deep breath.

'Yes, I have one question. It relates to the children we left behind at the Camp for Polish Children and Youth at Łódź ghetto. Those who failed the Aryan tests. I would like to know how they are getting on, if you have any information about them?'

She knew she was taking a risk asking Fräulein Koch for this information, but she couldn't think of any other way of finding out.

'We don't generally keep records of those children who have failed the tests. To us, they are unworthy of life, as you well know. However, I do recall being sent some information about some particular children at Łódź. One moment...'

She got up from her desk and went to a filing cabinet, shuffled through the racks and drew out a brown file. Then she returned to the desk and opened it.

'Ah, yes. I do recall now. The youngest child, Josef, was sent away first. He was too young to stay at Łódź, so he was sent to Auschwitz-Birkenau.'

Margarete's scalp tingled. 'But why would they send him there? It's a work camp, isn't it?'

'Not entirely, Nurse Weiss. Not entirely.'

'Poor, poor Josef...' Margarete muttered, thinking of the confused, innocent little boy. Whatever had happened to him in that great, alien place?

'And the others?' she asked, her voice shaking. She hardly dared ask the question. She held her breath.

'Well, the others were in some sort of bungled escape attempt, apparently. They managed to get out of a window at the factory they were working at. They were caught the next day, trying to board a train with a member of the Polish resistance. The woman was shot dead, but the children were returned to the camp.'

Margarete could feel the colour drain from her face, picturing the scene at the station, a brave, innocent woman dying of gunshot wounds on the ground. What about Marek? Would she find out what happened to him?

'Shortly after that, the two girls were also deported to Auschwitz.' Fräulein Koch looked up at Margarete and smiled. 'I have it on record here that the older child, Joanna Kaminsky, perished shortly after arrival.'

Bolts of shock went through Margarete like lightning.

'Perished?' she asked, barely able to form words. 'But why? How?'

'I wouldn't ask too many questions about that, Nurse Weiss. The Reich finds ways of ensuring that its most inconvenient subjects don't survive to trouble it for too long.'

Margarete stared at her. What was she saying? Had Joanna been killed? In cold blood? Was that what was happening in that camp?

Fräulein Koch closed the file.

'The other child, Lili? What happened to her?' Margarete managed to ask.

'The file is inconclusive. All I can see is that she was sent for some tests on arrival at the camp. I don't know what happened to her subsequently.'

'Tests?'

'Yes. That is what it says here. Now if that concludes your questions, I really need to get on. Do you have accommodation for tonight? If not, you can go straight to your new place of work. There is a room for you there. Here is the address.'

Fräulein Koch scribbled something on a piece of paper and handed it to Margarete.

Out on the street, Margarete could barely walk. Her legs and her whole body felt weak with the shock of what she'd just heard. She found a bench in some nearby gardens and sat down and took some deep breaths. She could hardly believe what Fräulein Koch had told her. Joanna had perished! The child had been healthy when Margarete had left her, but something told her from the way the woman had given her the news that Joanna hadn't died of natural causes: her death was deliberate.

How many more people were dying like that in those camps? She put her head in her hands and breathed deeply, trying to calm herself, trying to make sense of this unbelievable information. She had to sit like that, taking deep breaths, for a long time before her heart began to slow and she calmed down a little.

When her mind settled, she realised that she knew one thing for sure: she would have to write and tell Marta this information. But that wouldn't be possible for a while. Not for the time being, at least. She didn't want to break the poor girl's heart when she was almost certainly having trouble settling down to her new life. Perhaps, if she left it a few months, she would be able to find the right words to break the news to Marta. After all, the poor girl had a right to know the truth.

TWENTY-FIVE

MARTA

Munich, 1944

When Marta opened her eyes on her first morning in her new home, for a few seconds she had no idea where she was. She yawned and turned over onto her side, expecting to see Maja in the next bed, but Maja wasn't there, just some sumptuous pillows and embroidered bedcovers. Then it came to her: she was in that great, gloomy house in a wealthy district of Munich, living with two committed Nazis who were supposed to be her new parents.

She shuddered, thinking about the previous evening when she'd sat at a long, polished table in the huge dining room with its red velvet curtains, heavy furniture and paintings of Bavarian hunting scenes on the walls. Herr Fiehler sat at one end and Frau Fiehler at the other. Herr Fiehler had returned from his work at the Brown House at six o'clock and Marta had been called down into the living room to be introduced to him.

A big man, running to fat, with a florid complexion and a bushy black moustache, he bent down and peered at her. Marta had seen the hard drinkers who used to hang about the square in Jasło, and knew what a drinker's eyes looked like, puffy and bloodshot, and Herr Fiehler's eyes were just like that.

'Welcome to our home, Marthe, my dear,' he said, shaking her hand. 'I hope that you will soon feel that this is your home too.'

She was glad that he hadn't greeted her with a Heil Hitler salute, but after her first glance at him, she couldn't meet his gaze. In fact, she could hardly believe that here she was, shaking hands with a man in a grey uniform, with SS letters emblazoned on his collar, carrying his cap with the skull insignia under one arm. Not only was she shaking his hand, but she was going to be expected to call him Father.

However, she recalled grudgingly, in the first few minutes he'd been polite and kind. Unlike his wife, who continued to be frosty and hadn't smiled once since Marta arrived.

At the supper table, they were served by the maid who'd opened the front door earlier. She wore a black dress and white pinafore. She seemed timid, not once looking anyone in the eye. She dished out some sort of stew onto everyone's plates, complete with potatoes and green vegetables, and Marta eyed it in amazement. She'd never seen so much food on one plate. Not for years, if ever. She began to eat. The meat was very rich and she tried to hold back from eating too much. Her stomach wasn't used to food like this, and she didn't want to end up with stomach-ache on her first evening.

During the meal, Frau Fiehler asked her husband how his day had gone at work and he replied, 'It went well, thank you, my dear. It's such an honour, working at the Brown House, but you know I can't tell you much about it.'

Frau Fiehler smiled and turned to Marta.

'Herr Fiehler has a very important job, you know. He organises rallies for the Party and performs other important administrative tasks for them. One day, we hope to be able to take you a Nazi Party rally.'

Marta stared at her in horror. She had no words with which to reply. The thought of attending one of those rallies, like the ones she used to read about in Polish newspapers, with photographs of row upon row of uniformed followers marching and saluting in time to a marching band, appalled her.

Conversation was stilted after that. Herr and Frau Fiehler talked a little about the progress of the war. Since Marta had been kidnapped in Jasło, she'd heard very little about the conflict, but she'd got the sense that Germany wasn't doing too well. She had to hide a smile when Herr Fiehler said, 'The Allies launched an attack on Arnhem today. It seems they have started on a big putsch. It has a code name, apparently, Operation Market Garden.'

'Where is Arnhem, dear?' Frau Fiehler asked.

'It's in Holland, so, a very long way from Bavaria. You needn't worry, my dear.'

'Let us hope there are no more bombing raids on Munich, though, Heinrich,' Frau Fiehler said. 'They've already ruined so much of this beautiful city, the hateful brutes!'

Marta was tempted to speak up, to voice her support for the Allies, but she stopped herself. Was it really worth antagonising these people on her very first evening? She knew that there was no escape for her from this situation, not until the Nazis were overthrown. Perhaps she should just try to sit tight and not voice her opinions. At least for a while, until she understood how things worked.

Frau Fiehler turned to Marta.

'Tomorrow, you will go to your new school, Marthe. I have already registered you, in our name. You will have to change your name now, my dear, now that the adoption process has gone through. Your new name will be Marthe Fiehler – it won't be Kaplan any more, I'm afraid. It might be a little hard to get used to.'

'My name wasn't Kaplan in the first place,' Marta said, unable to bear the assumption that it was. 'It was Kaminsky.'

Frau and Herr Fiehler exchanged looks over the table.

'Those days are behind you now, Marthe,' Herr Fiehler said. 'You need to try to forget all about them. You are Marthe Fiehler now and you are a citizen of the Reich – and don't you ever forget it.'

Despite what she'd said to herself a few minutes earlier, Marthe felt tears stinging the back of her eyes. She swallowed them and put down her knife and fork. She could hold herself back no longer.

'But in my heart, I'm Polish,' she burst out. 'I'm Marta Kaminsky from Jasło and, whatever anyone says and does, I always will be.'

Neither of them answered her and the Fiehlers were subdued after that, eating their food in awkward silence. When they'd finished, Frau Fiehler said, 'We retire early in this house. We normally go up to bed at around nine thirty – we need to be up early for Heinrich to get to work. You are welcome to come and sit with us now, or if you'd prefer, you can go straight up to bed. It's your choice.'

'I think I will go up – I'm very tired from the journey,' Marta said stiffly.

'The maid will wake you at six o'clock. I asked her to set your uniform out on your bed, so please try it on when you go up. If anything needs altering, you can take it to her in the back scullery and she can sew it this evening.'

Marta stood up.

'Goodnight, Marthe,' the Fiehlers both said, without warmth. She said goodnight and went up to her room.

There, laid out neatly on the bed, was the uniform that Frau

Fiehler had mentioned. There was a navy-blue skirt, a white, short-sleeved blouse, short white socks, some black lace-up shoes and a red kerchief complete with a swastika brooch. Beside the uniform was what looked like a sports kit, laid out on top of a drawstring bag. It was an all-in-one costume with a little frilly skirt and white plimsolls.

Reluctantly, Marta took off the uniform that she'd worn all the way from the assimilation home and put the new school uniform on. It was uncanny how it fitted her perfectly, even down to the shoes. Perhaps Doctor Schiller had sent her measurements to Frau Fiehler in advance? One of the buttons on the skirt was loose though and it fell off when she tried to fasten it. She sighed.

She took the uniform off and put her own clothes back on, then, taking the skirt, crept along the landing and down the stairs, and across the tiled hallway. She hesitated, looking around her, unsure of where the back scullery might be. The door to the living room, beside the front door at the front of the house, stood ajar and she could hear voices: it was Frau and Herr Fiehler talking. Sensing that they were probably discussing her, Marta crept closer to the door and stood on one side of it so she could listen.

'At first I thought she was quite a well-behaved, compliant girl, but I must say I was surprised at her outburst about Poland,' Herr Fiehler was saying.

'Oh, I know, Heinrich. I couldn't believe my ears. I was mortified. I really hope she doesn't try anything like that at school.'

'Well, if she does, she will most certainly face severe punishment,' Herr Fiehler said in a self-satisfied voice. 'Such talk is a danger to society.'

'Didn't Doctor Schiller say she'd been fully Germanised?' Frau Fiehler asked.

'He absolutely assured me of it,' her husband replied.

'Hmm, do you trust him, Heinrich?'

'I thought so, but I'm not so sure now. If there are any other such demonstrations that the Germanisation hasn't worked, we will surely have to inform him. He did say we could send her away if things didn't work out.'

'Away? Back to Bruczków?'

Marta's eyes widened in shock, but what she heard next sent chills running right through her body.

'Oh no, they won't want her back there. The job of the assimilation home is done. If it hasn't worked, there isn't a second chance. No, such cases are sent off to places like Dachau and Auschwitz. The SS in charge there would certainly know how to deal with such anti-Nazi behaviour.'

Marta didn't want to hear any more. Stifling a cry, she ran across the hall and along the passageway to the scullery, where the maid sat in front of the stove reading a book. Marta gave the maid her skirt. The woman put her book down and took it a little huffily.

'Frau Fiehler said I should ask you if anything needs to be sewn. This button came off.'

'All right, I'll have it ready for you in the morning. I will leave it outside your door.'

'Thank you. I... I'm afraid I don't know your name.'

The woman looked at her, surprised. 'I'm Ada,' she said.

'Thank you, Ada.'

Marta had wondered if Ada might be an ally, someone to confide in, but she now realised that she probably wasn't. She got the distinct impression that Ada resented Marta's presence and the extra work it might cause her.

She left the scullery and went upstairs to bed, feeling miserable. She'd thought things couldn't get any worse than the assimilation home, but this already felt far worse. She'd never felt so alone before and the feeling left an empty pit in her stomach, even though she was full from the heavy food at supper.

She got into bed and switched off the bedside light. As soon as she closed her eyes, her mind started going over the events of the day. The conversation she'd overheard between the Fiehlers kept repeating in her mind. It had shocked her to hear how they spoke of her, but despite that she was glad she'd heard it. She knew now that she was on thin ice. Whatever she felt in her heart, she knew that on the outside she must appear to embrace everything about her new life without reservation. She must suppress her true feelings and put on an act. And if that act failed, she would find herself on a train to one of those terrible camps where people suffered, got sick and died.

In the morning, Ada knocked on Marta's door at six o' clock. She got out of bed and put on the school uniform, having collected the skirt from outside her bedroom door. Then she went downstairs to the dining room, where Herr and Frau Fiehler were having breakfast. They were both reading; Herr Fiehler was engrossed in the *Völkischer Beobachter* newspaper and his wife was reading *Frauen-Warte*, which looked from the cover to be a Nazi women's magazine. They both looked up when Marta entered and wished her good morning. Ada brought her some toast and indicated the pots of butter and jam on the table. She also poured coffee into a cup and orange juice into a glass.

'If you would like an egg or some ham, I can get them from the kitchen for you,' Ada said, but Marta shook her head. She didn't want to eat too much; her stomach was already churning with nerves at the thought of her first day at a German school. She could barely force down a piece of plain toast and butter.

'Today is an important day for you, Marthe,' Herr Fiehler said, 'and it is vital that you make a good impression. The fact that you have come from Poland and have been through the Germanisation programme is confidential, and I would ask you not to mention that to your fellow pupils – I will certainly hear about it if you do. You will soon settle down and I'm sure you will enjoy the lessons. I know from Doctor Schiller that you are a clever girl and that you are capable of studying hard.'

The school was a few blocks away from the house and Frau Fiehler walked there with her. Marta joined a class of around twenty girls of her own age. They all stared at her and giggled when Frau Fiehler brought her into the classroom. She wondered if it was because Frau Fiehler looked rather old and portly and was probably very different from their own mothers. The teacher, Fräulein Ingrid Bruckner, a young woman with kind eyes who reminded Marta a little of Nurse Weiss, welcomed her warmly and told her to sit at the front.

'That way, I can help you if you have any difficulties,' she said.

The lessons that morning consisted of an hour of history, followed by an hour of racial science and then German language for the final hour. They were similar to those she'd experienced at Bruczków, all of them aimed at indoctrinating the girls. The history lesson was focused on the greatness of the German people and their empire throughout history, and the racial science lesson repeated the mantra Marta was familiar with – the superiority of the Aryan race above all others.

She had heard most of this before from Herr Sturm, but she noticed that the pupils in this class were far more enthusiastic about the teachings than the children at the assimilation home had been. Here, the girls listened attentively and their arms shot up when the teacher asked questions. The girls seemed to compete against one another to be the first to put their hand up and to be the most knowledgeable. When they answered the teacher's questions, Marta noticed that they spoke in monotones, as if they were automatons reading from a script. It frightened her to be amongst so many committed Nazis and she wondered if she would ever find a friend here.

At the end of the morning, while the rest of the class were

trooping out to the dining room, the teacher approached her desk.

'Are you all right, Marthe?' she asked. 'How did you find this morning?'

Marta turned her eyes towards the teacher's. She realised that those gentle-looking eyes and that pretty smile might be deceptive, and remembered the conversation between the Fiehlers that she'd overheard the previous evening. She wasn't going to let her guard drop, not even for this friendly teacher.

'I found it very interesting,' she replied, trying to copy the tone that she'd heard the other girls use.

'Well, I'm glad about that. If you struggle with anything or have any questions at all, do let me know. I'm always available to talk. It must be difficult when German isn't your first language.'

Marta looked at her blankly. 'I can understand the language very well, thank you,' she said.

'That's good, but if you do start to struggle, I'm always here to help.'

'Thank you, Fräulein,' Marta said in the same flat voice.

'Now, hurry along to the dining room,' the teacher said. 'This afternoon, and every other afternoon, we have three hours of compulsory sport. This afternoon we are learning dance and rhythmic gymnastics. I think you will enjoy that. So, eat well, Marthe. You will need plenty of energy.'

In the dining room, she collected her lunch of sauerkraut, bread and salad and sat by herself at one of the tables in the corner. But she wasn't allowed to be alone for long. Two girls from her class came and sat with her, introduced themselves as Charlotte and Hetty and began to quiz her: what's your name? How old are you? Do you have any brothers or sisters? Where have you come from?

Marta struggled with this last question and simply said she'd been attending a boarding school a long way away. She would have been happy to tell them her story, but Herr Fiehler's words of warning rang in her head. If they didn't want her to reveal where she'd come from, and they were prepared to send her away if she stepped out of line, she would do her best to keep her past a secret.

In the end she told the girls that her mother and father were unable to care for her and that Frau and Herr Fiehler had adopted her. The two girls stared at her, silenced. She knew they wanted to ask her why her parents couldn't care for her any longer, but something stopped them. Even they had some sensitivity, she realised.

In the afternoon they went into the gymnasium and practised gymnastics and dance. This was new to Marta, but she was naturally graceful and had no difficulty in picking up the movements. It was a relief not to have to perform the marching and goose-stepping exercises that she'd been forced to do at Bruczków.

When school was over, Hetty and Charlotte came to say goodbye. Marta felt gratified that, although she felt as though these two girls could never be close friends, they were at least trying to make her feel welcome.

'Are you going to the BDM tomorrow?' Charlotte asked.

'BDM?' she asked, forgetting herself for a moment.

'You mean you don't know what that is?'

'Of course I do,' she said quickly, remembering.

'There's a meeting tomorrow evening,' Hetty said. 'Everyone has to go. It's compulsory, like the Hitler Youth.'

'Yes, I know.'

'Hetty and I could come and call for you at your house,' Charlotte said, 'and we could all go along together.'

'All right,' she said straight away. If she had to go to such a meeting, it would be better to go along with these two girls than with Frau Fiehler.

. . .

Marta looked in the cupboard for the BDM uniform that Frau Fiehler had put there. It resembled the school uniform in that it consisted of a blue skirt, white shirt and kerchief, but it was altogether more robust than the school uniform, and the shoes were stout marching shoes. On the second day when she came home from school, she went upstairs and put the uniform on.

'You look wonderful,' Frau Fiehler said with shining eyes when Marta came downstairs. 'Oh, if only I was young again. I would love to have a chance to be part of what you young people have on offer these days – it's all so exciting!'

Marta smiled a sickly smile and nodded. The doorbell rang. Hetty and Charlotte stood on the doorstep.

'So nice that you've already made some friends,' Frau Fiehler said as Marta left with the two girls. 'You're settling down very nicely after all.'

The BDM meeting was in a nearby community hall and was exactly as Marta had expected. Two zealous young women who were the local BDM leaders sat everyone down and gave them a lecture, focused on antisemitism, in hectoring voices.

'Our esteemed and enlightened Führer has instituted a policy of ridding the Reich of the danger of these people. He saw the truth without us even realising, that they were robbing us of everything – our wealth, our education, our institutions. Now we see them loaded onto trains and taken away to work camps in remote places. There, they can live useful lives, contribute to society with noble work, but they are unable to harm us any longer.'

Marta sat there, cross-legged like all the others, her eyes fixed on the floorboards. Everything she heard revolted her. She wanted to stand up and shout out how wrong this all was. She wanted to tell these gullible girls about what she'd seen in the Łódź ghetto – Jews forced to live in inhumane conditions, without proper shelter, adequate clothing or enough food, forced to work in sweatshops or starve on the streets. But she remained silent. She knew it would be madness to speak out and even if she did, they wouldn't believe her. These girls were indoctrinated, completely blind to any other point of view than the one that had been peddled to them by the Nazis since they were tiny.

After the talk, they were made to do some marching exercises in formation. After that, they sang some Nazi marching songs and were then given lemonade and cake.

While Marta was eating hers, one of the leaders came up to her.

'You're new to the group, aren't you? Welcome.'

'Thank you,' Marta muttered.

'There's a girls' camp next weekend in the mountains. I hope you'll come?'

'Of course,' she replied, her heart lifting a little. Perhaps that would break the tedium of life in that oppressive house with Frau and Herr Fiehler.

So, the following weekend, the entire BDM branch, of whom there were around fifty girls and two leaders, set off from Munich Hauptbahnhof by train, to the hills of southern Bavaria, carrying bedrolls, tents, cooking equipment, food, and everything they would need for a weekend in the country. Marta had wondered whether the weekend might present an opportunity to run away, but there was no chance of that. And even if she did manage to escape the clutches of the BDM, where would she go? She had no money and no friends to help her within a thousand miles. She would surely be caught and sent off to the very place she was trying to avoid.

They camped in an enclosed camping ground, with soldiers of the SS guarding the entrance and exit, and she was never alone. They spent the weekend singing songs, playing games, climbing trees and tending to the camp. She did her best to blend in, to appear to be having fun. On the way home on the train, sandwiched between Hetty and Charlotte, Marta reflected that the camp hadn't been unenjoyable, apart from the parts where she'd had to listen to Nazi doctrine or pretend to sing Nazi songs.

After that, life fell into a predictable routine of school, BDM meetings and homework. Sometimes at weekends, Frau and Herr Fiehler would take her to their chalet in the mountains, where Herr Fiehler would set off in his lederhosen and feathered hat with his rifle over his shoulder to shoot game, and Frau Fiehler would pluck it and cook it for the evening meal.

Marta quickly learned to completely suppress her true feelings. Her old self, Marta Kaminsky, lived buried deep inside, and the Marthe Fiehler who lived on the surface gave a good imitation of going along with what she was taught at school, what she heard at BDM meetings and elsewhere, while not embracing it or abandoning her true principles. That way, walking a dangerous tightrope, she learned to survive in this alien environment. And all the time she was poised like a coiled spring, waiting for the moment when she could break free and allow Marta Kaminsky to burst forth again. But there were times when something would happen to dent her spirits and make her think she would never be able to break free of this life.

One of those times was a few months after her arrival in Munich. One day, she happened to be in the hall when the daily post arrived. Marta was standing behind Ada as she received it from the postman. The maid shuffled the letters together quickly, but not before Marta had noticed one that she was almost sure was addressed to her: the writing on it looked familiar. Could it be from Margarete Weiss? Was this news of Joanna at last? How she'd waited for this moment!

'That's for me, Ada,' she said, and Ada held the letters to her chest and turned to her awkwardly, about to say something.

'Give that letter to me, Ada.' Frau Fiehler's cold voice came from the passage. She marched into the hall and held out her hand. 'I said, give it to me!'

Ada flushed and handed Frau Fiehler the pile of post. Frau Fiehler turned to Marta and said, 'There must be no influence from your former life coming into this house. I thought my husband made that crystal clear? And since you don't yet know anyone here who might write to you, this letter must come from your former existence, which you've now left behind. For your own good, I'm going to destroy this letter, whoever it's from. I'm not going to read it, I'm simply going to shred it, and we are all going to forget that it ever arrived.'

'But it could be news of my sister!' Marta protested, trying to snatch the letter from Frau Fiehler.

'How dare you, girl! Let me remind you – you *have* no sister. You are not that girl any more. You are Marthe Fiehler, our daughter. Now, go up to your room and calm down. I will overlook this outburst and I won't mention it to my husband, but let me tell you this – any other post that comes to this house like this will be destroyed in exactly the same way.'

Feeling wretched, Marta dragged herself upstairs, threw herself on her bed and sobbed her heart out. When six o'clock came round, she didn't go downstairs for supper, even though her stomach was rumbling with hunger. How could she sit at the table with these despicable people and share their food after such a display of cruelty?

She lay awake into the small hours and, when the house was quiet, she put on her dressing gown, crept down to the ground floor and let herself into Frau Fiehler's study. This was where she kept the papers for the Nazi women's committees she worked on and dealt with the household accounts.

Her heart hammering against her ribs, Marta put the lamp on and went to the waste paper bin and emptied out the contents. Sure enough, the shreds of a letter and an envelope were still there. She picked them up and examined them, but the pieces were so tiny, it was impossible to put them together, even though she sat there for over an hour trying to do that. Finally, she gave up, put the waste paper back in the bin and went back to bed. Hugging her knees for comfort, she sobbed herself to sleep.

TWENTY-SIX

JOANNA

Auschwitz-Birkenau, Poland, 1944–45

After the first day that Joanna worked sorting clothes in Kanada-kommando in the Auschwitz-Birkenau camp, every day was much the same, and the days and weeks all began to merge into one. Like everyone else, she was up before dawn after the sound of the first gong and if she had time she would queue for a quick wash in the washhouse, then return to the hut to eat breakfast if she'd managed to save some bread from the evening before. She would line up in the square with the others in her work detail and march to work in time to the band music. Then she would work alongside Eva and Zofia and the others sorting clothes and belongings from new arrivals. They would work for around eleven hours before returning to the camp in time for evening roll call at seven o'clock.

It was an exhausting routine for anyone, especially as prisoners were only issued with starvation rations, but for a ten-year-old girl it was punishing. The long working hours, the lack of food, the difficulty sleeping, the lack of hygiene were all very hard to bear. She knew she was getting thinner every day; her elbows and knees stuck out and although she had no mirror, she could feel that her cheeks had grown hollow too.

Once a week, the women were made to undress in the barracks and run naked down to the bath house and take a cold shower. As the weeks ground by, and autumn gave way to winter, the weather grew colder and colder – there was often frost on the ground and sometimes snow – but the rule didn't change. There was no soap and no towels, and they had to return to the hut wet to dry themselves on their uniforms, then put them on again.

Joanna had received a new uniform, a dress and kerchief like Eva's, during her first week at the camp. She was given no new underwear, though, and the dress didn't keep her warm on cold days. Once a month the uniforms were taken away for delousing and the women were issued with different ones. Sometimes they fitted and sometimes they didn't, but whatever you were given, you had to put up with until the next delousing session came round.

Sometimes, sorting clothes at the warehouses, Joanna would come across food that the owner had packed to sustain them on the journey or in the camp. The first time she discovered a loaf of bread hidden amongst the clothes, she unwrapped it and stared at it, her mouth watering at the thought of biting into it.

'Go ahead,' said Eva, who was working next to her. 'It's yours. You've found it, so you are entitled to eat it.'

'Do you want some?'

'Only if you can spare it,' Eva said, but Joanna could tell from her eyes that she was hungry and would love a bite, so she tore a hunk off and handed it to her.

'As you know, the SS never mind about us eating the food we find,' Eva said between mouthfuls. 'But if we did try to take anything else back to the camp, we would be severely punished.'

'Has anyone ever tried?' Joanna asked.

Eva nodded. 'Some of the women tried to bring warm clothes back under their uniforms. It was midwinter and, you'll soon find out, it gets bitterly cold here. They were caught by the SS and beaten with belts until they bled. I wouldn't want that to happen to you, my little one, so be very careful, please.'

'Of course I will,' Joanna said, then finished the bread and turned back to the task of emptying a large suitcase and putting the contents into different piles.

Knowing what she did now, it felt a terrible betrayal to be sorting through the belongings of someone who was about to die a senseless death in one of those forbidding buildings with the huge chimneys. And now she knew that the terrible smell from those chimneys was burning bodies, every breath she took sickened her. But she carried on; there was no choice. Every few minutes one of the guards would come past, with his dog straining at the leash, growling and snapping at the prisoners, to ensure that everyone was hard at work.

At that moment, a train's horn sounded in the distance and a huge, black engine appeared through the great arched entrance to the camp, pulling dozens of cattle trucks. They all squealed and ground to a halt at the station platform. These were the moments that Joanna dreaded, but still her eyes were drawn to the scene that was about to unfold on the platform. The SS guards and their prisoner workers banged on the doors of the cattle trucks with sticks, then they slid them open and the prisoners came spilling out, swarming onto the platform in all directions. Even from this distance Joanna could see that they were confused, that they had no idea where they were or what to do.

The guards pointed them to a spot to leave their luggage and soon they were herded into two lines, moving forward alongside the train towards the front, where the doctor had set up at a small table flanked by two guards. Joanna watched all this in horror. This was exactly what had happened to her and Lili when they'd arrived. No one knew, as they inched up the platform, that the doctor would decide with a flick of his hand whether they were to live or to die and that those who were directed to the left-hand side were walking towards certain death.

She wished she could warn those poor, innocent people; she longed to drop what she was doing, run over to the platform and yell at them to run for their lives. But she knew that she could never do that. She would be shot in an instant and, even if the people believed her and tried to run, the officers had guns and dogs. There was no hope of escape for anyone in this hellish place.

On Sundays there was no formal work. Those days seemed to drag more than the others, even though Joanna longed all week for Sunday to come around. She spent it with the others, tidying the hut, sitting at the table chatting with some of the women who could speak Polish or resting on the bunk, catching up on sleep. Some people received post from home and would lie on their bunks reading avidly. Eva never received letters. Now that Joanna knew about the chimneys and what happened to those selected, she was also sure that Eva's father and mother and her two children were dead. Her heart bled for poor Eva. It must be an impossible burden to bear and it amazed her that Eva managed to carry on each day as she did.

Joanna knew that she would never receive any letters either. No one knew where she was. When she started to think about that, her thoughts would go into a downward spiral. She would panic, wondering what would become of her, if she would ever see any of her family again.

Nobody knew how the war was progressing, but everyone hoped that the Allies were winning. Only that way would they ever be released from this hell. Sometimes planes would fly over and they would look up, willing them to drop bombs on the gas chambers.

One day, in September, when the weather was getting cold, there was an air raid. It was early evening and they had just finished roll call and were returning to their huts. Joanna heard the drone of aeroplanes overhead and shaded her eyes, to see dozens of aircraft approaching.

'Get inside, quickly,' Eva said, and they joined the panicked throng of women scrambling to get into the hut. Some crouched under the tables, others under the bottom bunk. The boom and crack of explosions rocked the hut, one after another, again and again. And then silence for a while, then more explosions in the distance.

Everyone got out of their hiding places and went outside to see. But although there were clouds of dust and smoke coming from somewhere within the camp, they could see nothing.

'Inside, everyone,' Ianina ordered. 'There's nothing to see here.'

The next day, they heard rumours that some of the barracks had been hit and that around three hundred prisoners had been killed.

'We all hoped they would hit the chimneys,' Eva said bitterly. 'Instead, they just took more innocent people. What a terrible waste!'

On Sundays, some of the women went to visit relatives or friends in other parts of the camp. Joanna wondered if she might be able to visit Lili on one of those days. When she and Eva were about to take their afternoon nap, Joanna asked Eva if she thought she would be able to visit her friend.

'Perhaps. Where is she? Which barracks, do you know?' Eva asked.

Joanna nodded. 'They said she was going to Block 16A.'

Eva sat up suddenly, banging her head on the ceiling.

'Block 16A? Are you quite sure?'

Her face had gone pale.

'What's wrong?' Joanna asked with dread.

'I don't think you should go over there. Visitors aren't allowed in that block. If you tried, you would certainly be punished.'

'But why? What happens there?' Joanna asked.

Eva looked at her, then she reached out with both arms and drew Joanna towards her, hugging her tight.

'My poor little one, how innocent you are. In that block, a doctor called Doctor Mengele uses the children who live there to test medicines. That's all I know. Nobody is supposed to know, just like we're not meant to know about the gas chambers, but how can terrible secrets like that stay secrets in a place like this?'

'Test medicines?' Joanna wondered what that meant.

'Yes, that's what I've heard. But I don't know any more than that. I'm sorry, little one.'

Joanna fell silent. Poor Lili. She wondered what medicines she might have had to take. She also wondered why visitors weren't allowed in Block 16A. Perhaps Eva was mistaken. Joanna thought that she would try to find out where it was anyway. Perhaps, if she found out where it was, and hung around outside it for a while, she might be able to see Lili going into or out of the hut.

She slid to the end of the bunk.

'I'm just going to the washroom,' she lied.

'All right, see you later.' Eva's voice was sleepy. She yawned and turned over and Joanna climbed down onto the floor quietly.

She left the hut and hurried away from it, walking between the other huts that housed the women of Kanada-kommando. Soon, she had left Kanada behind and was in another part of the camp, walking between other, different huts, all built along the same lines. The prisoners here wore different uniforms, blue and grey striped, and they were all men. Some stopped what they were doing and stared at her when she walked past. She carried on walking. She wanted to ask someone where Block 16A was, but didn't dare; nobody looked as though they wanted to talk to her.

She'd gone some way when she rounded the end of a building and came face to face with an SS guard and his dog. She gasped, then, without thinking, turned and ran. Terrified, she ran back in the direction she'd come from, her breath coming in gulps, her heart pumping. But the guard was quicker than she was and within a few paces he had grabbed her.

He yelled at her in German. He was red in the face, spit flying from his mouth. Joanna cringed, trying to get away from him, terrified of what might happen next. Then he spoke to her in broken Polish.

'Where is your block?'

'Kanada,' she managed to stutter.

'You are far from there. Where you try to go?'

'Block 16A. My friend is there.'

The man grew angry again. 'Nobody goes to that block,' he yelled, slapping her round the face with his hand, backwards and forwards, backwards and forwards. The slaps stung her and she cried out.

'You must never try to go to that block again,' he said, grabbing her dress and pulling her close. 'Let me take your number. If you go out of your area again, you will be punished. Do you understand?'

Joanna nodded and showed him her wrist. He wrote down her number in his notebook.

'You go back to Kanada now,' he said and started pushing her back in the direction she'd come from. He walked behind her all the way and when they arrived back at the hut, he went inside and spoke to Ianina. Joanna stood in the doorway help-lessly, watching them conferring.

After he'd gone, Ianina beckoned Joanna over.

'What were you thinking of, going over there?' she scolded, pinching Joanna's chin. 'Nobody is allowed to go near that block. Now they have your number and they've asked me to watch you and report back. So, there had better be no more trouble from you, do you hear me? You don't want the whole block to be punished, do you?'

Joanna shook her head miserably and went to her bunk. Eva was sitting up in bed, looking anxious.

'I was wondering where you'd got to. You didn't go and try to find your friend, did you?'

Joanna nodded and climbed onto the bunk. 'That guard caught me and hit me round the face lots of times,' she said.

Eva put her arms around her shoulders and held her tight.

'My poor, poor little one.'

Joanna couldn't stop the tears coming. She knew she'd had a lucky escape – she could have easily received more of a beating, or even something else, something far, far worse than a beating. Much as it pained her, she decided not to try to see Lili again, at least for the time being. And she promised herself that she would take Eva's advice in the future.

It was hard for Joanna to get up the next day and carry on. She couldn't stop thinking about Lili and what might be happening to her in Block 16A. The days dragged after that and, as Eva had predicted, the weather grew bitterly cold. Snow lay thick on the ground, but still the transports arrived at the platform and still she had to work outside alongside the other women, sorting through the belongings and packing them into bundles. They were each issued with a thin jacket to wear over their dresses, but still they shivered in the harsh Polish winter.

People had brought their best and most precious belongings with them when they'd packed to come to Auschwitz. Jewellery, family photographs, gold and silver ornaments, beautiful clothes, foreign currency, expensive spirits. It was still Joanna's job to find anything hidden in the seams or hems of garments, and she found many such items. Whenever she did, as instructed, she would take them to Kazia, who took them off to the office to be logged. Sometimes though a guard would wander past, see an item they liked in the piles of belongings, pick it up and pocket it.

'Why are they allowed to take what they want, but we are beaten if we try to take anything back to the camp?' Joanna asked Zofia, who was working beside her.

Zofia shrugged and laughed bitterly.

'Nothing is fair here. They aren't meant to, but nobody stops them. There are no rules for the SS here – they are as corrupt as they are cruel.'

Joanna had often been tempted to smuggle warm clothes or blankets back with her, now that the weather was unbearably cold. The brick pipe that ran down the middle of the hut provided some warmth, but it was still icy cold in there at night and one thin blanket wasn't enough to keep warm. But she didn't dare risk being discovered and receiving further punishment.

One day, when she was sorting belongings, she picked up a suitcase that looked vaguely familiar and her heart stopped. She stared at it, then at the label on it.

Maria Kaminsky, Floriańska, Jasło, Poland. She closed her eyes and covered her face, hoping it was a bad dream and that when she looked again, it would no longer be there. But when she opened her eyes the suitcase still stood there, taunting her. How could this be? She thought back to all the children who'd told her their parents had disappeared or been executed, especially those in the resistance. Perhaps Tata had been caught trying to help others escape, or doing something else the Nazis deemed a criminal act? Maybe he had been shot like the parents of the other children and Mama had been sent here? Horrified at the thought, she pictured SS officers coming to the house in the dead of night, dragging Tata out and taking him away, giving Mama five minutes to pack, then throwing her in a lorry, taking her to the train station to board a cattle truck.

She stood stock-still, unable to move, unable to take her eyes off the case. And then something dawned on her: did this mean that Mama could be here in the camp, in another hut somewhere, working, just like she was? A chink of light entered her heart.

An SS guard approached. 'Why aren't you working, girl? Get on with it,' he yelled at her. 'Get that case processed before I come back,' and then he moved on.

She bent down and undid the suitcase. It opened easily and, when she lifted the lid, a waft of Mama's familiar lemony perfume rose to meet her. She gasped and took a deep breath of it. The scent brought back the memories of her mother's arms around her, her smile, her laughter. With a heavy heart, she began to take out Mama's clothes and sort them into piles. Each dress she took out, each cardigan, each blouse was so familiar, even down to the places where Mama had darned holes in the fabric. Joanna could see her now, sitting in the corner of the living room, working under the light of a lamp, her face a picture of concentration, focused on the task.

Joanna didn't need to run her fingers along the seams and hems of Mama's clothes. She knew that all Mama's jewellery had been pawned to buy food, that she had nothing precious left. When she'd taken all Mama's clothes out of the case, there was one thing left in the bottom of it. At first it looked like a piece of card, but when she turned it over, she saw that it was a photograph of all four of them: Tata and Mama at the back, arm in arm, and Joanna and Marta at the front, smiling into the camera. They'd been to the studio in Jasło a long time ago to have that taken, when they still had enough money for some pleasures. Joanna picked it up and looked at it lovingly, tears in her eyes. Then she held it to her lips and kissed it. Despite the rules about taking things back to camp, she was going to take this with her, whatever price she had to pay.

TWENTY-SEVEN

JOANNA

Auschwitz-Birkenau, Poland, 1945

Luckily, that day she wasn't searched, although it was hard walking past the guards, trembling from head to toe, with her family photograph inside her underwear. Back in the hut, when she showed it to Eva, Eva looked at it for a long time.

'What a beautiful family,' she said wistfully. 'You must miss them so much.'

'I do,' Joanna admitted with a lump in her throat.

'You must hide that somewhere. I think it might be possible to slip it behind the frame of the bunk. You don't want an SS inspection to find it.'

Joanna peered into the tiny gap between the bunk and the wall. Eva was right – she might just be able to squeeze the photograph in there.

'You have to hold on to the hope that your mother is here in the camp,' Eva said. 'I will ask around for you.'

'Thank you,' Joanna said. 'I'm not allowed to go out of Kanada, otherwise I would look for her.'

'I know, my little one,' Eva said. 'I will speak to Ianina and ask her to speak to the other Blockältestes about recent arrivals. Try not to hold out too much hope. But even if we can't find her, it doesn't mean she isn't here – she could easily be in one of the other parts of the camp, or out working.'

The days passed and Eva and Ianina asked around the prisoners in other blocks to see if anyone knew a recent arrival, Maria Kaminsky, but time and time again the answer came back that there was no one by that name on their block. Every time Eva went out to ask, Joanna would wait anxiously by the door of the hut for her return, but each time Eva returned, Joanna was disappointed.

'Like I said, it doesn't mean she's not here, little one. Be patient.'

Joanna tried her best, but not knowing whether her mother was dead or alive, that she could be living in one of the huts within walking distance of Kanada, was tearing her apart.

One day, a couple of weeks into her search, Eva got sick. She woke up one morning with her body a furnace. Joanna could feel the heat of it radiating from her body, just lying beside her. Eva was shivering violently, her teeth chattering.

'Tell Ianina I can't work today,' she said, and lay back, exhausted from the effort of speaking.

When Joanna told Ianina, she shrugged. 'Probably typhus. We've had so many cases lately. It's carried by lice that live in the clothes – they never disinfect them properly. I'll tell the doctor.'

'Poor Eva,' Joanna muttered, not looking forward to the prospect of going to work without her.

'I see you're one short this morning,' Kazia said gruffly when only nine of them reported for work at the warehouse. 'The SS will be expecting us to do as much as we always do, so you'll all need to work harder today.'

They usually worked quickly, under the constant haranguing of the guards, but today they worked even faster than usual, sorting through and packing as many loads of clothes as they did when Eva was working. Every time she stopped working, Joanna glanced over towards the platforms at the railhead. It was strange; no trains had come in that day. In fact, now she thought about it, she realised that she hadn't seen any trains on the platform for a while.

'They've stopped the transports, didn't you notice, Joanna?' Zofia said, seeing her looking.

'I hadn't noticed before. But all these clothes... where have they come from?'

'There's a huge backlog. Thousands of people have been brought here, maybe millions. And they all brought luggage with them. And the Germans want to package it up neatly and send it back to the Reich to sell or use themselves. There's still months' worth of work for us here in these piles.'

After work that day, when Joanna returned to the hut and went over to her bunk, she was surprised to see that Eva wasn't there. The woman in the next bunk, Sonia, said, 'Someone said they took her to the medical hut. She was very bad apparently.'

'Poor, poor Eva! I will miss her so much. Do you think she will get better soon?' Joanna asked, sitting on the bunk, hugging her knees. She would miss Eva badly, especially at night when they snuggled together to keep warm.

'She won't get very good care in that place, if any. They've only taken her away because typhus is infectious.'

Joanna hoped she wouldn't get it herself, and was worried that there was no one now to look for Mama. Ianina had made some enquiries of the other Blockältestes but hadn't helped any further and Joanna didn't want to anger her by asking her again. Perhaps she would be able to persuade someone else in the block to help her, maybe Zofia, although Zofia frightened her a little and she wasn't sure she dared ask her.

That night, in the small hours, there was the boom of a great explosion somewhere nearby. It was so loud that everyone woke up, sitting up in their bunks and muttering to each other, wondering what on earth it could be. Perhaps it was the Allies, bombing the camp, Joanna thought, but she hadn't heard any aircraft this time. Aircraft had often passed overhead, but they'd never dropped bombs on the camp. Someone had said that bombs had been dropped at the chemical factory at the Buna camp, but since September none had fallen in recent months on Auschwitz-Birkenau.

The next morning when they went outside, the skyline had altered. One of the great chimneys that had belted out smoke since Joanna arrived at the camp was no longer there. It had been reduced to a mound of rubble.

'They've blown it up themselves,' muttered Hanna, one of the women in Joanna's work detail, as they lined up in the square to march to work. 'They must think they're losing the war, and they don't want anyone to find out what they've done.'

Joanna hoped it was true. Surely, if Germany lost the war, she and everyone else here would be released from the camp? They could go home. But then her heart sank. If Mama and Tata were no longer there, whatever would she do when she got back to Jasło?

The other chimneys were still belting out fumes at the same rate though.

'They're trying to finish their work before the Allies get here and see what they've done,' Hanna said. 'Just like I said. They're terrified of being discovered.'

When they returned to the barracks that evening, Joanna knew immediately that something was wrong.

Ianina was standing by the door. She was telling everyone who entered the hut, 'All prisoners are being evacuated from the camp. We leave this evening. After you've eaten, bundle up your belongings – your blanket, mug and bowl and spoon. We are setting off at ten o'clock.'

'Where to?' Joanna heard Sonia ask.

'To another camp in Germany. They want to take us away from the front line before the Russian Army gets here.'

'How far is it?'

'Hundreds of miles.'

'Are we going by truck?'

Ianina laughed a hollow laugh. 'You're joking, aren't you? We are walking.'

'Walking?'

'Yes, only the fit can go. The sick are staying in the camp but they will have to fend for themselves. There will be no guards staying behind to look after them. If you can't walk fast enough, be warned – you will be punished.'

'What about Eva?' Joanna asked, dread in her heart. And what about Lili, too? What would happen to them? She didn't know what was worse, being forced to march hundreds of miles or being left here sick, unable to care for yourself.

Ianina shrugged. 'She is too sick to march – she will stay here, of course. Now, go and get your things, then come back here to eat.'

Tears sprang to Joanna's eyes, at the thought of leaving someone else she'd cared for behind. But she had no choice. She did as Ianina had told her.

After a meagre meal of hard strips of an unknown type of meat and a piece of black bread, half of which Joanna kept in her pocket, Ianina told everyone to get their belongings and assemble outside in the square. Joanna bundled up her belongings in her blanket, took her treasured photograph out of its hiding place and slipped it into her underwear. Then she followed the others out into the square, where they normally assembled before work. The place was lit by floodlights and the air was freezing. Snow had begun to fall, settling on the ground. Joanna shivered in her thin dress and pulled her jacket tightly around her, but it had no buttons, so she knew it wouldn't stay done up once she started walking.

SS soldiers paraded around the square, their dogs snapping at the prisoners' ankles. It seemed an age before the march began, but when the order went up it was to start marching block by block and there was a further wait until it was their turn to march. It was a relief to start at last, to walk across the camp between the barracks and out under the pedestrian archway, beside the railway entrance where, months ago, she had entered in a cattle truck.

The march carried on, for hours and hours, along the long, straight road that led away from the camp, through a huge pine forest, through the thickening snow. SS guards walked up and down the column with their dogs and guns. The first gunshot came about an hour after they started walking. It rang out, piercing the night air.

'What was that?' Joanna asked Sonia, who marched beside her.

'I don't know,' she replied.

Someone behind them said, 'They shot someone and left her by the roadside – she couldn't keep up.'

After that, Joanna ignored her tiredness and ignored the blisters that were forming on her heels and toes from the ill-fitting clogs. There was no stopping at any cost and there was no bending down to adjust your shoes either. March, march, march, without relief, despite hunger, despite weakness, despite breathlessness. Joanna scooped up a handful of snow as she walked and ate it gratefully. At least they weren't going thirsty. Every so often the air reverberated with the crack of another gunshot: someone else had fallen behind and paid the price.

Joanna longed to stop, just for a moment, just to draw breath, but she knew that to stop or to pause, even for a second, was to die. To distract herself, she counted her steps under her breath. She often forgot where she was and had to start from the beginning again. Every one hundred steps was one hundred nearer to the end. The hours wore on and still they marched, on and on through the endless forest, then on across an endless plain. At last a grey light appeared in the sky followed by a weak yellow strip of sunlight over the distant horizon. It was morning – they had marched all night.

In the distance, a building loomed. It was dilapidated, an abandoned warehouse.

'You can rest in here,' the SS guards said, directing everyone in through the gateway. Joanna's legs were aching so much they'd almost seized up. If she sat down, she wasn't sure she'd ever be able to get up again.

Everyone crowded into the warehouse, where snow had piled up inside through holes in the roof and walls. Joanna found herself a spot beside a wall, ate her crust of bread and fell into a deep sleep the instant she closed her eyes.

In the morning, they were woken by the barking of dogs and the shouts of the guards. There was hardly time to wake up properly before they were ordered to their feet and were out in the freezing air on the march again, over the snow. Some people refused to get up, too exhausted, too defeated to go on. The guards drew their pistols and shot them where they lay. Joanna tried not to look at the bloodstained snow and the bodies as she passed.

'Move on, move on!' the guards shouted.

It grew dark and they marched on. Joanna wondered why they had to march at night. Was it so they wouldn't be spotted by enemy aircraft? Her feet were very painful now, with open blisters rubbing against her shoes; she winced as she walked, but she numbed herself to the pain. She wasn't going to stop for anything.

More shots rang out that day than on the first day. More people were too exhausted, too weak to go on. Some simply fell down by the roadside already close to death; there was no need for a bullet for them. The guards just kicked them to make sure and left them where they lay.

Joanna walked mechanically, on and on, Sonia by her side. Neither spoke; they had no breath, no energy, and there was nothing to say.

When dawn finally came, they were told there was one hour to go. Joanna didn't know if she had another hour left in her, but she carried on, one foot in front of the next. On and on.

'One hour to the station, then you will ride on the train,' the guards told them.

At last, they stumbled towards a village, a few scattered houses and a village station. There was a train standing beside the platform. Dozens of cattle cars, their doors open. Guards were directing people to the trucks. Joanna managed to climb up the station steps and pushed forward with the others along the platform towards the next truck. When they reached the door to the truck, the guard waved to Sonia to get up, but he pushed Joanna back.

'Not you. It's full. Go to the next truck.'

Joanna went to the last truck on the train and the guard waved her on board. She scrambled into the already packed cattle car and squeezed herself in amongst the bodies. She wished she hadn't been separated from Sonia, who she knew to be good and kind. How would she cope alone? She looked round at the strange faces – women and men, in their shabby, filthy uniforms, their faces grey and hollow, pictures of misery.

Her gaze settled on one face on the other side of the truck and her eyes widened, her heart leapt in hope. The face was far thinner than the one she'd known before, the cheekbones prominent, with hollows under the eyes, and the beautiful hair was now just blond stubble. But even so, she was almost sure.

She had to know.

Her heart racing, she started to push her way through the wall of bodies, but the other prisoners resisted.

'Get back there, there's no room this side.'

'What are you doing, girl?'

'I've got to get through,' she insisted, pushing past.

Just then the woman turned and looked her way and light shone in her deadened eyes.

'Joanna? Joanna? Is that really you?'

'Mama! Mama!' she said, pushing her way through the last people who stood between them. And then Joanna was in front of her, looking into her eyes, throwing her arms around her.

'I can't believe it's you! I thought I would never see you again,' Mama gasped, enfolding Joanna in her arms and holding her tight to her bony body.

Joanna clung to her, tears in her eyes, overwhelmed with emotion, never wanting to let her mother go.

TWENTY-EIGHT

MARTA

Munich, 1945

When Germany finally fell to the Allies and Allied soldiers swarmed through the cities, Herr Fiehler was terrified.

Marta watched him, with loathing, from her bedroom window as he burned his SS uniform and all his papers in a great bonfire in the back garden. What a coward he was, she thought.

One day, though, his past caught up with him and intelligence officers from the Allied forces came to arrest him. Marta stood at the top of the stairs as they burst through the front door. Herr Fiehler rushed upstairs and pushed past her; his face was red and he was panting. He ran into his bedroom. She followed and watched him as he tried to hide in a cupboard, but the soldiers swarmed up the stairs with their guns and he was dragged out, white-faced and shaking. Marta watched him being taken away in a black van, handcuffed, a pathetic figure. She felt no pity for him – in fact, she felt nothing at all.

She never saw him again. Years later, she found out that he'd been tried at Nuremberg and imprisoned for war crimes.

Frau Fiehler was hysterical after Herr Fiehler left. She couldn't cope without her husband, and she couldn't cope with the fall of the Nazi regime either. She'd been fully committed to the cause and had worshipped the Führer as if he were a living god.

Completely ignoring Marta, she went into a nervous decline, and the day he was arrested, she took to her bed. She began to rely heavily on medication and rarely emerged from her room.

One day, in September 1945, when Frau Fiehler had one of her hysterical attacks, she yelled abuse at Ada, the maid.

Ada called a doctor, who came and examined Frau Fiehler and immediately admitted her to a mental hospital. Marta stood on the drive and watched the ambulance draw away from the house. She'd loathed living with the Fiehlers and was glad that they no longer had power over her, although she did feel shocked and a little sorry to see Frau Fiehler in such a terrible state.

'What's going to happen to me?' she asked Ada.

Ada shrugged. 'I have no idea. They haven't paid me for weeks,' she said. 'There's no money left and I'm sure the house will be repossessed by the Allies one day. It belonged to a Jewish family before the Fiehlers moved in. I'm leaving right now, before that happens.'

That evening, Marta ate a few slices of stale bread in the kitchen and spent a sleepless night alone in the big, creaky old house. At school the next day, feeling wretched and alone, she told her teacher, Fräulein Bruckner, what had happened to Frau and Herr Fiehler. Fräulein Bruckner looked very concerned.

'So, you're all on your own in that great big house?' she asked.

Marta nodded. She was a little worried that Fräulein Bruckner might deliver her up to the authorities and that she would be put in an orphanage. She'd heard that there were many orphanages all over Germany full of children who'd been separated from their parents by the war. But to her surprise, Fräulein Bruckner had a completely different response.

'You must come home and stay with me,' she said. 'My parents won't mind. We have plenty of room and they are very open, generous people.'

'Really?' Marta was incredulous. It was the first act of kindness anyone had shown her since she'd left Bruczków and the caring Margarete Weiss behind her.

'Yes, absolutely. I'll come back with you after school to help you pack and then I'll take you home. As long as you want to come, that is?'

'I'd like that very much,' Marta said, feeling a huge weight lift from her shoulders.

So that day, Marta began a new chapter in her life. Frau and Herr Bruckner were enlightened and educated people; he was a lecturer and academic in literature at Munich University and Frau Bruckner was an artist. Her studio was on the top floor of the rambling house. She'd had to hide her work during the Nazi era because it would have been regarded as subversive. She liked to paint abstract, thought-provoking studies – very different from the classical art that Hitler favoured.

They both welcomed Marta into their home without asking any questions, and from that day on, Marta began to relax and enjoy life, despite the sadness that she harboured deep inside. She started to flourish both at home and at school. Gradually, over time, she found the courage to tell the Bruckners about what had happened to her and how she had come to be adopted by two fervent Nazis.

The Bruckners became the next best thing to her own family, and Marta was deeply grateful for what they had done for her. Frau Bruckner, whose name was Angelica, promised to

help her trace her family when things had settled down after
the war.

'We could go to Poland together,' she said. 'Back to Jasło.
See if we could find your parents there. And we can see if there
are any records relating to Joanna too.'

But as soon as the war was over, Poland came under the
control of the Soviet Union and it was impossible to travel there.
Marta had to give up her dream of returning, but when she was
a little older, she did try to find out what had happened to
Joanna from records in Germany. She quickly discovered that
she was up against a brick wall. Almost all the documentation
about the Lebensborn programme had been destroyed by the
Nazis in an attempt to cover their tracks and, although she
would gladly have travelled back to Łódź to try to find out what
had become of Joanna in the camp there, it was impossible to go
there as well.

After years of frustration, with the help of the Bruckner
family, she made a decision to put aside her search. She buried
herself in her studies instead. She discovered that she had a
natural ability at science and, because she'd always had a caring
streak and genuinely wanted to help people, Herr Bruckner
suggested she should become a doctor and encouraged her to
apply to medical school. In 1950, when she was eighteen, she
won a place at the University of Heidelberg to study medicine.

Marta realised, looking back on those days, that at university she'd studied hard but found it very difficult to socialise.
She was always afraid that she was different, terrified of people
discovering her past. Although she'd tried to tell herself it was
nothing to be ashamed of even if they did find out, she didn't
want to be different. She wanted to blend in, to be just like all
the other young women who studied hard and were committed
to their careers as doctors.

The same fears also stopped her from getting close to any
young men. One or two tried over the years. They were intelli-

gent, good-looking boys, whom she'd have loved to get to know better, but something inside stopped her from letting them in. She had a deep sense of self-loathing, stemming from what had happened to her during the war. She was afraid that if she fell in love, her true self would be exposed and once it was, she would quickly lose the other person, just as she'd lost most of the people she'd ever loved. She decided it was better to guard against that happening at all.

In 1989, when the communist regime in Poland fell and travel to the country became possible again, Marta gathered all her courage and booked a train ticket to Jasło. By that time, she was middle-aged, a well-respected specialist in diabetes, working in a hospital in Munich. But throughout those long years she'd never forgotten her family. The desire to find them burned as brightly within her as it ever had. Angelica Bruckner was dead by then and her daughter, Ingrid, Marta's former teacher, was busy with her own family, so Marta told no one about her trip. She just got on a train at Munich Hauptbahnhof with her suitcase and set off alone.

It felt strange returning to the country of her birth after so many years. She hadn't spoken Polish for decades but, despite that, she sensed it would return to her as easily as breathing. In fact, when the train reached the border between Germany and Poland, at the Neisse River, and an immigration official boarded and asked to see her passport, she was able to answer him in perfect Polish without the trace of a German accent. When she handed him her German passport, he looked at her quizzically.

'I thought you were Polish,' he said.

'I was once...' she admitted. 'It's a long story.'

'Ah... the war, I suppose,' he answered with an under-standing smile, and she nodded.

'That's right. The war.'

When she reached Jasło, she checked into a modern hotel near the station, left her luggage in her room and went out to walk around the town. She hadn't been prepared for the changes she saw all around her. The place had been transformed, and the modern streets she walked through now were worlds apart from the town of her childhood that she held in her memory. Whole streets had been replaced with modern buildings. It was almost unrecognisable as the place where she'd grown up. With trepidation she found Floriańska Street and walked along the road towards her old home. Like all the other streets she'd seen, it was unrecognisable. There was no trace of her old home; it had been replaced with a block of flats. Even the trees were no longer the ones she and Joanna had walked under as children. She stared up at the block of flats, trying to take in what had happened.

Disappointed, she returned to the hotel. She stopped at the reception desk and asked the receptionist, an elderly man, what had happened to all the old buildings.

'Didn't you know?' he asked. 'Well, it's a sorry tale. The Nazis razed the place at the end of the war. The town was on the front line. They expelled all the townsfolk first, then the Wehrmacht burned the whole town to the ground so there would be nothing left when the Russians arrived.'

She shuddered, trying to imagine an inferno engulfing the old buildings she'd known and loved.

'I lived here once, as a child,' she told him. 'I was taken away early in 1944. I came back to find my old home and to see if there's any trace of my family. Have you any idea how I might go about tracing someone?'

The man shrugged. 'You could go to the town hall and ask there – that's where they keep records.'

She did as he suggested and for five days remained at the hotel and followed up every Kaminsky with her mother or father's initials that she found in the local records. She tramped the town knocking on doors, steeling herself for a shock, but each time a door was opened by a stranger, she was disappointed.

Finally, she gave up and returned on the train to Germany and her old life, defeated, a hollow feeling inside. The place she'd known no longer existed and the people she'd loved had disappeared too. From that moment on, she buried herself in her work, trying her best to put the past behind her. But she never could quite forget everything, and the ghost of her childhood always lived on in her heart.

TWENTY-NINE

MARTA

Munich, 2005

Watching the programme on *Nachricht* 24 about Lebensborn and the kidnapping and Germanisation of children from Nazi-occupied Eastern Europe had been a painful experience for Marta. It had brought back so many memories that she was unable to sleep the night she'd watched the report. The next day, on duty at the refugee clinic, she couldn't stop her mind wandering back to that time. She realised that it was unlike her. Over the years she'd managed to discipline herself not to dwell on the past, and she'd always refused to give in to self-pity, but that day, when she was bandaging sprains, administering injections or examining patients, the past kept coming back to haunt her in many different ways.

At first, scenes from home in Jasło kept popping into her mind – Mama reading her a bedtime story, Tata sitting by the fire with Joanna on his lap, Mama and Tata taking the two of them skating on a nearby lake in winter. But those scenes were quickly replaced with less happy ones. Again and again, she pictured Joanna's face in the dormitory at Łódź the last time she'd seen her, peering out of the window as the truck pulled out of the yard. And she repeatedly found herself reliving the horror of the moment when they'd been snatched from the marketplace at Jasło, as well as the point at which they'd been told that Joanna had failed the Aryan tests and they would have to be separated. Just thinking about that time made her blood run cold. She had to breathe deeply and make a great effort to focus her mind and stay in the moment that day.

She knew that the next report about Lebensborn on *Nachricht* 24 was going to be shown that evening, and that Margarete Weiss was due to be interviewed by Kristel Meyer. How incredible it was, Marta thought, that Margarete was still alive and still trying to help the children she'd cared for, all these years after the war. Marta knew it would be a difficult experience to watch it, but she felt that she really must.

Some colleagues from the clinic were going to a bierkeller for a drink after work. They often did that, and Marta always enjoyed those evenings and the company of the other doctors and nurses, but this evening she declined the offer.

'Not tonight, thank you. I need to get home to see someone,' she said. It was only half a lie. She did need to get home, but, rather than for a visitor, it was to see Margarete on the TV.

Back at her apartment, she fixed herself a supper of steak and salad. There was half an hour or so before the programme began, so she sat down at the dining room table and ate it with a glass of burgundy. The wine might help her relax a little, she thought. But after a couple of sips, the memories started flooding back again. This time her thoughts strayed back to the assimilation home at Bruczków, the Camp for Polish Children and Youth at Łódź ghetto, and then to the Fiehlers, their stifling, opulent house and their strict, unyielding rules about how Marta should present herself and how she should behave.

She recalled then how everything had finally changed for her at the end of the war. Less than a year after Marta had gone to live with the Fiehlers, Germany finally surrendered. Allied soldiers were soon everywhere on the streets of Munich. She thought about how Herr Fiehler had been arrested, Frau Fiehler committed to a mental hospital, and how she herself had gone to live with Fräulein Bruckner and her parents, before eventually going on to study medicine at Heidelberg. She'd tried and failed to find out what had happened to Joanna and her parents, and she'd finally had to put her quest aside. There had been so many hurdles along the way. But she'd never forgotten them, never stopped longing for them, and now she was older and had more time to reflect, her childhood memories had taken on a new, even more vibrant quality than ever before.

With a deep sigh she took her plate and glass through to the kitchen and, glancing at the clock on the wall, realised that the programme must be beginning. She settled herself down in front of the TV in the living room and switched it to the correct channel. Kristel Meyer was already speaking.

'Today, I'm interviewing somebody who actually worked in the Lebensborn programme. Margarete Weiss trained as a nurse in the Charité Hospital in Berlin and was recruited to work in the Lebensborn programme in the late 1930s. Margarete took great risks, even risking her own life to keep records of the mothers and babies and later, the children in her care. It is due to her efforts that we have already managed to help so many people affected by Lebensborn, with the recent discovery of her wartime notebooks. Today, we are going to talk about Margarete's work in the assimilation, or Germanisation, homes, both in Poland and in Germany.'

The camera panned round to a frail old woman sitting in a chair opposite Kristel. Her hair was white, and her face heavily lined, but when the camera zoomed in for a close-up, Marta immediately recognised the expression in those eyes and the shape of the old lady's face, with its fine bone structure.

Margarete's beauty still shone through despite her advanced years. Marta gasped, transfixed.

'Margarete,' Kristel began, 'thank you so much for joining us this evening and thank you, on behalf of the network and also all those who've so far been helped by your notebooks, for your bravery and dedication.

'We've talked before about your work at Schloss Schwanburg in Bavaria with babies born into the Lebensborn programme, but today, we're going to talk about another, terrible aspect of the Nazi policy in that area – the kidnapping of children from occupied countries and Germanising them to be adopted by Nazi families. How did you first come to have anything to do with this aspect of the programme, Margarete?'

'I had just come back from managing a Lebensborn maternity home in Norway and I was ordered to go to Poland and work in an assimilation home there. But first I was told to accompany a group of children to Kraków to go through some preliminary tests for Aryan qualities, then on to Łódź for further tests there, then on to Bruczków in Poland, where an assimilation home had been set up in a former children's home.'

'And what can you remember about those children, Margarete?'

'There were around twenty of them, aged between three and around twelve. They were all terrified. They'd been snatched off the streets by SS soldiers, ripped away from their families. I saw it as my role to help them through that terribly difficult time. I tried to be kind to them.'

'Did you never worry that you were participating in some terrible crime, the kidnapping of innocent children, and that in effect you were facilitating it?'

Margarete looked pained. 'Of course, of course I did,' she said. 'All the time. But I had to weigh up my options. If I ran away, I would have been caught and put into a concentration camp. I would never have been permitted to walk away from the programme. I knew far too much. Alternatively, I could stay and I could do my best to minimise the harm the children were subject to. I could try to make things better for them.'

'And did you succeed in that?'

'I did my best. I think I did in some cases. I tried to stop the beating of children for speaking Polish in the common parts of the building. I forbade my nurses from doing that and from punishing them for things like wetting the bed. Although the doctor in charge brought in other staff to go above my head, I believe my actions had a good influence. I also did my best to show the children affection and kindness. I hope, if any of them are watching, they will remember that I did that.'

Marta nodded. 'Yes, I remember, Margarete,' she murmured.

She was transfixed by Margarete's voice, which had hardly changed down the years, and by her words. They transported her straight back to Bruczków. She could suddenly remember everything about the place, from the smell of food cooking in the kitchens to the sound of children's voices in the corridor, to the bitter winter wind biting into her when she worked in the gardens with Agata.

The interview continued, and Margarete was asked to describe the tests the children had to pass, the Germanisation programme they were put through, what the other staff were like in the homes she worked in. Listening to her, Marta recalled Margarete's kindness to her personally, how she had stood up for her twice with Doctor Schiller, how she had probably actually saved her life.

The programme was drawing to a close and Kristel asked one last question.

'I'm wondering if you are able to tell us if you have any regrets from that time. If there was something you would have liked to do but were prevented from doing for some reason?'

Margarete thought for a moment, and then she said, her

voice barely more than a whisper, 'Yes, without a doubt, one of the most harrowing things that happened during my time with the Germanisation programme, and something I think about daily, concerned two young Polish sisters. They were aged ten and twelve. I met them in Kraków in 1944. I was struck straight away by how close they were, how the older girl looked after the younger one.'

Margarete paused and swallowed, composing herself.

'It turned out that they were actually half-sisters and the tragedy of it all was that one of them passed the Aryan tests and the other, the younger one, failed them. We were forced to leave her behind in Łódź with the others who had failed the tests. The older one came to Bruczków and was traumatised by the separation. Her behaviour was challenging for a time and the doctor in charge of the home wanted to punish her. I tried to stop him. Eventually she was sent to live with a German family in Munich. I found the separation of those sisters one of the hardest things I had to bear the entire time that I worked with the Lebensborn.'

'Do you know what happened to the younger girl?' Kristel asked.

Margarete was quiet for a second and then she said, 'I did make enquiries and discovered some information about her. I wrote to the older girl to tell her about it, but she never replied. I'm not sure if she ever got the letter. I'm not going to give that information out on air in case she is watching this.'

Marta stared at the screen, tears blurring her vision. The pain of her separation from Joanna was as fresh and painful at that moment as it had been the day it happened. She watched, hardly listening, and as Kristel wrapped up the report, she was reliving those terrible, life-changing moments from 1944.

'If you were one of those children who was taken from your family and Germanised during the war years, we'd love to hear your story. We might be able to help you trace your family, or at least to point you in the direction of resources to help you. All you have to do is to call this number. Calls are confidential and lines are open twenty-four hours per day.'

A number flashed up on the screen and the credits for the programme started to roll. Marta had no hesitation this time, not now she'd seen Margarete's face and knew that Margarete remembered her with such clarity. She knew now that Margarete held the key to discovering what had happened to Joanna. She fumbled for her mobile phone in her handbag and with shaking fingers, dialled the number.

THIRTY

MARGARETE

Munich, 2005

To speak on camera about her work in the Germanisation homes had taken all Margarete's emotional courage. She was talking about things that had lain buried for sixty years and that she had thought she would never want to tell a soul about, let alone thousands of viewers. She no longer worried that people wouldn't understand and would judge her for her part in it all, though. Kristel Meyer had managed to convince her that her story would be far better out in the open than hidden away and she'd already seen with her own eyes how many people had been helped after the discovery of her lost notebooks.

Kristel had asked her to come and stay in Munich in her apartment while they made the recordings, and Margarete had been glad to stay for a few days with Kristel and her Italian partner, Lorenzo. She was so pleased they had fallen in love and that they were so happy and contented in each other's company. It made her heart sing to see them together.

The interview had been recorded over the course of two days and she went into the studio on the evening the programme went out on air. Watching her interview was almost as difficult as giving it had been. She felt drained when it was all over and the programme had come to an end.

Kristel came over and kissed her on both cheeks.

'Thank you, Margarete,' she said. 'I know how much courage that took – you're so brave.'

Margarete clutched Kristel's hand and swallowed a lump in her throat.

'I couldn't have done it without you,' she said.

'I just asked the questions, Margarete. It was all you. There is one other thing I'd like to ask you, though,' Kristel said, pulling up a chair to sit beside Margarete. 'You've done so well in the interviews, and they have been so well received, that I'd like to do one last one with you, if you'd consent to do that?'

Margarete hesitated. 'But I've told all there is to know about Lebensborn,' she said. 'I don't know what more I have to tell.'

'Well, there's your own life, Margarete. You haven't told people how *you* were affected by the war, how you lost your family, how you lost Tomas and your baby. I think people would be very interested to hear your personal story before we bring the series of reports and interviews to a close.'

'*My* story?' Margarete was astonished. 'Why would anyone be interested in that? So many people were affected by the war, lost loved ones, lost their homes and everything they owned too. My story is no different to that of thousands of others.'

'People would be very interested,' Kristel said. 'You have really struck a chord with people. An ordinary woman caught up in an evil regime, forced to work for them but doing their best to be true to their ideals and doing what they could to alleviate suffering. It's a dilemma that everyone can relate to. I'm sure those people would be very interested to hear your own personal story too.'

Margarete wasn't sure she could bear to speak about her own loss, even after all these years, but Kristel had been so good to her. After all, it was only through Kristel that her diaries had been discovered and that she had been able to fulfil her lifetime's wish of uniting the mothers and babies she'd nursed.

At that moment Nicole, Kristel's assistant, came through with a notebook.

'Kristel, someone called Marta Fiehler has called. She's a retired doctor living in Munich. She says she was one of the sisters that Margarete was speaking about in the interview that was broadcast this evening. She said she desperately wants to know what happened to her younger sister, Joanna, and that she'd love to meet Margarete again.'

'Marta!' Margarete gasped, and then, remembering what she knew about Joanna, her spirits fell. 'I didn't want to say it on air, and I really don't want to have to tell her the truth about her sister.'

'What is the truth, Margarete?' Kristel asked gently.

Margarete swallowed. 'Her sister tried to escape from the camp at Łódź with another girl. They were both caught by the SS and sent to Auschwitz. I understand that Joanna at least perished there within a few hours of arrival.'

Kristel's hand flew to her mouth. 'Oh, how terrible,' she said. 'I can see why you don't want to have to give her that news, but doesn't Marta have a right to know what happened?'

'I suppose I do owe it to Marta to tell her the truth,' Margarete said. 'She obviously never got the letter I sent to her towards the end of the war. I don't want to tell her over the phone though,' she added.

'We can ask her to come to the studio to meet you,' Kristel said. 'Do you think you could arrange that?' she asked her assistant.

'Of course. I'll go and call her now.'

'So, Margarete,' Kristel said, 'what about that interview?'

'All right,' Margarete agreed. Hearing about Marta had

given her more strength. 'If you think people would want to hear it.'

'I'm sure they would, and thank you so much,' Kristel said, squeezing her hand. 'We can make a start on the recording tomorrow, while you're still here in Munich.'

Recording that last interview was even harder and more emotionally draining than the ones Margarete had previously given about the Lebensborn programme. Those interviews had been emotional enough, but the pain of her own loss was still raw and immediate, and incredibly hard to speak about.

First, Kristel asked her about Tomas, and she found herself giving voice to some of the thoughts she'd had about him but had kept to herself for many decades.

'He was the kindest, most principled, bravest man I ever met. He came to Schloss Schwanburg to help Doctor Finkel and we quickly became allies. He had such courage – he was prepared to risk everything to help those babies.'

Kristel asked her to describe some of the things Tomas did for the babies and Margarete talked about how he helped the young women giving birth, how he tried to ensure babies were adopted by lower-ranking Party members rather than members of the SS, and how he'd also been prepared to risk everything to save babies who'd been marked for euthanasia.

'The policy was to send any babies that were less than perfect to Aktion T4, the euthanasia programme in Munich where they were killed by lethal injection. Tomas faked the documentation to ensure babies weren't sent there. He also ensured the mothers were offered painkillers during the birth and that they were able to hold their babies and show them love. He was even prepared to help one young mother escape, but unfortunately that plan was thwarted by Doctor Finkel.'

'You have told me that you became lovers during the time

he was at Schloss Schwanburg and that you became pregnant with his child. Did you plan a future together?'

'Yes, of course. We were in love, but because we were colleagues we would have been punished if we'd been found out. So, when my pregnancy began to show, Tomas arranged for me to go home to Berlin. I never saw him again after I left the castle,' Margarete said, her voice cracking with emotion. 'He never saw his baby daughter.'

'Could you tell us what happened to him?' Kristel asked gently.

'The fact that Tomas had been faking documentation was somehow discovered,' she said slowly, 'I don't know how. Perhaps it became obvious that no babies had been sent to the Aktion T4 programme while he was in charge. He was arrested by the Gestapo and sent to Dachau while I was in Berlin. I believe he died there.'

'That must have been a terrible time for you, Margarete.'

Margarete nodded. 'It was. I had to return to work with the Lebensborn after my baby was born. I had no choice. I was summoned back and they would have arrested me if I hadn't gone. They posted me to Norway to run a Lebensborn home there and I had to leave my baby in the care of my mother and sister in Berlin.'

'And how long were you in Norway?'

'Not too long, just a few months. Once I'd set things up there, I was called back to Berlin.'

'And I understand that when you got back, you made a terrible discovery about your family?'

'That's right.' Margarete took a deep breath. This would be the hardest part. 'When I went back home, I discovered that our apartment block had been destroyed in an air raid....' She faltered, unsure whether she could utter the next words, but Kristel's understanding eyes were on her face, encouraging her gently to carry on. She opened her mouth and no words would come out, so Kristel asked her another question, this time taking her back a step.

'So, whereabouts in Berlin was the apartment, Margarete?'

'Oh, it was a square not very far from Anhalter station. Most of the buildings around it were destroyed in that raid.'

'That must have been an unbelievable shock for you.'

'It was, absolutely terrible. There didn't seem to be any survivors. I asked around in all the hospitals, but there was no sign of any of my family – my mother, my sister, Alicia and my baby daughter, Tomasina. They had all been killed when the building collapsed.'

'That's truly, truly terrible, Margarete.'

'When I reported into the Reich Main Office, they confirmed that my family had all been killed in the air raid. It was then that I discovered that my sister Alicia must have been watched by the SS or the Gestapo. She had worked for the resistance, helping Jews hide from the SS, for years.'

Kristel asked her several more questions then, about how she coped with the loss of her family, how she eventually escaped through the Brenner Pass to Italy at the end of the war and how she made a new life for herself in her adopted country. Those questions weren't so hard to deal with. Margarete was happy to describe her journey on foot through the mountains in Austria and how she found a job in an orphanage in a convent in northern Italy and devoted herself completely to the children there.

'It was a way of making amends for the past. I gave myself up to the work and had no life at all outside the orphanage. I suppose it was a way of forgetting too, everything and everyone I'd lost.'

Kristel drew the interview to a close then and thanked Margarete profusely for telling her story.

'We will edit the film and it will go on air tomorrow evening. That way we will be sure to keep the interest of those who've tuned in daily to hear the reports on the Lebensborn we've been broadcasting – I don't want to leave it too long.'

Margarete felt drained. Speaking about that time had taken all her energy. She was glad when Lorenzo came to collect her to take her back to the apartment. Once she was there, she fell asleep in an armchair, and, when she finally woke, Kristel was already home from the studio.

'Margarete,' she said, her face alight with excitement, 'something incredible has happened. Someone called Joanna Kaminsky called the studio. She said she'd seen your interview on satellite TV in Poland, that she is alive and well and wanted to meet you. She wondered if we were able to put her in touch with her sister, Marta. I was able to say that we've arranged for Marta to come into the studio tomorrow. Joanna is getting a flight in the morning and will arrive at the studio while Marta is there.'

Margarete blinked at her. 'Joanna? But I was told that Joanna had died in Auschwitz. Are you quite sure?'

'Of course. This is definitely the same woman. Your information must have been wrong.'

'Thank God,' Margarete breathed as the news sank in. 'Thank God for that. I won't have to break the terrible news to Marta after all – but more importantly, the sisters will be reunited after a lifetime apart.'

THIRTY-ONE

MARTA

Munich, 2005

Marta's nerves were making her stomach churn when she approached the building where *Nachricht 24* had their studios. How incredible, she thought, that she'd probably passed this unremarkable office block a thousand times in her life and had never even noticed it before. She'd been oblivious to the fact that one day it would play such a momentous part in her life.

She went up in the lift to the fifth floor, checked in with the receptionist and was asked to wait on a plush leather sofa, in front of a floor-to-ceiling window with a fabulous view over the city. There was a pile of magazines on the coffee table, but Marta had no interest in those – she was far too churned up to concentrate on anything. She just sat there, twisting her hands, taking deep breaths. She kept telling herself to calm down. That had always worked in the past when she was about to take an exam, to give a presentation, or to face a difficult meeting at work. Learning the truth about Joanna was so much more important to her than any of those things, she thought, and tried to forgive herself for feeling so nervous.

'Doctor Marta Fiehler? Hello, I'm Nicole, Kristel's assistant. We spoke on the phone.'

Marta looked up. 'Yes. Oh, hello,' she said to the pretty, dark-haired girl with the clipboard, who was approaching with a friendly smile.

'Would you like to come this way?'

Marta got up and followed the young woman through some swing doors and down a long passage, through some more double doors and into a large, high-ceilinged room. She looked about her. There were spotlights on the ceiling. Was this a television studio? She couldn't tell. Kristel Meyer was already striding towards her, her hand outstretched, smiling broadly.

'Marta? Very pleased to meet you. I'm Kristel.'

Kristel looked a little taller and slimmer in real life than she appeared on TV, but Marta was reassured by her presence. She felt as if she already knew her.

'Nice to meet you, Kristel,' she said, relaxing a little as she shook the woman's hand.

'If you'd like to come and sit down over here, Margarete is waiting and is looking forward to meeting you... again.'

Marta followed Kristel to another part of the studio, where Margarete was sitting in a wheelchair. She looked just as she had done in her interviews on TV, a frail, white-haired old lady, but she still had the same look in her eyes that Marta recalled from all those decades ago in Bruczków. They were full of kindness and compassion.

When she saw Marta, Margarete held out her arms. 'Marta!' she cried.

Marta went over to her, bent down and put her arms around the old lady. Tears sprang to her eyes and, in that moment, she was that vulnerable young girl again, back in the assimilation home in that forbidding old house in Bruczków, and Margarete was the only person she could trust and who was prepared to stand between her and an unjust and harsh punishment.

'Thank you,' Marta kept repeating. 'Thank you for saving me. I've never forgotten your kindness.'

'It was nothing. There is no need to thank me. I've never forgotten you either,' Margarete said.

Dabbing her eyes, Marta sat down in a seat beside Margarete.

'I came here because I wanted to meet you again, and I wanted to know what happened to Joanna,' she said. 'I know you tried to write to me, but the Fiehlers destroyed the letter.'

'Ah, yes,' Margarete said. 'I realised something like that might have happened. I thought that I was going to have to give you some bad news about Joanna today, but in the past twenty-four hours, something new has come to light.'

'Yes,' Kristel chipped in. 'There's someone in the studio who wants to talk to you, Marta.'

'Sorry?' Marta was confused. What was Kristel talking about? Why didn't they just let her know the news? She didn't like games. But Kristel was already standing up and beckoning someone to join the group. Marta watched as a woman, a little younger than Marta herself, approached them. She was a similar build to Marta, tall and slim, and she moved in a way that reminded Marta powerfully of someone from deep in the past. Suddenly it clicked and, her heart soaring, she leapt to her feet.

'Joanna!' She stood transfixed, staring at the woman who was walking towards her with her arms outstretched.

In Marta's mind's eye, Joanna had stayed forever young. Why hadn't she realised that Joanna would have aged, just like her? But despite the changes wrought by the passage of the years, it was definitely her sister. Those eyes, which were brimming over with tears of emotion, just as she knew her own eyes were, were unmistakably Joanna's.

Marta took two steps forward and the sisters fell into each other's arms. They stood there sobbing, clinging to each other, both too overwhelmed to speak. Finally, they drew apart. Kristel handed them both tissues and they dabbed their eyes.

'I can't believe it's really you. I hoped against hope that you were alive, but thought you must have died during the war,' Marta said.

'I very nearly did. I thought I would never see you again either,' Joanna responded.

They wandered to two easy chairs a little way away from the others.

'Where are you living?' Marta asked. There was so much to ask and the question sounded trivial.

'In Kraków. I've lived there since the end of the war. At first, we went back to Jasło, but the whole town had been destroyed. We decided we couldn't live there after that.'

'I know. I went back to Jasło myself in 1989. But... wait a minute, you said "we". Who is "we"?'

'Mama and me. I met Mama at the end of the war, just by chance. I'd been in Auschwitz, you see, and it turned out that she had too. During the evacuation I got onto a transport train and there she was.'

'Mama? How incredible! So, she actually survived the war?'

Joanna nodded, beaming all over her face. 'We were both very weak, but we helped each other survive through the final days. I couldn't believe I'd found her and that she was alive.'

'And now?'

'She's still alive, Marta! She's ninety-five now, you know. She lives in a care home just round the corner from us. Me and my husband, that is. My son and daughter are grown up now. I didn't tell Mama I was coming to meet you, but you must come and visit as soon as you can. Her health isn't good now, sadly.'

'Of course!' Marta was stunned. 'I'll come straight away.'

There was so much to take in. She could hardly believe that her mother was alive and had been living close to Joanna since the end of the war. She would be able to see her again, to hold her hand, to kiss her cheek. How many times had she dreamed of that happening? And then she remembered what Joanna had said about how they met. She turned back to her sister, frowning.

'Auschwitz – you said you were in Auschwitz?'

'Yes. I tried to escape from the camp at Łódź with another girl. The SS caught us and sent us to Auschwitz. I was due to die, but by some miracle had an incredibly lucky escape. I ended up working in the camp until January 1945, when the whole camp was evacuated and marched to Germany.'

'Oh, Joanna!'

Marta could hardly believe what she was hearing. For years she'd wondered if Joanna had been sent to Auschwitz, and once, after her disappointing visit to Jasło, she'd even travelled to Bad Arolsen in Germany, where records of the Holocaust were held. There, she'd searched for every permutation of Joanna's name she could think of, but hadn't found anything.

That thought had always been in the back of her mind though, and, getting ready this morning, she'd wondered with dread if that was the news that Margarete had to tell her. It was partly why she'd been so nervous when she arrived at the studio.

Marta held out her hand and Joanna took it. They sat there in silence, holding hands. There was so much to say, so much to ask, but there was plenty of time for that. Just being together was enough.

But there was one important question Marta still had to ask. 'What about Tata?' she said. 'What happened to him?'

'He was executed, Marta,' Joanna said quietly. 'Not long after we were taken away. The SS discovered that he'd been helping Jews to escape and to hide, and they took him away, with others from the resistance, and shot him in the woods.'

Marta stared at her, shock pulsing through her. She'd long

resigned herself to the fact that Tata must have been killed by the SS, but having it confirmed was still hard to bear.

They sat together and talked for hours. Outside the building, the light was fading, but neither sister noticed the passing of time. Marta gradually realised that her stomach was rumbling and, when Kristel came over to ask if they'd like to go to a restaurant and carry on their conversation there, they both agreed.

After a tearful goodbye to Kristel and Margarete, with promises to keep in touch, they walked to a quiet brasserie Marta knew in the next street.

Over the meal, Marta told Joanna about her career as a doctor and how, even though she was now retired, she still worked at a clinic helping refugees.

'I knew you would do something like that,' Joanna said, smiling proudly. 'Remember how you used to care for Mama when she was sick?'

'Yes, you're right,' Marta agreed. 'Do you know, I've never thought of that before. Perhaps that's what inspired me. How extraordinary! And what about you, Joanna? What did you do?'

'I became a teacher. A history teacher. It wasn't always easy under the Soviet regime, we had to teach what we were told, but now things are much freer. I retired a few years ago, of course.'

'And family? You said you were married and that you have grown-up children?'

'Yes. A boy and a girl. My son is a doctor too actually, and my daughter works in IT. And I have a husband, Lukas. Another teacher. I met him when I was studying. He is a good man, Marta. He can't wait to meet you. I've talked about you so much over the years. But what about you? Did you not marry?'

Marta shook her head sadly. 'No. I never met anyone I cared for enough. I found it hard to let myself love, I suppose.'

Joanna squeezed her hand on the table. 'There could still be time,' she said, her eyes dancing, and they both laughed.

Then Joanna said, 'I'm going back to Kraków tomorrow. Why don't you come back with me? You could meet the whole family and see Mama.'

'I'd love to,' Marta said instantly. 'Now that we've found each other, I don't think I could bear to let you go. And I don't want to wait any longer than necessary to see Mama.'

The care home was a large, white-painted house set back from the main road a few kilometres from Joanna's apartment in Kraków. Marta and Joanna had flown from Munich that morning and had arrived at the apartment in time for a lunch that Lukas had prepared for them. He had greeted Marta warmly and Marta felt instantly at home in his company. He seemed kind and caring, and witty too. She could see how Joanna had fallen for him.

'You know it was just by chance that we watched the *Nachricht* 24 programme,' he told Marta.

'Me too,' she said. 'I just happened to be watching one evening when Kristel's report came on the TV.'

'We'd only just got cable TV and I was flicking through the channels,' Lukas told her. 'When I saw that there was a programme about the Lebensborn, I called Joanna through from the kitchen to watch. We were so moved by the stories that we watched all the reports. And in the last one, it was instantly clear to Joanna that Margarete was talking about you two. That's when she knew she had to phone in.'

'Me too,' Marta said. 'And I'm so glad I did!'

After lunch of delicious *pierogi*, Polish dumplings, Joanna said, 'Are you ready? I normally visit Mama after lunch, and she'll be expecting me. Especially as I didn't go yesterday.'

'Of course,' Marta said, thrills of excitement and anticipation rushing through her. She couldn't wait.

'Do you want me to drive you round there?' Lukas asked.

'No, thank you. I think it would be nicer to walk,' Joanna said.

They put their coats on and set out in the chilly winter air. Marta put her arm through Joanna's. There was ice underfoot, so they had to tread carefully.

'It's even colder than Munich,' she said, shivering, but she soon warmed up when they started walking.

She couldn't wait to get there. 'Do you think she'll know who I am?' she asked Joanna, suddenly nervous.

'Of course. I knew who you were instantly.'

'Yes, but you were expecting to see me, weren't you?'

'She'll know. You just wait and see,' Joanna said, smiling and patting her hand.

Marta felt a little apprehensive as they walked up to the front door of the building, went into the reception area and signed the visitors' book.

'Where's Mama today?' Joanna asked the receptionist.

'She's in her room,' the woman answered. 'She was a little tired and didn't want to go into the day room after lunch today. She's looking forward to seeing you, though – she missed you yesterday.'

'I'm looking forward to seeing her too,' Joanna said. 'And I have a surprise for her today.'

The receptionist smiled. 'That will be nice for her.'

They walked through a glass door and down a corridor lined with doors. Joanna stopped in front of one about halfway along.

'Are you ready?' she said. Marta could hardly speak for nerves. Her mouth had gone completely dry. She nodded and Joanna gave her an encouraging hug before knocking on the door.

'Come in?' The voice was fainter, more tremulous, now, but it was still the beloved, gentle voice that Marta remembered from childhood.

Joanna stepped into the room and Marta followed.

'Mama, I've brought someone to see you. Someone we haven't seen for a very long time,' Joanna said.

'Who is it, dear?'

Marta stood beside Joanna and looked down at her mother. She was small, shrunken and white-haired now. She looked even more frail than Margarete. An overwhelming feeling of love flooded through Marta at the sight of her mother, and her legs went so weak, she thought they might collapse under her.

'Come forward, so I can see you,' Mama said, leaning forward in her chair and peering at her.

Marta did as she asked.

Mama looked up into Marta's eyes and for an instant she frowned. Then her face cleared and she gasped and held out her arms.

'Marta, my darling girl! I knew you'd come back to me one day.'

Marta bent down and hugged her mother and felt those beloved arms around her at last, pulling her close. She buried her face in the old lady's shoulder. The years unravelled and she was that little girl once again. She sobbed with joy and love and gratitude.

THIRTY-TWO

MARGARETE

Trento, Italy, 2006

Margarete was back at home in Our Lady of Mercy care home in Trento, sitting in the bay window in her room, looking out at the snow-covered mountains. She'd been back from Munich for two days now, having left straight after her final interview had been broadcast. Kristel had invited her to the studio to watch the programme being aired, then Lorenzo had driven her back to Italy, through the Brenner Pass in the snow. He was taking the opportunity to visit his parents in Trento before driving back to Munich. As they'd driven through the pass, Margarete had looked out at the forbidding peaks of the Dolomites, remembering how, as a young woman at the end of the war, she'd trekked through those mountains alone. It was amazing how those years were still vivid in her mind, more real somehow than anything that happened in the present.

She could relax a little now, she reflected. She would no longer have to think those nagging thoughts that had plagued her for years about all the mothers and babies she'd failed along the way. Her notebooks and Kristel's programmes had brought so many people together. Tomas had been right all those years ago when he'd said, 'Your notebooks will be useful someday, you'll see.' She was only sad that Tomas himself wasn't there to see his words come true, but she could sense that he was still with her, watching over her, even now.

Bringing all those people together had been wonderful, and it had brought tears to Margarete's eyes to see Joanna and Marta reunited after decades apart. Moments like that made everything worthwhile. But still, in the depths of her heart, the sadness of her own losses remained. She knew it would never leave her as long as she lived.

Watching the road outside the window and the front drive of the care home, she noticed a familiar red Fiat turn in at the gate and draw up in the drive. She leaned forward, peering. Could it really be Kristel? When the driver's door opened, she saw that it was. Kristel got out of the car, pulled her long winter coat around her, shut the car door and approached the front door of the house.

Margarete waited impatiently, wondering why Kristel had made the journey all the way from Munich. Perhaps she couldn't bear to be away from Lorenzo for another night and had driven down to Trento to see him? But if that was the case, what was she doing coming here to Our Lady of Mercy?

Soon there was a knock at the door and Ginetta, one of the senior carers, put her head round. 'You have a visitor, Margarete,' she said, smiling, and the next moment Kristel strode into the room.

'Good afternoon, Margarete,' she said, coming straight over and kissing Margarete on the cheek.

'Hello,' Margarete said. 'This is a surprise.'

'I'm sorry to burst in on you like this,' Kristel said, 'but I have some important news for you, and I didn't want to tell you over the phone.'

'Oh, Kristel,' Margarete said. 'Thank you, but the phone

would have done just as well. It's such a long drive, especially in this weather. You must be exhausted.'

Kristel took her coat off and hung it on the back of the door, then pulled up a chair opposite Margarete's.

'No, Margarete, the phone wouldn't have done. Not for this news.'

'Really?' Margarete's interest was piqued. Whatever could have happened?

'I'll tell you,' Kristel said, sitting down and focusing her attention on Margarete. 'Are you ready?'

'Of course.' Margarete was intrigued. She wished Kristel would get on with it though, whatever it was. She hated being kept in the dark about anything.

'After your last interview was broadcast, two days ago, we had several calls, but someone in particular phoned the studio. It was a woman called Esther Bloch. She lives in Switzerland now but was originally from Berlin.'

'Oh?' Margarete asked, wondering what Esther Bloch might have to do with her.

'Esther is Jewish. She told us that both her parents were deported at some point in late 1943, but that a kind lady called Alicia Weiss helped the girls. Apparently, Alicia arranged for Esther and her sister Rachel to be hidden in the loft at the top of her apartment block to avoid them being deported too.'

'Alicia did that?' Margarete marvelled. She knew that her sister had helped many Jewish people avoid deportation, but she had no idea that she'd actually hidden children in their own apartment block. How incredible! For a fleeting second, she wondered why Alicia hadn't confided in her about it and felt a twinge of sadness that her sister hadn't felt able to trust her, then she pulled herself up. Alicia was probably under strict instructions not to tell anyone outside the resistance network, and, particularly as Margarete herself worked for the ministry, she would have been regarded as high-risk.

'When the apartment block was bombed, in 1944, Esther and Rachel somehow managed to survive with just cuts and bruises. The roof beams somehow sheltered them. They crawled out of the building in the dust and rubble. They were about to walk away when they heard a baby crying. They searched amongst the debris and eventually found the baby. She was screaming but unharmed. She was lying right next to Alicia, who they were shocked to find had been hit by falling masonry and sadly passed away.'

Margarete gasped and her hand flew to her mouth. 'Poor, poor Alicia! But was that baby Tomasina?' she said. She hardly dared hope.

'It was a baby girl. A few months old. They picked her up and took her with them. They knew they had to get away quickly in case the SS should come along. They wandered through the city, which was in a chaotic state after the bombings, and eventually turned up at a hospital. Esther doesn't know which hospital it was, but it was likely to have been the Jewish hospital. A doctor there, knowing the danger they were in, took Esther, Rachel and the baby into his own home, then handed them over to the resistance.

'They stayed hidden in an apartment in Berlin for several weeks, but then they were taken by road, concealed in the back of a lorry, to the Swiss border, where they were smuggled through. In Switzerland they were placed in an orphanage, where they remained for two years until a generous Swiss family, the Blochs, adopted all three of them.

'They had always assumed that the baby girl was Jewish, until they heard your interview the other evening. In it, you mentioned the bombing of the apartment block, your sister Alicia, who helped them and who they remembered, and the fact that Alicia was looking after your baby girl.'

'And Tomasina?' Margarete asked tentatively. 'Does she know about all this?'

Margarete could hardly process what she was hearing. How could this even be possible? She'd thought for so long that her beloved baby girl was dead. Was this a dream? Was she about to wake up to the cruel truth that none of it was true?

'Yes,' Kristel said, 'She does know about it, although Tomasina isn't her name any more. The girls didn't know the baby's name and she was called Emilia by the family who adopted them. She and Esther are coming to Trento tomorrow to see you. Emilia has offered to take a DNA test to discover the truth. She's always wanted to know about her parentage and is very much looking forward to meeting you.'

'Oh, Kristel!' Margarete was lost for words. 'How can I ever thank you?'

'There's nothing to thank me for. It was your interview, Margarete. When you told your own story, that's what inspired them to call.'

'But *you* got me to do it. I was reluctant to.'

'But you did it, Margarete. And that's what's important.'

What if I hadn't? she thought in a sudden panic. She'd been so close to refusing to do the interview at all.

'Don't think about that now,' said Kristel gently, squeezing her hand. 'Think about meeting Emilia.'

'What if she isn't Tomasina after all?' Another wave of panic washed through Margarete.

'Just think about it logically, Margarete. Your sister was holding the baby when the bombs hit the apartment. What other baby could she possibly have been holding?'

'I suppose you're right,' Margarete admitted, still terrified that she was going to be disappointed.

'So, just focus on tomorrow. They're going to arrive at about eleven o'clock.'

'I don't think I'll be able to wait until then,' Margarete said.

'That's why I've come. I'm going to stay with you for the rest of the day. We can chat and play cards if you like?'

'What about Lorenzo? Don't you want to see him?' Margarete asked.

'Oh, his father has asked him to help out in the café today, but he'd said he'll come along later on to collect me. He will drop in and see you then.'

It was just after eleven the next morning when Margarete saw the taxi draw up on the drive. She and Kristel were sitting in the window, both on tenterhooks. Margarete hadn't been able to eat any breakfast. She was so full of pent-up excitement that she wondered if she'd be able to speak when the moment came.

She leaned forward in her chair and peered at the two woman who got out of the taxi. Both had dark hair and were dressed smartly, one in a red coat, the other in a navy-blue one. Both wore winter boots. That was all she could see; their faces weren't visible, so she couldn't see their expressions, but she could tell that they were close. They linked arms as they walked to the front door.

'I'll go down and show them the way up,' Kristel said and left her alone.

Then there was another agonising five minutes to wait while the visitors signed in at the desk and came up the stairs and along the corridor. When Margarete heard the door open, she was so keyed up she couldn't help jumping.

Kristel came in first, then the two visitors. While they were walking upstairs, Margarete had worried that she wouldn't know which one was Emilia, but now as they both came towards her, smiling and saying hello, she knew instantly. The older woman came forward and took her hand first. 'I'm Esther Bloch,' she said. 'Thank you for seeing us, Miss Weiss.'

'Thank you for coming,' Margarete replied in a cracked voice.

'And this is my sister, Emilia,' Esther said, and the younger woman stepped forward and took Margarete's hand and leaned forward to say hello.

Emilia looked very good for her sixty-odd years. She was slim and lithe, her face only a little lined and her dark hair was lustrous. Margarete looked up into her eyes and for a few moments was unable to speak. She had such a powerful sense of connection with Emilia that she felt as if electricity was passing between them, because looking into Emilia's face it was as if she was looking straight into Tomas Müller's eyes. The shape of his face, the colour of his eyes, the curve of his cheek, they were all replicated here in the face of this beautiful woman they had made together. In that instant there was no doubt in Margarete's mind that this was her daughter, and it was as if all the heartache and waiting of a lifetime was cancelled out in that second.

'Tomasina,' Margarete said when she was able to find her voice. She held out her arms and she felt Tomasina put her arms around her. 'You came back to me.'

A LETTER FROM ANN

Dear reader,

I'd like to say a huge thank you for reading *The Stolen Sisters*. I hope you loved reading it as much as I loved writing it.

If you'd like to keep up with my latest releases, please sign up for my newsletter. Your email address won't be shared, and you may unsubscribe at any time.

www.bookouture.com/ann-bennett

If you enjoyed the book, I'd be very grateful if you could write a review. I'd love to hear what you thought of it, and reviews help new readers discover my books for the first time.

I love hearing from readers, so do get in touch via social media or through my website.

Thanks,

Ann

facebook.com/annbennettauthor

x.com/annbennett71

REFERENCES

The following are some of the sources of inspiration and information for the series.

Books

Boyd, Julia, *A Village in the Third Reich*

Fallada, Hans, *Alone in Berlin*

Hagen, Louis, *Ein Volk, Ein Reich: Nine Lives Under the Nazis*

Hall, David Ian, *Hitler's Munich: The Capital of the Nazi Movement*

Levi, Primo, *If This Is a Man*

Lukas, Richard C., *Did the Children Cry? Hitler's War against Jewish and Polish Children, 1939–45*

Lukas, Richard C., *Forgotten Holocaust: The Poles under German Occupation 1939–1944*

Milton, Giles, *Wolfram: The Boy Who Went to War*

Rees, Laurence, *The Nazis: A Warning from History*

Wiesel, Elie, *Night*

Television

BBC, *Auschwitz: The Nazis and the Final Solution*

BBC, *Rise of the Nazis*

Web Resources

Arolsen Archives, *85 Years of Lebensborn*

Holocaust Encyclopaedia, *Lebensborn Program: Łódź*

Institute of National Remembrance, *German labour camp for Polish children on Przemysłowa Street in Łódź* (1942–1945)

Jewish Virtual Library, *Stolen Children: Interview with Gitta Sereny*

Warfare History Network, *Hitler's Lebensborn Children: Kidnappings in German-Occupied Poland*

Wikipedia, *Lebensborn; Kanada warehouses, Auschwitz*

Yad Vashem, The World Holocaust Remembrance Centre

Hope Keeps you Going – The Story of Marta Weiss

Take the Girl – The Story of Holocaust Survivor Shela Alteratz

Thank God You Are Here – The Story of Gita (Giselle) Cycowicz

The Death Marches – Herta Goldman and Lea Frank Holitz

YouTube

DW Documentary, *The Warsaw Ghetto; The Kidnapping Campaign of Nazi Germany*

Doobie Does the World, *Auschwitz Children: Block 16A*
Herman Wouk, *War and Remembrance*

HMTC, *Survivor Testimony: Escaping the Auschwitz Gas Chambers – Rachel Gleitman*

Jewish Broadcasting Service, *Witness: Gena Turgel*

ACKNOWLEDGEMENTS

I'd like to thank the wonderful team at Bookouture for their constant support and dedication, especially my fantastic editor, Lydia Vassar-Smith. I'd also like to thank my family for their encouragement and support, and everyone who's championed my writing down the years by buying and reading my books.

PUBLISHING TEAM

Turning a manuscript into a book requires the efforts of many people. The publishing team at Bookouture would like to acknowledge everyone who contributed to this publication.

Audio
Alba Proko
Sinead O'Connor
Melissa Tran

Commercial
Lauren Morrissette
Hannah Richmond
Imogen Allport

Cover design
Emma Graves

Data and analysis
Mark Alder
Mohamed Bussuri

Editorial
Lydia Vassar-Smith
Lizzie Brien

Made in United States
Orlando, FL
13 December 2024

55596755R00188